DIRECT LEGACY

Author's Other Works

Fiction

A Question of Time: The Snake Eater Chronicles, Book 1

Appointment in Tehran: The Snake Eater Chronicles, Book 2

Non-Fiction

No Moon as Witness: Missions of the SOE and OSS in WWII

Masters of Mayhem: Lawrence of Arabia and the British Military Mission to the Hejaz—The Seeds of British Special Operations

Special Forces Berlin: Clandestine Cold War Operations of the US Army's Elite, 1956–1990

The Horns of the Beast: The Swakop River Campaign and World War I in South-West Africa, 1914–15

DIRECT LEGACY

THE SNAKE EATER CHRONICLES 3

JAMES STEJSKAL

CASEMATE
Philadelphia & Oxford

Published in the United States of America and Great Britain in 2022 by
CASEMATE PUBLISHERS
1950 Lawrence Road, Havertown, PA 19083, USA
and
The Old Music Hall, 106–108 Cowley Road, Oxford OX4 1JE; UK

Copyright 2022 © James Stejskal

Hardcover Edition: ISBN 978-1-63624-119-7
Digital Edition: ISBN 978-1-63624-120-3

A CIP record for this book is available from the British Library

Printed and bound in the United Kingdom by TJ Books

Typeset in India by Lapiz Digital Services, Chennai

For a complete list of Casemate titles, please contact:

CASEMATE PUBLISHERS (US)
Telephone (610) 853-9131
Fax (610) 853-9146
Email: casemate@casematepublishers.com
www.casematepublishers.com

CASEMATE PUBLISHERS (UK)
Telephone (01865) 241249
Email: casemate-uk@casematepublishers.co.uk
www.casematepublishers.co.uk

Note:
This book is a work of fiction. Names, characters, places, and incidents either are the
product of the author's imagination or, if real, are used fictitiously.

The lyrics to "We're Off To Dublin In The Green" are used with acknowledgment to the
Irish marchers of 1916.

"The world is what it is;
men who are nothing,
who allow themselves to be nothing,
have no place in it."

—V. S. Naipaul

Ireland, 1980s

This story is set during the waning years of the Cold War. It takes place in Northern Ireland during "The Troubles"—a polite term for an ugly sectarian conflict between two groups with long-simmering grievances: the loyalists who wished to preserve the status quo and the republicans who wished to unify the North with the Republic of Ireland. While the historical details of Lord Mountbatten's assassination and the killing of British soldiers of 2 Para at Warrenpoint described herein are generally accurate, readers will struggle to identify the other personalities encountered in this story. That is because they do not exist, and the actions attributed to them—for the most part—never happened.

"Just remember, we're not here to make friends."

—Anonymous

Prologue

Tell me again why I volunteered for this shit.

Stavros felt truly helpless. There was a small army of trolls pounding on the inside of his head with pickaxes. His tongue told him that they must have marched in and out of his dry mouth with filthy boots. His gut burned from his stomach to his esophagus and he felt like a hot metal spike had pierced his brain from over his left eye to behind his right ear. He struggled to clear the sticky fog that permeated the deepest recesses of his brain. This was the worst hangover he'd ever experienced.

He could barely move. The coarse manila rope ground into his wrists like rough sandpaper. He cursed his cover story—a writer of pacific, social interest articles—otherwise, he would have had a blade hidden in the waistband of his pants. If he'd been wearing pants. Those seemed to have disappeared along with his shirt. Now all he was wearing were his shorts and a tee-shirt. Even his socks were missing. No wonder it was cold.

The air was heavy with the acrid smell of smoldering peat. It filled his nostrils with a pungent, thick odor that stung. It was difficult to breathe anyway, with a heavy burlap bag over his head. The hood couldn't mask the depth of the blackness that surrounded him. There were other things in the air, the smell of damp wood and very faintly, a rotted sweetness—maybe potatoes. Taking the smells together with the cold, still air and hushed darkness, he decided he was in some sort of underground cellar.

Day or night? Not a clue.

He rubbed his left wrist on the chair, trying to feel his wristwatch. Not that he could read it but it would reassure him. It wasn't there.

From time to time, footsteps shuffled on the floor not far above his head. The sound of wood scraping on wood as someone sat and repositioned a chair. A muffled laugh came from somewhere, the low murmur of voices, sounds unintelligible to his ears. Then silence. He didn't like the silence; you couldn't figure out what was happening if there was no sound.

Recalling events as best he could, Stavros tried to reconstruct how he had ended up in this position. The last thing he could remember was drinking a beer in a crowded pub and talking to that pretty dark-haired woman he had only just met. Then nothing.

Whatever she used must have been quick and powerful. *How do I know it was her? It just had to be.*

He had been in similar situations over the years but those had all been training—SERE, for Survival, Evasion, Resistance, and Escape, they called it. He'd trained with everyone but the Marines and doubted they had much more to teach him. It was all quite simple and straightforward. Survival for learning how to eat bugs, deal with snakes, and make signal fires out of nothing. Evasion for the tricks best used to elude trackers, dogs, and circling helicopters—a breeze for someone who'd spent his youth as an aspiring teenage criminal. Resistance was a dark subject—learning how to avoid answering questions directed at you at the end of a stick, or a fist, or while stuffed inside a wooden box two sizes too small, or at the end of three days with no sleep. Escape was the best segment: getting away from it all without being recaptured. Of course, their jail-breaks never succeeded because they were expected and on a schedule, but trying is half the game.

How long have I been here? They'll be coming down to question me before long.

He assumed they must be letting him stew first, building up his anxiety, but then he wasn't sure if whoever was holding him had a clue about interrogation techniques or even if they knew he was awake. As it was, he didn't know who or what to expect, and that worried him.

I'll find out soon enough.

Before then, he knew he had to remember: Who am I? Why am I here?

Slowly, painstakingly, he recalled his cover story. He remembered the details of a life that he knew but had never actually experienced and went back to schools he never attended. It was all close to his real life, but just different enough.

Mentally, he was free to roam and it was better that way, to be away from where he was. Physically, it was another matter. Trying to get some slack in the ropes that held him, he squirmed, but as he did the restraints seemed to tighten even more. The walls he couldn't see started to feel like they were closing in. It didn't make sense, but in his pitch-black world, the air seemed to press down on his chest and ears. His pulse started to throb; he could feel it in his temples and neck. He was getting hot despite the coolness that surrounded him. He breathed in and couldn't get enough air. The coarse cloth mask made damp by his breath fought his efforts. What air he got was stale and heavy. He inhaled long and deeply several times and tried to straighten up in the hard chair. It was his way of preventing an episode. The episodes almost always happened at night, usually a couple of hours after he lay down. But he could feel one coming on now.

Breathe deep and relax.

He went back five years to Walter Reed Army Hospital, lying in his dark room trying to sleep. Sterile, fluorescent green light spilled in through the open doorway from the hall. He had demanded they leave it that way. With the door shut, the room closed in on him. The pain was immense. A compound tibia and fibula fracture, the result of a bad parachute landing; his leg hurt like nothing he'd experienced before. Surgery followed, metal rods through his bones, an external brace, and more pain. He'd wake up and feel like he couldn't get enough air. At first, he became anxious; panic followed, then came an overwhelming fear of suffocation. Panic, but not hysteria.

He would sit up and take rapid deep breaths—it was not enough— he had to move and move quickly. Only when he slid out of the bed into his wheelchair and propelled himself down the corridor could he find relief. He would race around the ward's halls, laid out in a rectangle with nurses' stations in the center, pumping the wheels as hard as he could. He rolled past the rooms at Mach 1, while the officer nurses and enlisted medics hanging around the counter just watched him fly by at three in the morning. After several nights, they had seen him enough not to wonder. Finally, he told his doctor what he was feeling.

"Took you long enough to ask," she said.

The pain killers precipitated anxiety attacks, she explained. After that, he consciously tapered off, pushing the button on the IV or taking the pills only when the pain got unbearable. Even so, long after the hospital, the attacks continued, suddenly, unexpectedly, sometimes in small or crowded spaces. He never talked about them again with anyone. Instead, he tried to manage them by himself through exercise and meditation.

This time, he couldn't move. He had only his mind to calm the storm. Breathing deeply and rhythmically, he concentrated on that neutral moment between inhale and exhale. Nothing else. In, out, in, out. Slowly, slowly, he relaxed and then slipped into a welcome sleep.

1

Shadow V, a 30-foot wooden lobster boat, rocked gently in the sparkling sapphire waters of the harbor as its crew prepared to get underway. Paul, a strapping young teenager, a local villager who maintained the boat, coiled and stowed ropes under the gaze of a tall man with a regal, military bearing—the boat's owner.

The owner, even at the age of seventy-nine, looked in charge—appropriately enough, because he was Prince Louis Francis Albert Victor Nicholas of Battenberg, better known as the 1st Viscount Mountbatten of Burma or simply, Earl Mountbatten. His service in World War II had brought him his title, although some—Canadians, in particular, who remembered him from the Dieppe disaster—hated him.

There were four others on board; all relatives of the earl, expecting a quiet day on the water, maybe some fishing, but mostly just relaxation.

Mountbatten took the wheel in hand as the boat slipped its moorings and turned toward the open water of the bay, out of Mullaghmore Harbour. He steered toward a line of lobster pots and cut back on the throttle so the boat glided silently up to and alongside the first marker buoy. The boat bobbed a bit in the light swells as it inched forward. John, Mountbatten's son-in-law, leaned over the gunwale, snagged the buoy's anchor rope with a gaff hook, and began to pull up the trap.

"Lord, it's heavy! We're going to have some lobster tonight!" he said to no one in particular while continuing to pull in the rope. Paul came over to lend a hand.

About a thousand meters away, a man standing by his car on the coastal road watched the scene through his binoculars. He was relatively young, late twenties, with dusty, reddish-brown hair. Except for his eyes, which were coal-dark and expressionless—almost dead, one might think—it was an unremarkable face that would be hard to place after a casual encounter.

He looked around to make sure he was still alone and then took a small plastic box from the front seat of the car. Pulling out a long silver antenna, he pointed it toward the boat and waited a moment until he saw the orange flag marker on the lobster pot's anchor line appear through the binoculars. Then he flipped a red safety switch and pushed a button.

A flash of yellow and orange and a geyser of water erupted under the boat, tearing the hull apart, shards of broken oak, teak, and brass fittings shooting skyward. A ball of black smoke billowed outward and upward. By the time the sound of the explosion reached the man several seconds later, he was already in the driver's seat and starting the car. He had to admit, thinking to himself, that the engineer's idea to put the bomb in the lobster pot was brilliant. They had avoided the constables guarding the boat and most of the evidence was now on the bottom of the bay.

The 10 pounds of gelignite exploded a couple of meters under the boat, and the resulting shock wave and water plume tore the boat and the people on board to pieces. The dead and wounded floated in the water along with the rest of the flotsam. Other boats in the bay turned their prows toward the blast site to see if they could help.

A solitary circular wave rolled out from the smoking hole in the water. Above, on the bluff overlooking the bay, the man drove south, stopping after thirty minutes on the road. He got out and walked to a public telephone standing next to a shuttered public house.

He dialed a telephone number from memory. When someone on the other end of the line picked up, he said, "The package was delivered," and returned the receiver to its hook. Turning back to his car, he pulled a cigarette from a pack. He lit it with a match, waved the flame out, and flicked the stick into the gravel. Taking a long draw, he exhaled slowly and focused on the horizon. He slid back into the driver's seat and continued, stylizing himself as belonging to the band of warriors in the great hall of Valhalla.

But I'm not dead yet.

***

Several hours later and 190 kilometers away on the eastern side of the island, a dark green Land Rover followed by two Bedford lorries filled with soldiers from the 2nd Parachute Regiment roared past a group of gaping, staring children in a park who had stopped their bank holiday play at the village edge to watch. On that hot Monday afternoon, the convoy rolled out onto the tarmacadam A2 and accelerated into the countryside. The Warrenpoint Road lay close upon the frontier between the province of Northern Ireland and the Republic. It followed the Newry River, which ran along one side; on the other were farms delineated by ancient rock walls. It was a dangerous stretch of road for the army to use, prone to ambushes as it was, but there weren't many good choices when you needed to move. So, it was risk versus gain and besides, they were many and well armed. In any event, the route was chosen because it hadn't been used in a while. The A2 was a narrow but well-maintained track, as were most military roads in the North, and the trucks were able to keep up a healthy clip as they rolled to the northwest.

The men of 2 Para had begun their tour of duty in the North not long before and had only recently returned from service with the

Allied occupation forces in West Berlin. For the soldiers, rotating from that mission of standing ready to repel a Warsaw Pact invasion to one of serving as an internal security and counterinsurgency force with Operation *Banner* was quite a change in scenery and operational focus.

Ahead, near the appropriately named Narrow Water Castle, a pair of eyes watched from across the river. The man was as close to the road as you could get to the North and still be in the Republic. He heard, then saw, the convoy approach and readied himself.

There was a turn-out where the road widened briefly. The lead vehicle passed a trailer loaded with straw bales parked along the road. The British commander didn't give it a thought until he felt the thunderclap of the blast and saw the dull gray day ahead illuminated by the flash from behind them. The first lorry driver saw nothing: he was instantly shredded by the shock wave and metal shrapnel traveling at nearly 3,000 meters per second. He was definitely dead, the cab engulfed in flames where he sat, his pelvis welded to the melted seat.

The driver of the Land Rover almost lost control but managed to come to a sliding halt about 60 meters ahead. The blast blew out the rear windows, spraying tiny bits of plastic through the interior, luckily without much damage to the occupants who jumped out to see a scene of utter devastation. The first lorry had been ripped apart and tossed on its side by the force of the blast. Five hundred pounds of ANFO—ammonium nitrate fertilizer mixed with fuel oil and set off with a primer block of plastic explosive—had done its work. Bodies and parts of bodies lay scattered about the burning heap, in the trees, and along the water's edge. There was human detritus on the river; it sank to the bottom or floated with the current down to the sea, no longer of use to its owners.

The second lorry had been far enough behind that it only lost its windshield in the blast. The driver, his face cut to pieces by the flying glass, was covered in blood. He was too stunned to move.

"Get HQ now!" Major Reid yelled at his signaller. "Report and get us a medevac."

The corporal was already on the radio, yelling into the handset because he couldn't hear his voice. He was deaf and would be for the next three days. The wounded from the second lorry were being pulled off the road by the still able-bodied, and the single medic began to triage and treat the wounded as best he could with his meagre supplies.

A few men sat on the road or wandered dazed, but the majority set into action, scanning the surrounding woods and fields, fully expecting to be attacked. A couple of rifle shots were heard, cracks that seemed to come from across the border. The Paras fired back over the river into the woods at two figures. One crumpled to the ground; the other sprinted off into the brush. It became quiet except for the crackle of burning metal, oil, canvas, and flesh, mixed with the shouts of those who took charge in the chaos.

Within fifteen minutes, two helicopters came flying over the scene, the rotor wash making the smoke and bits of hay fly about crazily as if caught up in a whirlpool in the sky. A big Wessex for the wounded and a little Gazelle settled onto the pasture. The Gazelle carried the rapid response force commander from the Queen's Own Highlanders and his radio operator. Jumping from the chopper, Colonel Peters took charge and set up a command post a ways down the road in a gate house that led to a country home. The scene became somewhat settled as he took charge and reeled out a string of orders. His signaller was taking notes and talking on the radio at the same time.

Exactly thirty-two minutes after the first blast, the gate house, now command post, disappeared in a huge fireball. The men inside, including Peters and his signaller, were vaporized as the granite structure was blown apart. Huge stones, turned into projectiles, hammered down on the helicopters. The Gazelle was destroyed and the Wessex took serious damage but managed to get off the ground and away with its precious cargo of wounded. One of Peters' rank epaulets would be found 100 meters away, the only evidence of his death.

The terrorists had guessed correctly that the army would set up there and hid a second bomb—another 800 pounds of ANFO—in milk cans next to the house. Twelve more soldiers were dead. The total was eighteen men. Eighteen British soldiers. Across the water, the man belonging to the eyes behind the binoculars disassembled his remote control, put it into his pouch, climbed onto a bicycle, and rode off down the track, away from the North, away from the carnage, his deadly errand done. He couldn't believe his luck: he'd expected maybe a single vehicle. He too would make a call to report his job accomplished. It was 5:12 p.m., five hours since Mountbatten had died.

***

Fifty kilometers away, the man on the telephone sat back. He was older, late forties, his hair thinning all around but especially on top. As he lowered his glasses, a thin red scar under his left eye became visible. It cut from high on his cheek bone and angled down straight toward his nose as if he'd been cut with a sharp knife, which he had.

He was content; the packages prepared by the engineer had worked. He was sure he would find out soon enough from the press reports what kind of damage they'd done. For the moment he closed his eyes and smiled.

It's a great day. Bloody Sunday is avenged.

But there remained an even bigger enemy to destroy.

2

Kim Becker walked down the hall consciously oblivious to everything and everyone around him. The *International Herald Tribune* he was slapping against his thigh was the indirect source of his anger, and he tossed it onto the communal table in the team-room as he entered with a bit more force than necessary. So much force that Nick Kaiser sloshed the coffee from his cup as he pulled it out of the way. Becker stood facing the map on the back wall with his hands on his hips, fuming.

Fred Lindt, who knew how to read angry team sergeants, broke the tense silence that his fellow teammates had adopted.

"What going on, boss?"

A moment passed as everyone held their breath, fully expecting to be sent on a three-month mission to Norway to learn how to be reindeer muleskinners.

"Bastards," was the only response.

"What happened?" said Stefan Mann.

Kaiser, who had a better grasp of the geopolitical than most and could see the headline on the paper, said, "Ireland?"

"Those bastards killed Mountbatten and they ambushed 2 Para."

"Jesus," said Mann.

"Which bastards?" asked Logan Finch. Finch was reading an intel summary on the *Rote Armee Fraktion* and had difficulty switching subjects sometimes, even if it involved two similar terrorist groups.

"The IRA. I heard a little about it on RIAS, but no details yet," said Kaiser.

Becker turned around, a look on his face somewhere between malevolence and grief. "Around twenty Paras were killed along with five of Mountbatten's family," he said.

"Why the hell did they kill Mountbatten?" Lindt said.

"They've been looking to whack a royal and he must have been an easy target. They killed him in the Republic."

"In Ireland? That's a cheap shot." Mann shook his head trying to grasp the whole complicated picture that was "the Troubles."

"Who in the Paras? Anyone we know?" asked Lindt.

"No names yet. I just hope it wasn't the guys we trained with," Becker said. His face had changed, showing that he had decided on anger.

"What a mess. They are never gonna get their shit together over there," Mann opined.

"The Brits have more experience at colonial policing than most countries, especially with MI5 and the SAS at their disposal," said Becker.

"These things never go well. Look at how things in Kenya and India went," Lindt pointed out.

"Those were different situations," Becker said. "Those people were trying to gain independence."

"And the republicans aren't?" Lindt countered.

"They're in the minority up North."

"Maybe we should offer the Brits our assistance?" said Finch.

"That wouldn't go over well in Washington, I think," said Becker.

"Why not? We do counter-guerrilla warfare." Finch looked about the team-room for support of his new crusade.

Paul Stavros looked up from the newspaper he'd been studying, his deep brown eyes refocusing on his teammates.

"Because it's not our war to fight," he said.

3

The engineer was taking a break after several hours of work and stood in the door of his small cottage sipping his tea. The dawning sun was beginning to cut through the early morning chill and a light mist was rising off the grass. He rarely slept through the night, much preferring to take short catnaps throughout the day. He had spent much of his time studying his collection of unexploded ordnance disposal reports, which gave him ideas on how to design and build bombs that would frustrate the engineers who tried to defuse them. That was how he had come up with the lobster pot bomb—he had read a military report that described how the Viet Cong used an underwater device to destroy bridges during their war with the Americans.

He had a big task ahead and a good concept of how he would put the package together. What he envisioned was complicated. Not only did it need to be effective and deadly, it needed to be difficult to detect and nearly impossible to disarm. The diagramming was almost finished and he was at the point of gathering the necessary materials to build the system. That was always a difficult proposition. He had to acquire everything without leaving a trail. Not only did he wish to evade detection, he didn't want to leave clues about his design as each device was unique. Unlike vanity bombers, he refused to leave tell-tale traces like a bit of spare wire wrapped in a ball as a mark of ownership. His signature was the damage the bomb inflicted on the enemy.

The sun felt warm on his face as he watched it come up over the trees. Suddenly, there was the sharp shatter of breaking porcelain and he felt the teacup go to pieces in his hand. Startled, he looked down at the remains of the cup and then at his chest where a red stain started to spread across his shirt, already soaked with his morning tea. He felt no pain; he didn't feel anything. He leaned on the door frame. When the second bullet hit him, he didn't hear a thing. With its impact, his vision began to blur. He swayed a bit and then fell backwards into his house and onto the floor. Two and a quarter seconds had elapsed.

The small-caliber, high-velocity bullets expanded on contact, their copper jackets blossoming like deadly flowers. They pierced the skin and shredded the organs and blood vessels in their path. The ballistic pressure wave did the rest. Even if someone had been there to help, nothing would have saved him. The destruction to the man's internal organs was massive and he would bleed out in a matter of minutes.

Two figures dressed in drab clothing, carrying empty kit bags, hustled out of the nearby brush and into the cottage. Stepping over the body, their trainers shrouded with surgical covers, their hands with gloves, they took photographs of the scene and began to gather papers, documents, and other interesting things for exploitation, including samples of the engineer's blood and hair. It was all rather quick, but since the engineer had used only paper and pencil in his work, it was simple. Finishing up, they exited the way they had come in, checking that they had left nothing behind. They moved quickly toward the woods where they met a heavily camouflaged sniper team at the edge of the forest, 150 meters away. The two ghillie-suited marksmen picked up their kit and all four scurried off deeper into the woods. They had a rendezvous with a lorry several hundred meters away and then needed to make it across the frontier and back to Ulster and relative safety.

***

The news of the execution took several hours to reach Desmond Reilly. Reilly was the IRA's regional chief and directly responsible for sending men across the border for operations. He had also planned the Mountbatten and Warrenpoint ambushes after receiving his guidance from GHQ—"the Bosses" as he preferred to call them.

Any regret, sadness, or anger he felt about losing a comrade was quickly overshadowed by the implications of what had happened. He was in a quandary. He had tasked the engineer to produce a device for a very important event. It was work that could not be handled by any of the local boys. He sat back and considered his options. Frowning, he returned to the newspapers he devoured every morning when an article jumped out at him. He didn't even read it but the word "Boston" stood out.

He had an idea and an old smuggler friend in the States who might help him find someone who could bring his vision to fruition.

4

Neil Fitzpatrick casually walked into the taverna. It was not far off the beach in Faro, Portugal. He headed toward the alcove in the back that his instructions had described. As he moved, he carefully took in the room's small size and noted the lack of exits other than the way he'd entered. It was a bad location for a meet, but he didn't have an alternative. The IRA man in Boston had told him the time, location, and where his contact would be sitting. The alternate was the same location two hours later—all of which was not very original or clever planning.

Fitzpatrick's impeccably forged passport said he was American, which he was. It also said his last name was Barry, which it wasn't. But Irish he was still. No way to change his DNA that he knew of, not that he wanted to. He had classic Irish features, the legacy of a father who had emigrated from the island and a mother born unto immigrants in America. His face was long and angular; a determined jaw thrust forward seemed to point the way wherever he looked despite the beard that was beginning to fill, and sparkling green eyes signaled humor as well as mischief. He was tall, six feet one, lean with long arms and legs and no more fat on his body than a silver dollar pinched between two fingers. But his hair was his most striking trait. It was long, flowing, and fiery red like Spencer Tracy's, but he didn't like being compared to a former Squid even if the man did have an Academy Award. Unseen, however, was a physical speed and agility that generally only showed itself when he was angered—at which point it was too late for the unfortunate person who precipitated the outburst. Luckily, those occasions were rare.

There were few customers as it was early in the evening and most Portuguese ate much later. In fact, to find an open restaurant at all was difficult. A young couple sat near the front door, foreign tourists who were totally engrossed in themselves. A waiter dressed in a black shirt, black pants, and a long white apron glared at him as he walked past, looking like his break had been rudely and abruptly cut short. Sitting close to the entrance at a small table, a wizened Portuguese man, his face creased by wrinkles and burnt by the sun, studied a tumbler filled with what appeared to be red wine.

Not a threat, Neil thought.

He had seen many bars like this one. In the back alleys of Fayetteville and Lake Charles, one or two in Panama, several near the *Bahnhof* in Frankfurt—they were all much the same: painted and decorated when they opened, then falling into a terminal spiral of deterioration until the owner skipped town or died.

The walls were pale green, or was it faded turquoise? He could see the chipped and blistered paint, ravaged by humidity and years of wear, slowly oxidizing and falling into a chalky pile of dust on the floor. A three-year-old calendar showed the month of *Outubro*; several cheaply framed pictures of places not even remotely related to Faro hung haphazardly. A faded advertising sign for frozen desserts hung above a broken, glass-topped refrigerator. A ceiling fan turned slowly, its base wobbling against the ceiling with each useless rotation of the blades.

It didn't take much to identify his contact. Only one man was near the table that had been described in the plan. Neil didn't speak to him but sat at an adjacent table with his back to the wall. He dropped his *Herald Tribune* onto the table, his left hand lying on top of it. The man looked at him briefly and stood up, carefully shifting a chair in Neil's direction as he moved. A small leather pouch lay on the seat. The man turned and walked toward the front, noisily engaging the waiter to pay his bill while Neil tossed the newspaper over the bag and pulled the chair closer to him.

Long after the contact disappeared, the waiter grabbed the bar's tattered menu and sauntered back to where Neil sat. He flipped the menu onto the table and didn't bother to speak Portuguese. Neil's clothing, hair, and complexion marked him as a foreigner. Not many of his kind had spent much time in Faro, at least not since Napoleon's Irish Legion.

"*Cerveza*," Neil said. It wasn't Portuguese but close enough.

He was neither a wine nor a port drinker and he had no intention of remaining in the restaurant long. Watching the waiter walk back to the front of the shop, Neil gathered the pouch from under the newspaper and stuffed it into his canvas shoulder bag. At the same time, he picked up the paper to cover his movements and catch up on the week-old news.

He had sixteen hours to kill before his flight. His plan involved drinking beer, a dash to the hotel for a nap, and then to the airport with his bags. A flight from Boston straight to Ireland would have been a simpler route, but the boyos were worried that a young American-Irish gentleman traveling alone might pique the security folks' interest. So Faro was chosen as the place to pass the package before continuing the trip.

The security controls in Faro were lax for outbound flights. He didn't expect any trouble with the £50,000 he was now carrying. Dublin might pose a problem, but he had been told that his arrival was expected and hopefully screened by friendly customs agents.

"Just try not to look like a druggie," they said.

He had arrived in Portugal two days earlier and, citing a hotel and the names of "friends" obtained from an Irish-American-owned travel agency in Boston, passed through the border formalities without a hitch. He spent his days at the beach cabanas, drinking and occasionally flirting, but never going over the line. There were plenty of girls to chase, mostly Brits and Germans. But he didn't want to advertise his prowess at charming women, so he held well back. He needed nothing to burden his mind. His long-term track record with women was nothing to speak of anyway. Instead, he spent his time reading the books he had brought with him. A portable Kipling, Tolkien, and two of the *Flashman* series were a small part of his esoteric collection on leadership, strategy, and war.

As he sat in the almost empty taverna, his thoughts went to considering his new employers. He wasn't sure that what he had seen so far of the IRA was very impressive as clandestine organizations went. He knew that most of the IRA's American sympathizers in Boston were wannabe amateur "Plastic Paddies" who would never get into the fight no matter their proclaimed toughness and bravado. He hoped the guys on the island weren't clowns. He'd spent too much time getting to this point, perfecting his skills, working with some of the best in the business, to get tripped up by the stupidity of others. That said, he suspected they weren't that bad. After all, the IRA had sixty years of on-the-job training.

He was still wary; it was his nature. A couple years ago in Berlin, a Turkish businessman—a smuggler actually—told him he had eyes in the back of his head. After Neil threw out a low-ball offer for a stolen Rolex, the Turk accused him of worse.

"*Du bist ein Ganove!*"

"Asshole, I'm no God-damned swindler!"

It all turned out well, for Neil in any event; the Turk didn't notice that the bank notes were counterfeit. Damn fine quality they were, confiscated from an East German intel officer who had been arrested on another op.

Swept back into the present, he checked the time. The Rolex was holding up rather well, he thought. He rustled the newspaper into shape and took a sip of the lousy Portuguese beer and went back to reading. The news looked more or less normal: some foreign prime minister had resigned, unemployment was bad, and the Super Bowl was over.

Who cares.

Nothing appeared very exciting in Ireland at the moment, which was quite fine with Neil. He wanted everything to be normal when he arrived on the Emerald Isle.

5

As Neil had been told, arrival in Dublin wasn't a problem. The lone immigration officer looked at his passport and stamped it without a word. The customs officials sat on the bench and waved him through the checkpoint while they continued to chat. Then he was in the arrivals area where he exchanged some of his cash. That money, along with his carrying fee for the bundle entrusted to him in Portugal, would tide him over for a while. After that he'd have to transfer money from the *Bundespost* account he maintained in Germany.

As he walked through the crowded terminal, he saw a number of *Gardaí* officers. Instead of looking away, he returned their stares with the sure conviction that he belonged where he was, that he had nothing to hide. He was just an Irishman coming home.

Neil walked outside and stopped at the edge of the sidewalk. If he smoked, he would have lit a cigarette and scanned the area but he didn't, so he just stood and looked about with his shoulder bag sitting on top of a well-worn duffel at his feet. He was, more or less, among his people. They spoke his language and many looked like him; some might even support his politics but he didn't dwell on that. It wasn't his first trip to the island. Neil had been here years ago as a young man with his mother, when she returned his father to the home he loved. On that trip, father had been poured from a polished metal urn, a gray cloud of ash whipped away across the green fields where he had been born. Forced to leave Ireland for a crime he'd committed but didn't believe was truly a crime, he had become a refugee. His father always maintained that he'd just done his duty as an Irishman.

Neil was a couple of days early for his meeting. He stood with his jaw confidently set, hair rustled by the breeze, deep green eyes observing. Observing the traffic, the people, the security, and the tension in the air. Feeling none, he relaxed a bit. He too was, after all, not guilty of anything. Yet. He flagged a taxi and headed into the city with nothing more planned than checking out the neighborhood. He'd get acclimatized to his new surroundings before he jumped into anything.

The son was back.

***

Two days later, Neil was bored. He'd played tourist, visited the sites of family memories that he'd been told about but couldn't begin to remember, and done what any operative does when first arrived in country. He studied the maps, cased the routes, memorized the transport system, learned the neighborhoods and where the locals liked to go and where they didn't. It was called area study and it was mandatory if you really wanted to survive an undercover life.

Along the way, a modest amount of beer and maybe a whiskey or two (Irish not Scotch) were consumed as part of the acclimatization process. He wanted to establish his tolerance of the local brews as he knew his drinking abilities would be tested by the locals, intentionally or not.

When contact day came, he felt minimally prepared for action according to his standards, but he knew enough of the city to be able to run a tight counter-surveillance route to the meet site: a pub in the inner city of northern Dublin.

As the sun bedded down in the western sky, cold, gray shadows extended across the streets. Neil walked into the area and saw it wasn't much different from some areas of Southie. The hair went up on the back of his neck. It wasn't so much his training but his life experience that kicked in. He knew he was in a bad area. On this final segment, he walked from the canal along the quay, up Commons, through a park, and then onto Crinan Strand, taking advantage of natural look-back points to quick-check his six. No one of interest was on the street behind or in front of him. Passing a chip shop that seemed to be operated by a Chinese family, the full blast of steam and exhaust smoke that vented out onto the street smacked him forcibly in the face. The smell of frying cod made him hungry after three hours of walking and bussing himself about the town.

Finally, he came to the locale he was looking for and crossed the street with one last scan of his trail. He was still clear as far as he could tell, and it was too dark for anyone to see him when he walked into the pub.

He first thought that it was a lovely place as far as dives went. It didn't smell too bad and there seemed to be a variety of beers on tap. Shelves of hard liquor framed the requisite mirror behind the bar. As his eyes grew accustomed to the dim light, he could see the men in the room were all interested in the newcomer.

Neil walked to the counter where the publican awaited him and asked him for a pint. When it was delivered, he followed up with his parole, "I'm looking for Danny Monahan. Would he be about?"

As he toweled off a glass, the publican nodded his head toward the corner where two gentlemen sat in animated conversation. Between them and Neil were two tables occupied by several watchful pairs of men; behind him were several more. He therefore moved slowly across the room with his beer in one hand and the other hand in open view. He presented himself before the table and waited for acknowledgement. When they looked up at him, he said, "I'm Neil and I'm looking for Danny," and waited.

The man looked the part of a mob heavy. Even while sitting he was coiled and ready for a fight. A large round face, slightly pink from the whiskey he was drinking, stared at Neil intensely.

"You've found him. Sit," he said, motioning to an empty chair. Neil sat while the Irishman regarded him for a long moment before speaking. "So, you've come for the job, have you?"

"I've come to help out if I can. Your friends said you might have a spot for me."

"We might if you're up to it. What made you decide to support us now?"

"I'm Catholic and Irish and I've been supporting the cause for a long time. A portion of my allowance has been coming this way since I was three."

"What's your specialty?"

"I'm an engineer." Neil stayed vague. He was still unsure whom he was talking with.

"So, you build things?"

"Or take them down," he said, "quickly."

Danny nodded. "And I think you have something for me. A pouch with the letter 'M' on it, perhaps?"

"I do." Neil pulled it from inside his leather jacket and dropped it on the table. Danny's description confirmed he was talking to the right person. "I've taken my carrying charge per our agreement. The rest is all there for your widows and orphans fund."

Danny smiled as he hefted the pouch and then slid it over to his companion to put away.

"No need to count it. We know how to find you," Danny said.

"I'm sure you do."

"Well, now," Danny continued, "we'd like to take you to another location to talk more in detail and to determine how you fit in.

You're staying downtown at the Fleet, right? Pretty nice place for a student."

"Former student, plus you're paying for it."

"Whatever, give us your key. We'll collect your stuff because you'll be leaving from here."

"I figured that might be the case. There's not much there, one bag, already packed. I have my important stuff with me."

"A Boy Scout too. Are you always prepared?"

"It comes from my army days. Always expect the unexpected. Now, I hope I can enjoy my beer before we leave."

"Before *you* leave. But, yes, enjoy the ale which never lets you grow old. Of course, none of us may grow old. *Sláinte!*"

"*Sláinte agad-sa,*" Neil responded.

"Ah, you speak our language."

"It's mine too, my friend."

6

The occasion was unusual. The prime minister rarely met personally with the director general of the Security Service to discuss internal problems. The prime minister didn't like to mix with the front-line people, the people who actually got their hands dirty. Normally she dealt with them through the home secretary, who was nevertheless present and quietly listening to his subordinate speak in the high-ceilinged spaces of COBR, the Cabinet Office Briefing Room.

The DG was not a line officer, although he had been at one time. Now he was an administrator, a bureaucrat, at most a dispatcher who directed others to do the dirty things he'd once himself done. Much of his time was spent in his well-appointed office waiting for results. The rest of his time consisted of receiving and delivering status reports and making excuses for why things didn't go the way they should have. Only rarely did anyone in Her Majesty's Government acknowledge their wins.

Director General Davies-Jones began his quickly practiced brief with the bottom line up front.

"The American Embassy legal attaché came to us with information that a former soldier of theirs, an expert in demolitions, may have volunteered for the Provisional IRA," he said.

"And how is this a problem for us?" said the PM.

"We removed one of the Provos' senior bomb-makers from the pitch last autumn and we know they don't have the depth on their team to replace his expertise. That, along with some indications of an upcoming major play, may mean there is a connection." The DG often talked in sports metaphors to cultivate his image as a sportsman, a trait that few who knew him took seriously.

"What else did the Americans say?"

"They know the man left the United States and believe him to be in the Republic or up in Ulster. They want him back."

"They want who back? The soldier?" the PM snapped.

"Yes, they want to get him out of there unharmed and back to the States without him being implicated in any terror activities."

"He's already implicated himself now, hasn't he?" said the home secretary.

"Indeed. What do they want us to do? Coddle some sympathizer, and for what reason?" the PM demanded, irritation punctuating her usual well-enunciated cadence.

"I imagine it's a political thing. I doubt the new US president wants any bad publicity to affect his Irish base. He is Irish, you know."

"I can't imagine one man would be greatly missed, especially if he's tied up with terrorists," said the PM.

"One wouldn't think so, but support for the IRA is big in New England. Besides, the attaché said the ambassador was quite insistent. Apparently, he hinted at holding back on some special assistance if we didn't agree."

"Blackmail, is it?"

"Yes, Ma'am."

"Any ideas?"

"Just one. We put some of our people onto finding and capturing him without a fuss, the biggest problem being that we're not sure where he's located."

"Let me consider this. Thank you, Director." The PM turned toward a white board hung on the wall of the briefing room and stood contemplating some photos pasted to it without really looking at them. Davies-Jones looked at the home secretary who dismissed him with a curt nod of the head. When they were alone, the home secretary approached the PM.

The PM looked at the ceiling intently as she spoke.

"Find this American," she said. "I want you to work with SIS and the army on this, not MI5, cut Davies-Jones and his people out of it. He seems to think his work is some sort of sport and sport usually involves fair play. I don't believe in that. And, for that matter, the secretary of state for Northern Ireland is not to be informed. And last, on no account do I want this matter to go in front of any other members of my cabinet. This must be handled as an extremely sensitive operation."

"Of course, you know these things are very tricky and never go quite as planned," the home secretary said.

The PM turned to her minister and stared at him with a piercing gaze. Her dark blue-gray eyes narrowed. A theatrical pause.

"That's exactly my point. These bastards murdered Lord Mountbatten and eighteen of our boys. I have no wish for any of them to escape justice and that includes anyone who helps them."

The PM paused for a moment, either to ponder the next thing she would say or just for effect, the home secretary wasn't sure.

Then she continued: "So, I want you to tell the Americans we will do all possible to find him. In fact, why don't we invite some of their people to assist in the search. Then, if anything were to go wrong, they could hardly blame us. Are we understood, Home Secretary?"

"Completely, Madam Prime Minister, I understand completely."

7

The water seemed to stand on the side of the steep hill. Paul Stavros had never seen the like before, but here it was doing just that. Another reason to dislike the place. His boots had long since soaked through and he imagined his feet looked like white prunes. A glance at his Seiko Diver told him that it had been just over fifteen hours since he had begun the march, about six since he hit the mid-way point.

A cold rain was falling hard now; the almost-frozen drops, driven sideways by a brutal wind, stung his face. Tight tufts of grass made walking the hills treacherous. You stepped on top of the mounds or between them, but not both. You risked twisting your ankle, which, with a heavy rucksack on your back, was bad. His leg felt fine though; much therapy and rehab had brought him back to peak fitness. He was fit. Not football-player bulky or basketball-player tall as he found out in high school, but strong and long of legs. He found he was well suited for aquatic sports, qualifying as a civilian scuba diver even before he got his driver's license and doing crew with an eight-man scull during his short academic tenure in college. He even contemplated joining the SEALs after seeing a film called *The Men with Green Faces*, but realized he didn't fancy cold water as much as he did dry land. Besides, Special Forces had its own combat diver training. But for the moment, he was thinking about the now.

The previous afternoon, they had tumbled out the rear of a big lorry and stood next to the road looking up a long narrow track. The road sign said Bryn y Fedwen, which matched a tiny spot on his map, but he still had no idea where he was other than somewhere in Wales.

Stavros and the thirteen other candidates were clustered around the jump-off point waiting tensely until their names were called. Each was checked off the list by two SAS cadre who made sure the man's Bergen rucksack weighed 55 pounds. They had to weigh at least that much at the end or it was an inglorious trip home, the so-called RTU or return to unit.

When they finished with Stavros, he heaved the ruck up onto his back in one well-practiced motion and jockeyed it into the most comfortable position. He cradled his L1A1 Self-Loading Rifle in his arms before looking at the men again. One of the Brits checked his watch and nodded his head as he noted the time on the roster.

"Alright mate, off you go then."

He slogged off up the long slope.

It was hours since the start, and there seemed to be more uphills than down. And all the downs were over bad terrain or through thick undergrowth. Maybe he was just choosing bad routes, but there weren't even sheep tracks out here.

Along the way, he ran into a patrol of four already-badged troopers who were taking the same walk just to stay in shape. They had stopped and were sitting by the edge of the woods brewing up their tea. He stopped for a second to chat but moved on again quickly. He didn't want to be drawn into their circle. He had to walk alone, and the more time he spent with them, the more he would delay.

A well-trained team's march dynamic is different from a solo walker's. When one man's energy ebbs, the others sense it and rotate positions to take up the slack, flowing like a skein of geese. He didn't have that luxury; he had to deal with it himself, he was always on point. He had to keep his attention and focus on the end goal and not on taking a break or looking for excuses. There were no excuses out here.

He didn't like tea anyway.

He looked out over the terrain they called the Brecon Beacons. A desolate landscape, not at all inviting at that moment. Visibility was shit. Through breaks in the weather, he saw thin, horizontal streams of mist whipped by the wind sailing over and around the tips of the crags. He rechecked his compass and studied the landscape to choose a route that would get him where he needed to go as quickly and sanely as possible. His map was folded in a square about ten inches across. It was about four inches thick. If he unfolded it all, it was almost as long as he was tall. And he was just short of six feet.

"This is today's walk. Forty miles. Twenty-hour limit." The squadron sergeant major had announced this with a barely concealed smile on his lips. Everyone knew it was the final challenge. They—the candidates and the cadre—were standing in the open bay of an old wooden barracks in Bradbury Lines. "We'll truck you out to the start point and you can get going after we weigh your Bergens."

Stavros watched as the grizzled senior sergeant pointed out the start and end points and then the mid-point while holding the Ordnance Survey map with one hand over his head. The other end touched the ground, but then the sergeant major was short and built like an ox. Not someone to tangle with.

Forty miles straight line, maybe. More like fifty after all the ups, downs, and arounds. The previous walks had been relatively easy, requiring simple navigation and straightforward physical conditioning like the Fan Dance, 24 kilometers of climbing up, over, and down the highest peak in south Wales: Pen-y-Fan. The march he was on now was called, with good reason, the Long Drag. It was about endurance, both physical and mental endurance. The will to succeed had to be absolute and Stavros was having second thoughts.

Tell me again why you thought this was a good idea? he asked himself as his boots continued to soak up more cold water.

Several weeks before, his own sergeant major, Jeff Bergmann, had called him into his office. Bergmann was always a come-straight-to-the-point leader and asked Stavros if he wanted to try out for one of a couple of training slots with the Special Air Service. No guarantees, just a chance. Take a couple of physical tests, make some long walks and, if you're selected, you spend a year with the Squadron, training and participating in their exercises. Only two Americans a year get the chance.

"It would be one hell of a career move," Bergmann had said.

Instead of jumping at the offer like most, Stavros asked, "Why me?"

"Because I have good judgement is why," Bergmann shot back. The sergeant major rolled his cigar back and forth in his fingers before taking a long pull on it. He paused and then slowly exhaled. It was a form of punctuation.

"You're one of the best shooters in the unit, you're in good shape, and young. Too many older guys go but they're not around long enough afterwards to share what they learn. You'll be around for a while. Most importantly, you're a good operator. What you did in Tehran speaks for itself."

Bergmann took another draw off the Montecristo and savored the flavor. He purchased them by the box in East Berlin, cheap.

With a wave of the cigar, he left no option for Stavros when he said, "Now get out of here and get ready. You've got just over a week to prepare yourself."

A stream of smoke followed Stavros out the door.

***

Standing with the rain dripping off his boonie hat, he thought back a couple of hours. On one particularly bad section of the walk he almost regretted accepting Bergmann's challenge, but that was a while ago. Now he was determined to finish and finish well. He shoved the plastic-bagged map back into his jacket, hiked his Bergen rucksack up, and plowed on, a catchy rhythm running endlessly, annoyingly, through his mind,

Half a league, half a league, half a league onward ….

He was wet and cold. It wasn't a question of quitting, but there was always the question of his body continuing to function. Keep moving, keep warm. He leaned forward and was off again. He was alone. He couldn't see any of the other men. There was no encouragement, no hints at what came next, just the bleak landscape and the lure of the finish line.

***

Across the valley, two men stood just inside the dark green protective curtain of the forest called "Half Way" on the maps. One of them had a pair of 10×50 Zeiss binoculars up to his eyes and was watching the distant figure.

"What do you think, Boss?"

Major Reed dropped the binoculars and continued to study the progress of the ant on the far hill.

"He's strong and it looks like he'll make it in good time. His personality is solid. Quiet, but pretty intense. I think I like him."

"He's young," Sergeant Major Andy Wilkins said, ever the contrarian.

"That's what we want. As long as he's technically, tactically proficient, and has stamina. We don't want a guy who appears too military. The others have 'soldier' written all over them."

With a shrug to shake off the cold, Reed turned back into the forest.

"Let's see who makes it to the collection point on time."

8

Neil came out of his sparely furnished room early. He hadn't slept much, out of both curiosity and test anxiety, not that he was really worried. There was coffee on the stove. He poured a cup and drank it black. He wondered whether they had bothered to use a filter as it was strong, bitter, and a bit chewy. The grounds filled about a quarter of the cup, reminding him of Turkish coffee except that it tasted like burnt instant.

He looked out the windows through the gauzy lace of the curtains. Having been warned off going outside for the obvious reasons, he contented himself with scoping out the neighborhood from the only vantage points he had. Neil had determined from the drive time that he was probably about a hundred kilometers from Dublin. It could be closer but not much.

The back door squeaked open and Seamus entered. "About time that you're up. Let's go out to the shed."

Seamus looked to be a countryman. Dressed roughly in wool pants and shirt. Wellington boots beat to hell. He was at home here. All business, not a word of welcome, thought Neil, or even an offer of breakfast. He hadn't eaten much at the bar and he was famished.

"I'm going to need some nourishment before long or I won't be able to function," he said. Seamus ignored him and walked outside and through the grass to another large building, more of a barn than a shed.

It was just after dawn and the moisture on the ground was not even thinking of evaporating despite the sunlight; the air was yet quite cold. Walking into the barn, Neil felt a bit warmer. He stood before a stout man, not short, not tall, mid-forties. He didn't look like a farmer, more a city man wearing a dark green vest buttoned closed with tarnished gold toggles, but he did look like he knew how to use his hands.

"Call me Rourke. I'll be checking your knowledge today with a couple of tests. If you pass, we might be keeping you about."

"If I don't?"

"Then you can enjoy Ireland as a tourist before heading home again."

On the table was an early Sten submachine gun, a Mark II to be specific.

"Take it apart. You've got a minute," Rourke commanded.

Neil picked it up, removed the magazine and cleared the weapon before beginning to tear it down. Almost by muscle memory, he quickly spun off the barrel assembly, removed the skeleton stock, buffer, and cocking handle before emptying the bolt and spring onto the table.

"You want me to disassemble the trigger group too?"

"No, that's good enough. Now make it ready again."

Neil looked at the man and then picked up a nearby trash pail before returning to the table. With a deft movement he swept the small parts into the pail and then dropped the receiver in with them.

"Done," he declared.

"What's that supposed to mean?"

"You wanted it ready. It's ready as it'll ever be. That gun is a piece of shit. I hope you have something else to shoot with."

I'm off to a good start.

32

Rourke was fuming.

"Alright funny man, try this." He whipped a big, ugly submachine gun out from underneath a blanket.

"Ah, we're swimming in antiques. The Irish Sword, a M1928 Thompson, Winston liked these. I think Michael Collins did too, but then his must have been a 1921 model cause he got killed in 1922, didn't he? Brings back memories …."

And he began to hum a tune and broke out into words,

"Where the bayonets flash and the rifles crash, to the echo of the Thompson Gun …."

He paused, enjoying the incredulous looks on the two Irishmen's faces. They were beginning to consider him a madman.

"Catchy tune, eh? So, what do you want me to do with this?"

"Same thing, take it apart." Rourke was clearly irritated.

Neil dropped the magazine on the table and cleared the weapon. He placed the safety and selector switches in their proper positions and flipped the gun over. Pressing a detent, he pulled the frame off the upper receiver. The buffer and spring came out, then the bolt handle, followed by the bolt itself. He placed the parts neatly on the table.

"Bolt and trigger mechanism too?" About forty seconds had elapsed.

"No, that'll do, Now, put it back together."

Reassembly went just as quickly and then Neil went through a function check before setting the weapon back on the table.

"You know I'm not a weapons specialist, right? My specialty is demolitions."

Rourke looked at Neil for a second and shook his head.

"We've got that covered. Come over here."

He turned to a second table that was draped with a cloth and turned on an overhead lamp. Rourke picked up a stack of cards and gave them to Neil.

"Put these in sequence from low order to high."

Neil saw that on each card was written a type of explosive or chemical, ammonium nitrate, RDX, nitroglycerine, dynamite, and TNT among them.

"Some of these are redundant. Dynamite is usually based on nitroglycerine and C4 contains RDX," he said as he laid out the cards based on their explosive power, "and others, like ammonium nitrate, need to be combined with something to be effective as an explosive."

When he finished, the tester checked them against a crib sheet and nodded his head.

"Okay, next thing. Draw a firing circuit with an anti-handling device."

Neil took up a pencil and sketched a battery-powered electrical circuit with several switches, then drew in the symbol for a sensor.

"What's that?" Rourke pointed at the symbol.

"An x-ray sensitive photodiode. If the device is x-rayed, it goes off. Tends to deter the bomb disposal people."

"Will it work?"

"It requires a pretty specialized sensor, which might be difficult to get. A standard light or movement detector would be easier."

Rourke simply said, "Okay, one more." He removed a sheet over a smaller table and revealed a box without a lid. A pair of wires came out of the box and were attached to what looked like a block of explosive.

"Tell me what's right or wrong with this."

Neil looked at the device. The block was dark gray, not the right color to be C4 or Semtex. But it could be some other explosive. He bent over and sniffed at the block.

"Clay. So, it's a dummy." He looked closer at the box. "Are there anti-handling devices?"

"No. It's just a simple bomb."

Neil slowly extracted the blasting cap from the clay and let it rest on the table still connected to the box. "The cap is real though." He moved the clay block away from the cap in spite of himself.

"Only one initiator. It would be better if it was dual primed."

The wires were attached to a copper lead placed in the face of a simple alarm clock and to its metal case. When the hour hand of the clock touched the lead, a connection would be made and the cap would explode. A basic 9-volt battery powered the system.

"The leads on the clock are poorly done, you might get a connection, but probably not. That is, if they don't fall off while you're transporting it. There's no safety switch and where the hell did you get these wires?"

"What are you talking about?"

Neil disconnected the battery and lifted out one of the wires to show Rourke. "This is vintage cloth-wrapped wire, maybe twenty years old."

"So, it still works, doesn't it?"

"Actually, no, it won't," Neil stated matter-of-factly. "Look at the herringbone weave. The 'V' in the pattern should be pointed in the direction the electrical current needs to flow. This is installed backwards; it's impeding the circuit. It won't work!"

"What? Bloody Hell! I didn't know that!" Both the tester and Seamus were leaning in close, staring at the offending wires. Neil stood up straight and watched the two for a moment.

"You guys are new at this, aren't you?" he taunted.

"Whaddaya mean?" Seamus' face was creased with irritation and confusion.

"I just fed you a crock of bullshit, is what. Electrical wires aren't directional; you ate that right up."

Rourke stared at him hard. Neil wasn't sure who he was annoyed with but pressed on regardless.

"Did I pass?"

Rourke allowed a bit of a smile and said, "I think you'll do, lad." Then he dismissed Neil and Seamus with a gruff, "Go get some breakfast."

When they were gone, he picked up the phone and placed a call. Reilly answered only with the last four digits of his phone number and then listened.

"The boy did alright. I think he's got what we need."

Reilly was pleased. His plan could go forward and he was beginning to weave a bit of extra web into it. As he was spinning his thoughts, he reminded himself to send a thank-you gift to his friend in Boston.

9

Stavros was tired but fully alert as he walked towards the intersection of two tracks in the grass. He saw a big Bedford lorry in dark green and black NATO camouflage parked near the tree line in front of him. A couple of men clustered around it talking and paid him no attention. They were in clean uniforms and sand-colored berets so he deduced they were the reception party. No one with a rucksack was nearby. He plunged forward to the checkpoint and called out his codename when he was close. Only then did the troopers deign to take notice. One grabbed a clipboard off the truck's wing and glanced at it while rustling through the pages.

"Drop your Bergen, Yank." He continued to stare at the papers before finally saying, "Get your map out. Prepare to copy the coordinates for your next leg."

Stavros deflated on the inside. This was supposed to be his end point. He should have known the previous controller's comment was a lie. He dropped his ruck and copied down the new location while looking at the map to see where it was. It was about eight clicks away to the south over more rough terrain.

"I have it."

"Let me see your plot." The trooper checked his work and nodded. "Any questions?"

"No."

"Alright then, no duff. Walk on."

Stavros picked up his rucksack and hefted it into a comfortable position and then, cradling his rifle, he turned to go. Redundant, but checking to make sure, he asked, "I'm good to go, then?"

"Yes, get on with it."

Stavros plodded down the track following his compass shot and headed for the point where his track headed off up another hill. He figured it would take him around two hours, less if he could keep up a good pace. Arrival would be just before nightfall. The track swept left and disappeared into the trees. He planned to get off of it and continue straight on into the woods. As he came even with the turn in the road, he glanced to the side and saw the same stocky sergeant major who'd given the instructions back at the base before the start.

The distant figure whistled and waved Stavros over before turning toward a small building half concealed in the trees just off the track. With relief, Stavros recognized he had just been subjected to a ruse. Just when you think it's over, you get hit with another trial. Some just lose heart and quit. The determined ones continue on and find out it was a trick, as he just did.

Stavros was walking toward the building when a door opened and two more men came out. He could see that one was an officer, he wasn't sure what rank, but from this distance he could see a single device on each shoulder. That meant either lieutenant or major. The man was older, must be a major.

They stood waiting for him and when he reached them, the major told him to drop his pack, which he was happy to do.

"Well done, Sergeant!" The sergeant major reached out and shook Stavros' hand. "That's it, you're finished."

Almost too tired to talk, Stavros exhaled with no small amount of relief. *You got that right.*

"A nice walk in the woods." He managed the words and smiled for the first time in a day.

The major shook his hand as well.

"Drop your kit and rifle here and come with us." The major put his hand on Stavros' shoulder and guided him to a dark green Land Rover sitting behind the building. He could see there was another man sitting in the back seat. The rear door was open and the major guided him to it. He climbed in while the other two got in the front seats.

Stavros was surprised when he saw the man's face. "Sergeant Major!"

"Well done, Paul," he said, as he too shook his hand.

Stavros knew something was up.

"I didn't expect to see you here," was all he could muster.

"I imagine you didn't," Bergmann replied, "but we have some pretty important things to discuss before you continue."

Bergmann gestured to the front seat. "This is Major Reed, commander of 'A' Squadron, and Regimental Sergeant Major Andy Wilkins. I think they should give you the verdict."

The truck lurched forward as the sergeant major started the engine and drove them down the track toward parts unknown.

Reed turned in his seat to look straight at Stavros. "You did a good job on all the tests. We'd like you to serve with us, but what we have in mind requires you to volunteer. And then do a bit more training."

Stavros was a little puzzled and said so. "I thought my trying out was my volunteer statement?"

"It was, partially, at least for the selection bit. But there's another piece that we couldn't discuss until we knew you were in." Reed handed the conversation back. "Jeff?"

Bergmann took a moment before he spoke, maybe for dramatic effect, maybe just because the subject was sensitive.

"Remember Fitzpatrick?" he said.

"You mean Neil? Of course, we were on the same team. Damn, what has he done now?" A light came on when Fitzpatrick's name was mentioned. Stavros never did completely understand why Neil had decided a college degree was so important.

"Hopefully nothing yet, but what I am about to say stays with us. Whether you accept this offer or not, it is a matter of national security. Our involvement was directed by JCS and it's classified. Understood?"

"Yes, Sergeant Major. I understand."

"Good. Now, Neil was planning to go back to school but he didn't. Seems he returned to New York and got diverted somehow. The FBI was surveilling some Irish Aid Society members in Boston when Neil came up on their radar. He was seen in a bar with a known weapons smuggler who's tied to the IRA. The Bureau started a trace but he disappeared off their scope faster than usual, despite the fact that the FBI had the Society well penetrated. It was almost as if he had experience at eluding surveillance … obviously, we trained him well." Bergmann had mixed feelings about that. On one hand, one of his soldiers was being sought by the Bureau; on the other, Neil had eluded them on their home turf.

He continued, "Then an informant tells the Bureau that a 'Green Beret' is going to Ireland to help train the Provisionals. One thing leads to another and they end up tracking Neil to Portugal where they lose him again. And he probably is using a fake passport but they don't have the details. That was a couple of months ago. They think he's either in the Republic or in Northern Ireland."

"Christ." Stavros stared out the window as the trees whizzed by, a blur of dark green. He was putting together the information and its implications. He knew Neil to be passionate about "the cause"—he had been perpetually in an argument with Ewen McKay, the unit's only expat Scot, about Ireland—but he never would have thought Neil would personally get into the fight.

He had seen Neil taunt Ewen and he was good at it, which drove the Scot crazy. Stavros remembered the arguments, which usually started with something like, "You and your damned loyalists."

"What are you talking about?" Ewen would exclaim, turning a predictable crimson color, which for a guy with white hair was a memorable sight.

Ewen always yelled. He never spoke softly when he drank, which was often and quite usual. The bar would go quiet for a moment as everyone looked at the two. Then, slowly, the raucous roar returned.

"The loyalists and your army are oppressing and murdering the Irish!"

"They're not Irish, they're *fooking* British!" Ewen would yell.

"You're not British! You're a God-damned Jock!" Neil would retort.

Neil looked like he was ready to kill, but it was an act. He would just smile as Ewen spun into a rage. Neil had more self-control, and shortly thereafter, his nemesis would fall asleep in a corner.

Turning back to Bergmann, Stavros asked, "Where do I come in?"

"We want you to help find Neil so we can bring him back. Nothing else. Major Reed will fill you in on the operational details but I have to be sure you're willing to volunteer to help. The question is: Will you volunteer to conduct a clandestine surveillance operation in Northern Ireland and the Republic of Ireland to find Fitzpatrick?"

"No disrespect, Sergeant Major, but wasn't there a specific reason you chose me for this?"

"Everything I said stands, but you know Neil better than most. Handing the Brits a photo wouldn't do it. You know what he looks like, how he thinks, and what he's capable of better than most."

Stavros did know Neil, just as Neil knew him. They were friends, had drunk far too many beers and fired too many rounds down range together not to know each other.

"And when I find him?"

"He'll be apprehended if he's in Ulster. If he's in the South, the US government will ask the Irish government to extradite him."

"And if he resists?"

Reed chipped in, "You don't have to worry. First, we don't want you to confront him, just spot him for us. Second, Her Majesty's Government has agreed not to treat him as a terrorist. We'll arrest him and deport him. End of story."

Bergmann continued, "We have set up direct liaison with the British through their Special Forces Headquarters. The embassy's army attaché and the FBI Legat in London will pass any information to you through that connection. On the ground, Major Reed's people will maintain contact with you. Otherwise you'll be acting totally independently."

"No Agency folks?"

"No, they don't want to get involved because Neil's an American and they don't work in Northern Ireland. Besides, the Bureau has better contacts with Special Branch and MI5."

"Good. After Iran, I don't much like dealing with the Agency anyway. What are my ROE?"

"None, other than you can defend yourself if threatened but don't do anything stupid. You won't be armed—at least not initially. No offensive action; you're going in as a civilian but we'll give you a new identity. If you go into the Republic, we won't have much coverage on you, but there's always the embassy if you need help. Just let us know where you are."

"I think I heard that in a movie once," Stavros said. "'You're on your own, son!'" He paused. "I imagine there's nothing for me to sign?"

"Good call. As far as anyone knows, you're off training with the SAS somewhere."

"And our other guys?"

Reed jumped in again, "One's off to Belize for a couple of months and the other is going back to Berlin."

"There'll be a bit of jealousy back home, but that's normal," Bergmann added.

"If they only knew. Picking off leeches in the jungle or chasing angry leprechauns," Stavros said.

He stared out the window while mulling things over. It was one thing to be training with the SAS and another to actually be going into action with them in a war that wasn't exactly his to worry about. Before he met Neil and Ewen he had known little about the Troubles or the Irish. Years ago *The Quiet Man* introduced him to Hollywood's idea of the Emerald Isle, fake accents and all. He had never heard of the Black and Tans, Michael Collins, or much else Irish besides Guinness. Or leprechauns.

Now he knew too much, especially after training a bit with 2 Para back when they were doing their rotation through Berlin. He had listened to them bitch about Ireland while, ironically enough, drinking with them at the Irish pub in the Europa-Center. He was saddened when he heard the reports of Warrenpoint: a couple of those men were his friends.

Neil and Ewen's nightly debates in the local *Kneipe* left Stavros with the impression that Ireland was another nearly intractable insurgency. It reminded him of something his Vietnam veteran buddies said: "We were fighting the long defeat." True enough, but then, he didn't sign up thinking he would be able to pick and choose his conflicts. The "Troubles" were an issue that truly didn't affect Americans unless they were of Irish descent. Even then, most Irish-Americans didn't have a clue what it was all about. But one of his comrades was involved, which superseded all politics or national insanities. His Greek-American heritage would make him a stranger there, a trait that could be a benefit; he would have no need of affiliation or allegiance to the country, its religions, or people.

Finally, there was the fact that this would be a live mission and he would be operating independently. Although he loved his team, he preferred being a singleton and working alone. He also admitted to looking forward to the adrenaline rush that would come with working undercover and be a welcome escape from the routine. He had already planned on being away from Berlin for a while. The city wouldn't miss him, but Sarah might still complain.

That's what relationships are all about. He'd just have to convince her it was all part of the master plan.

Decision made, he turned back to Bergmann. "OK, I'm in, Sergeant Major. You did say this would be good for my career … that is, if I come back alive."

"There you go." Wilkins laughed.

Stavros had doubts.

Suspension bouncing and tires squealing, the Land Rover broke out of the forest and onto the paved country lane. Wilkins pointed them back toward Hereford.

10

Inside the plushly appointed room, the older man worked behind his massive wooden desk. The term "work" was somewhat subjective as he was the senior officer of a well-known, but entirely undeclared office of Her Majesty's Government that kept its offices in a building known as Century House, a location unknown to anyone in London except taxi drivers and the KGB. The man's role was simple: he reviewed the ongoing antics of his little band of operatives, approved the projects he liked, closed down those he believed to be a waste of time and resources, and in his spare moments thought up diabolical projects to thwart the enemies of the realm, which unfortunately were myriad. He also drank single-malt whiskey.

He was distinguished looking. He wore an impeccably tailored, dark blue tropical worsted suit, with a medium blue, short-sleeved, sea island cotton shirt (he hated dirty cuffs), black casual shoes (and abhorred laces, so dangerous), a thin black grenadine silk tie, and a Rolex Oyster Perpetual watch to top it off. The tailoring complemented his physique, which was fairly good for a fifty-eight-year-old bureaucrat. He hadn't always been bound to an office, but few people knew his full background, which some hinted was military while others spoke of postings in far-flung reaches of the Empire. In any event, his records had either been expunged or disappeared long ago. He was known by the single initial "C" with which he signed all his official correspondence in green ink, a practice that harkened back to the outfit's first director.

"C" placed the single sheet of water-soluble onionskin that he had been reading down on the desktop and thought for a moment. The paper carried the return address of Number 10 and was stamped MOST SECRET. He tapped his pipe out in the ashtray and began to refill it with a tobacco mixture that had no need of flame to be aromatic. He lit it anyway and sat back in the leather chair to savor the moment. The smoke curled about him, but he hardly noticed.

He pushed a button on his desk. Despite the door's tufted-leather soundproofing, the distinct sound of scurrying, rat-like creatures could be heard on the far side. A head belonging to one of the director's support staff poked in.

"Yes, sir?"

"Lionel, come and take a message."

Lionel trod lightly across the carpet like he was afraid he would leave a footprint. Rumor had it that the huge blue and white silk Isfahan was a prize of some long-forgotten expedition of the Great Game but no one was quite sure how it made its way to England; maybe on the back of a Bactrian camel and over the steppes of Central Asia. Lionel took up his position in front of the desk and readied his pen and notebook. He wore the look of a dedicated but downtrodden civil servant who aspired to more than he was capable of physically or mentally.

"This is to go exclusively to ARGON."

"Belfast, then," Lionel said.

"Lionel, have you always been such an idiot? That's why we have codenames. Codenames hide what, who, or where we are talking about, so we don't have to say them out loud. You're lucky this is a secure facility and that your father is a friend of mine. Now just take the message and get it there via secure link. Right?"

46

"Yes, sir. Sorry, sir."

"Take this down: 'As of today, you have complete freedom to conduct all necessary actions in your assigned territory or the adjacent state to eliminate the QUEST threat to the Crown. Recommend use of OUTSIDER to accomplish the task, especially with regard to QUEST's facilitators. Final disposition of OUTSIDER and QUEST et al are left to your discretion and best judgement.' That's it. Read it back."

Lionel read the message back succinctly. He was, after all, well trained to take notes.

"But sir, may I ask what or who are OUTSIDER and QUEST?"

"C" drew on his pipe and contemplated his dim-witted assistant for a moment as he slowly exhaled the blue-gray smoke. School-chum connections aside, he decided Lionel had his uses.

"Have you forgotten what I said about codenames?" Without allowing Lionel to answer, he silently chuckled at the thought that OUTSIDER was an American they were using to find QUEST, another American. Instead all he said was, "Just give it the usual 'BIGOT' and 'Destroy after reading' caveats and get it off right away."

Lionel was no clearer on the meaning of the message than before but nodded his head and disappeared off to the communications center code room with a mumbled, "Right away, sir."

11

When operational approval came down from London, Sergeant Major Wilkins turned Stavros over to Captain Rhys Brown at the Headquarters building on Bradbury Lines. Brown, a very relaxed officer, had started out at the bottom and worked his way up. Simply put, he lacked the ego most officers carried in their luggage.

Stavros dressed in British Army fatigues with a wool commando sweater but no insignia. No one could decide what headgear he should wear, so he went without. No one else wore their beret around the compound anyway and, besides, the sergeants major knew who he was and ignored his infractions, especially his overly long, curly brown hair.

They had just finished discussing the outlines of the mission when the door opened and a young woman walked in. Stavros saw a hard-edged female who had crafted herself into a dangerous weapon, not the attractive woman she was. She was wearing worn jeans with the thick-soled combat boots that the punkers in London loved.

Doc Martens, he remembered.

A black leather jacket on top of a dark sweater added to a picture that said "keep away." Most striking was her brown hair. It was short and spiky with blonde tips.

At least it's not purple.

Brown made the introductions: "This is Hunter. She'll be your primary contact."

In his secondary role as dispatch officer, Brown had to assemble the moving parts of the operation. He would soon believe he was herding cats.

Hunter didn't move. She looked at Stavros with her brilliant blue eyes as if she was assessing him with hostile intent.

Stavros stood up. "I'm Paul."

His outstretched hand went unacknowledged so he dropped it back to his side and turned to Brown. Stavros had never worked with a woman before, but he was familiar with being played off and he felt confused by Hunter's obvious animus.

"How's this supposed to work again?" he asked.

"You two need to develop a contact plan before you go in. Hunter will already be on the ground. She'll deploy back into the area a couple days before you go in. What do you think? How will you be able to connect?"

"I'm working as a freelance journalist," Stavros began. "How would we get together? What's her cover for being there?"

"Hunter?" Brown tried to push her, knowing full well he had little control over what might happen next.

"I don't have a specific story. I use whatever makes sense at the time. I don't get into details."

Stavros wasn't fully clued into how Brown's section operated, but he did know a solid cover was needed if you wanted to survive long in hostile territory.

"Where do you live?" he asked.

She glared at Stavros for intruding into her space. "At our team house with my section. It's a secure facility."

"So if you're followed home, everyone knows who you work for?"

"I don't get followed; our operating procedures make sure of that."

49

There was a short pause as Stavros processed her answers and the person in front of him. *She's a hard case*, he decided and then pushed forward, probing with his questions.

"OK. So, if the IRA suspects something then loses you a couple times they might wonder who you are?" Stavros was digging deep and expected the reaction.

"I told you, our methods cover all that. You'll see soon enough."

Frustrated, he paused and tried a calmer voice. "Where do you meet your contacts?"

"Usually quick meetings in out-of-the-way places: parks, trails, and the like. I'll tell you when we are to meet."

"What if we need to talk over operations, maybe have a longer conversation. You ever meet in a pub or a cafe?"

"Short meetings. I call the shots."

The tension returned, although it had never really left. It was evident in Stavros' tone.

"That won't work. I need to meet as soon as I have information, not wait for a schedule."

Hunter's dander was up; her hands went to her hips, her eyes narrowed. "Boss, who's running this thing?"

Brown was trying his best to be diplomatic. "This is a joint op. You two are partners and have to figure it out together."

Hunter, like a cat tiring of the game, spoke first. "So you want to meet me in a pub? We don't do that—it's the kiss of death for an informant."

"I am not an informant."

"Maybe not, but you don't know the environment."

"I'll figure it out quick enough. I've worked in some pretty difficult areas."

"Right, but you don't have time to figure it out, and I already know it."

Stavros let his anger slip. "And I'm supposed to trust your judgement?" He pointedly looked her up and down dismissively.

Hunter saw his look and her well-hardened shell closed down; her face flushed red.

"Why is it that every damn male of the species questions my capabilities based on what I'm wearing or the color of my hair? Yank, you have no idea who you're dealing with and where we're going. You're gonna either listen to me or I'll drop you like a hot potato." Hunter spun on her heel and walked out, slamming the door hard.

That went well, thought Stavros. What had he failed to see when she came through the door? What had he said to set her off? He doubted he'd ever understand the female of the species.

Brown hung his head for a moment. "Do you always piss off your mates like that?"

"Sorry about that, but she lost me at the handshake. She seemed too sure of herself and has a very hard edge about her—she stands out by choosing to look like a member of the fringe. People won't think she's military, but they'll remember her. She should look plain vanilla like every other normal person if she doesn't want to stand out. Most importantly, I need to know whether she's going to get me killed. I've worked with guys who had that same 'I am a badass' attitude. They can be dangerous."

"Vanilla … never heard that one before." Brown paused and then admitted, "She is intense, but we don't recruit Jane Austen debutantes. And she probably thinks the same of you, just another hot-shot American."

"I'd settle for Miss Moneypenny or, better yet, Emma Peel."

"Emma Peel is not vanilla. More importantly, John Steed knows how to work with her personality. They understand each other. You need to do the same with Hunter."

"Yeah, I get it." Stavros considered his options before continuing. "I may have been a bit hasty with my judgement."

"You think?" Brown admonished. He was not unsympathetic, but he knew effort was required to hold a team together.

"I get it," Stavros said, his voice harsh, a bit abrupt. He paused, thinking. "Sorry, Boss. I have to figure out how to make this relationship work. You told her about my background?"

"She's wary and a bit jaded. Since she got here she's put up with a lot of guys who think she's just a bit of fluff. That's why she doesn't want to work with you. You're an unknown and unproven as far as she's concerned. We've got a ways to go before all our male operators get that."

It was Rhys' turn to pause for a moment before continuing.

"She's not fluff, she's a good operator. You need her more than she needs you."

"Understood, I need a good teammate," Stavros said.

"I think you're going to have a wee bit of work to do there."

12

Stavros reflected on his situation as he stared at the off-white-washed walls of his barracks room without really seeing them. He knew that he was not the smoothest operator with women and Hunter's reaction to his outburst had generally confirmed that. It also wasn't the best way to build team solidarity. His first work day with the Brits was not going the way he would have liked.

After the Tehran mission, he'd visited his girlfriend, Sarah Rohan, who was in the midst of her own training at a place in Virginia called the Farm. It was only through the ministrations of his contacts within the Agency that she was set free from training to meet him during his short visit. It wasn't that difficult to break her loose. With her background, languages, and street experience, the graduation certificate with her name on it was already printed and waiting. Not to mention that Stavros' new friends were two of the most senior officers in the outfit.

They had spent the first day in the nearby village, wandering about the places that Sarah knew like the back of her hand. Which was just as well because she couldn't see her hand, it being tightly entwined in his.

As they walked down a cobblestone paved street, Stavros took in the sights and sounds without a word. He read the heritage signs on the old and very old buildings that remained where they had stood for hundreds of years. Rambling around the city like tourists, Stavros felt his muscles relax. Tonight he wouldn't sleep with one eye open.

It put him back in touch with what he considered the real world. Although he liked Berlin, living and working in that isolated outpost was never normal and his last missions had emphasized that. Sarah sensed his mood and moved silently in tandem with him.

Finally, Stavros spoke. "I'm hungry. Wanna find a place to eat?"

"I see you are back with me and, yes. There's a place up the road a bit," she said. They walked on.

"What are you thinking?" she asked.

"A little bit of everything. I realized I've missed the States a lot. For the most part, everything is calmer, more understandable here. The rest of the world is a bit crazy."

"So I've noticed. What else?"

He stopped and turned to Sarah. "I missed you a lot."

"That's good to hear. All the time or just when things were bad?"

"When I had time to think and sometimes when I didn't. Did you miss me?"

"Hardly ever." She looked up into his dark brown eyes and smiled coyly.

He wondered if he was being played but then she pulled him close and kissed him full on the lips. A shiver climbed up his spine as his synapses fired in rapid order. His brain was dumping chemicals into his bloodstream and the fireworks began. It was just like the first time he kissed her all over again.

Nothing he felt about Sarah had changed. Nothing.

Several seconds later, she pushed him away, a demure but all-knowing look on her face.

"Let's go," she said, dragging her somewhat dazed partner down York Street. They jumped up the stairs into a place called Rampell's. Anyone who saw them had no doubt they were a pair.

Rampell's was an old colonial tavern that had seen much history, tapped many barrels of liquid courage, and plated many meals for the local population and, more recently, tourists.

The woman at the front showed them through the main room and seated them on the veranda. The evening was pleasant; the oppressive heat of the South would come later in the year. The table stood alone, far enough away from the bustle but close enough not to be forgotten by the staff. Seeing Stavros' questioning look, Sarah explained. "The woman who owns the place is a friend and I knew we were coming here."

"Recruiting assets already?"

"Isn't that what life is about? A little quid pro quo and you're set."

"What did you give?"

"I sent them some business and made sure they knew it came from me. Didn't cost me a dime."

An effeminate waiter, historically outfitted in leather breeches, long white socks, a dark red vest embroidered in gold over a linen, balloon-sleeved, band-collar shirt, took their order after Sarah interrupted his prepared monologue on the famous guests that had been served in the establishment.

Stavros watched the waiter retreat with their order, then asked, "Should you have told him that you're a relative of the Marquis de Lafayette?"

"Why not? It's the same story I gave the owner. I even have proof."

"What proof?"

"One of the technicians at the Farm helped me forge a parchment that looks vintage. I wrote it in old French script so no one can read it, but I told her it's a letter from Lafayette to his cousin, who was my great, great grandmother."

"I thought your family left France in the seventeenth century."

"They did, but I forgot to mention that."

The tavern was a rustic affair. A small wood fire in a big stone fireplace in the corner of the veranda threw light across the floor while candles burned on each table. The light was so dim that it was possible to sit back and disappear into the dark. Stavros didn't want to disappear; he leaned in to look at Sarah closely in the flickering candlelight, finding the things he had remembered of her and missed while they were apart. Her dark, coffee-brown hair, dark, mysterious eyes. And there were things he hadn't noticed before, but now did. Like how her mouth curved up slightly at the ends, giving her a subtle smile … unless she was pissed off. There was no mistaking her mood then.

She wore no lipstick, no eyeliner, no anything; she'd stopped wearing it altogether in training. She said she didn't want to look fashionable for the instructors or the students anyway. One of the instructors—a misogynistic Ivy Leaguer, long retired from the field—had made the mistake of criticizing her lack of make-up.

"It's unprofessional," he said.

"Why don't you wear it then?" she had inquired.

The challenge was dropped and conversation went downhill from there, but her class standing didn't suffer.

Dinner came. Crab soup followed by a seafood muddle for Sarah, while Stavros stuck with something he knew, clam chowder and grilled brochettes of shrimp, scallops, and swordfish. When he wasn't watching Sarah eat, he scanned the faces of the couples and families who filled the tables around them. He assessed them as he often did when he was in public; they were ordinary people who had no clue that he and Sarah were anything other than a young couple and probably didn't care.

Sarah stopped and put her utensils down on the plate at four and seven; a theatrical pause, it seemed. She swirled her wine, a dry white Sémillon Graves, and watched Stavros as he looked around.

"Are you happy to be back? You seemed a bit tense today. At least until a few minutes ago."

"Yes, very much so. I was thinking that I'm always happy to be home after a mission is over."

"I'm beginning to understand that now. The other students are all stressed out but most of them haven't experienced anything close to what you or even what I have. For me, it's a vacation compared to Berlin or Prague."

"Or Iran." He almost kicked himself for bringing it up.

"I read everything I could about the raid and the accident at Desert One. It sounded terrible, but you weren't there at the crash were you?"

Her face betrayed nothing, yet she had stated the fact with such assurance that she must know, Stavros thought.

"Your friend Hans told me," she said. "He said he drove down with you and told me a bit about the operation."

"He said he was writing an after-action report. How did you meet him?"

"He talked to a few of the army people a couple of days ago. He pulled me aside and told me that you two worked together there. I remembered seeing him in Berlin."

"Anything else?"

"Just that your part was very difficult but you pulled it off."

He took a bigger drink. He had tried not to think about the Iran mission much since he left Turkey. It was his first solo tasking and he had stuck parts away in a memory closet. He wasn't ready to open that door yet.

"It was kinda hairy at times, but I learned a lot. There were moments," he said.

"That's enough, say no more. You came back and that's all I wanted. But what happens next?"

"Back to Berlin to finish my tour and then I was hoping to get a job near you."

"Funny you say that. I may be headed up north to a new unit that Hans told us about. He wants to talk to you too."

"He told you all this?"

"He kinda wanted me to recruit you first."

Sarah avoided his eyes as she dove back into her food while Stavros processed the news.

"What is it for?"

"I don't know much, but it's new and it's about doing intel work for special operations."

"That shit-head. He didn't say a thing on the way down here."

"Like I said, he wanted me to do the dirty work."

"Does it have a name? Where up north?"

"He didn't tell us the name. It's in Vermont. A place they've nicknamed Camp Nitrocellulose."

Stavros sat back, realizing that Sarah had just pitched him.

"So, is this dinner a recruitment or what?" A trace of anger laced his voice.

"Kinda. It's a two-phase thing, one part is work, the other isn't."

"What's the second?" He left the "it better be good" unsaid.

"The second part is about us. I wondered if you might want to team up—a two-person team—just you and me."

"For work?"

"More for play, I hope."

Stavros paused and fell back into Sarah's eyes. He had been pitched, just not how he expected.

"*Se agapó*," he said.

"What's that mean?"

"It's something you should learn before you meet my mom."

They stared at each other for a long moment. Stavros saw golden flecks in her eyes he hadn't seen before, then realized it was reflections of the dancing candlelight. Sarah touched his check gently and a sizzle of electricity coursed down from his brain, lighting up his senses.

True to form, the waiter appeared to interrupt the moment.

"How about some dessert?" he said.

"No." Sarah's voice was firm, but as she looked at Stavros, her eyes softened. "Let's get out of here."

"I thought you said you wanted dessert?" said Stavros.

"I do, but they don't serve what I want."

"What's that?"

"Strawberries, crème anglaise, and you."

13

The next morning in Bradbury Lines after several dreams of Sarah, Stavros revisited the plea he intended to give Hunter. He knew that sometimes it was necessary to prevaricate to succeed. But first, he would have to grovel.

As he approached Hunter in the open quadrangle, he saw she was talking with another guy in civilian clothes. He could see she was watching him walk toward her. He did a quick assessment of her companion. He looked like a junior officer, fit but not SAS, too clean-cut, more an intel type.

He stopped just out of Hunter's reach: "Hi." She just stared at him.

"I wanted to apologize. I was baiting you and I went overboard."

"It's alright," Hunter said to her companion. After he moved off, she turned to Stavros while she field stripped the cigarette she'd been smoking.

"You did. Go on, Yank."

"I prefer Paul, but whatever. I think you are not an easy person to know, but I want to work with you. This job is important to me. The guy we're looking for was my friend and I want to get him out."

"It was his choice. He's gone over to the wrong side. He has to live with the consequences."

"We'd kinda like the consequences to go our way. If he gets killed, the paperwork would be tremendous. Not to mention the bad PR for both the UK and the US."

"Like I said, it's his choice. You think he's worth it?"

Stavros stared at her for a minute, not sure if she understood what he felt. "He's a brother. He's worth it."

She didn't speak but left a gap for him to fill.

"Listen, I know you have your way of doing things and I can handle that. I know your background, I've done the same. So has Neil. I am supposed to give you guys the edge because of that. But I need your help. Tell me what you want from me."

"Meet me here tomorrow morning at eight. We have things to sort out." With that, she turned and walked away.

Stavros watched her disappear into another building and then turned to see Captain Brown watching him. They met halfway.

"At least she didn't kick you in the bollocks."

"I was waiting for that. She may have decided she's stuck with me, sir."

"She *is* stuck with you. And call me Rhys. We're not much on formalities here."

"Or anything else that's shiny. That's good. That's why I got away from the regular army," Stavros said.

"Let's go and see the boss. He'll be wanting an update on how your courtship is going."

Stavros laughed, "I'm going to say we're at the divorce stage right now."

As they walked, Stavros asked questions. He wanted and needed to know more about the group he was to be working with.

"How did you get involved with this outfit?"

"Very simple, really. I wanted to be a Para and then one thing led to another. When I was a sergeant, I did selection and was badged. I served a couple of years as a trooper and when I had the

61

opportunity to become an officer, I took it. I was commissioned as an intelligence officer and was asked to come back to work on this project. And now I'm the commander."

"What is 'this project,' if I may ask?"

"Since you're going to be with us, I can tell you. But I have to warn you, just like your unit, our existence is classified."

"Understood."

"When the Regiment first got involved in Northern Ireland, it had to rely on its own personnel to conduct close surveillance of targets. When the load got too much for the operational tempo, they began to use folks from outside the unit to do the work, but they weren't up to doing everything quite as we wanted it done. So, we organized our own internal section—it's named the Element—and, eventually, we reached company strength and have a full complement of operators. They go through selection and are trained in all the esoteric skills needed for the work: surveillance skills, photography, driving, fieldcraft, clandestine entry, shooting—not quite to our counterterror Pagoda Troop standards—and most importantly, close target reconnaissance. And we're more diverse as you've noted with Hunter."

"Who handles the training?"

"The squadron does the hard skills, then specialists handle most of the technical subjects, locks, photography, things like that. MI5 helps out from time to time especially on exercises. We're starting to use our own instructors now that we've been at it awhile."

"Similar to us then, except all of our folks come from inside. Everyone is fully qualified and then our unit-specific training kicks in. I imagine most all your work is in the North?"

"Actually, we call it Ulster, and right now, all of our ops are there. We might expand our operations to other parts of the world if the need arises and we can convince the brass we won't bugger it up."

Arriving at Major Reed's office, Brown rapped on the door frame. Seeing the commander immersed in reading, he motioned for

Stavros to follow him, walked into the room, and waited in front of the desk.

Finally, the major looked up. "How's it coming then?" The question was directed at Stavros.

"Not too bad, sir, except that I have already alienated my partner."

Reed looked to Brown, who simply said, "Hunter." Her name conveyed the story well enough.

Reed laughed. "There's always some tension when new guys come in. Especially foreigners, even if you are a cousin. There is suspicion until proved otherwise."

"So I am finding out. We've agreed to continue on and will do our first sessions together tomorrow. We shall see."

"I'm confident you'll work it out. Our women have had some difficulties being accepted by more than a few of the men of the Regiment. I suspect she wants you to know she can handle herself. That said, she knows you're an integral part of the team."

Changing subjects, Reed gestured toward a map of Ireland.

"We've had some reports from Stormont that indicate the nationalists may be planning something big. Nothing specific yet, but we took out one of the IRA's senior bomb-makers a while back and the evidence we pulled out of the site showed he was working on some very sophisticated bombs that might have been intended for something special. It might be that your friend was recruited and brought over for this operation as a result of our success."

"What's Stormont?" Stavros asked.

"MI5 Headquarters in Belfast."

Stavros was still skeptical. "I find it hard to believe that Fitzpatrick would participate directly in IRA operations, especially a bombing campaign. Something must have happened to push him in that direction. He never came across as a hardcore supporter of the republican cause—certainly not the Provos. Has there been anything on his whereabouts?"

"Nothing. We still don't have whatever name he's using, and he has either been playing it very low key or his minders are keeping him under wraps."

"That would not be difficult for him; he knows how to disappear."

Stavros was looking at the map and its now somewhat familiar names when he suddenly stopped.

"Although to be truthful, we've had a few guys go bad. One of the guys I went through selection with disappeared suddenly after training. He showed up later as a member of FALN, the Puerto Rican Liberation Army. Not quite the same as Neil, but it just popped into my mind. Too strange to forget."

Rhys had to make a point: "You Americans do have a tendency to rebel."

"I suppose. But, it shows the regard the bad guys have for our training."

Reed contemplated the soldier in front of him for a moment.

"Frankly, I'm not sure the IRA really wants to end this problem. Anyway, hopefully, we'll catch up to Fitzpatrick before he gets in too deep or does something we might all regret."

"Hopefully. I don't want to think about failure."

14

"Welcome to Camp Jericho" was all the sign declared at the front gate. A slightly overweight civilian guard rolled out of the security booth to check the driver's identification. He looked at the passengers with little curiosity as he leafed through the manifest before waving the bus through. Another twenty minutes of driving took them to an isolated set of buildings. The compound sat in a clearing cut out of the tall dark green fir and spruce trees that surrounded it. Mountains, some still covered with snow at their summits, peeked over the trees to the east. This camp within the bigger camp was basic, unlike the training that went on inside. The 1st Special Service Force had spent time here before they deployed to Europe during World War II, practicing alpine warfare techniques. It was the main reason the place had been built and its isolated location was ideal for its present purpose. The sub-camp was isolated from view at the ground level as well as from Soviet surveillance satellites. There was no reason to give the KGB or GRU any indication that this was one of the most sensitive areas in the United States—sensitive not because of its technology, which was rudimentary, nor its weaponry, which was more or less standard, but because of the people who worked there. It wasn't that they looked different; they didn't look like soldiers, but they were also not your normal civilians. They had unique talents, and what they lacked in certain special skills, they were about to learn.

The twenty-seven people who got off the bus looked like a cross-section of New York City, a study in diversity. They could have been a university group doing a weekend seminar in the woods. Sporty, fit, outdoorsy men and women in their mid- to late-twenties, a few in their thirties. None wore a uniform and the men's hair was long. Their whole point was not to look military; they were operators trained to move in and out of hostile places without anyone noticing. The only oddity was that a number of the group wore leather boots that had been scuffed clean of all color, a sign that they had been well used and abused recently.

A man who looked to be in charge because he had a clipboard in hand came out of the end building to address the group. Everyone clustered around him as he read off the building and room assignments and his assistant handed out the keys. They picked up their luggage and moved off to their assigned spaces. One might have also noted that military terms were not used for anything. There were bathrooms not latrines, buildings not barracks, and rooms but not billets. And no ranks. It might be Mister or Miss, but never sergeant or captain. Not that it mattered, since none of the names they used were real either.

The bus pulled off from the drive to disappear back into the main camp as the last of the group disappeared into the buildings. One member of the group remained peering off into the distance, taking in the crisp air and the green beauty of the surroundings. It was not unlike parts of her native Czechoslovakia but without the boundaries, without the restrictions.

After hearing a distant "crump" and feeling the earth shudder under her feet, she looked to the south. A small pillar of dust rose over the trees a couple of miles away.

That's why they named it Camp Nitrocellulose. What fun.

Happily, Sarah Rohan—now temporarily known as Ruth Simon—shouldered her two civilian duffel bags and trudged off to find room C21.

15

Stavros met Hunter in the quadrangle the next morning. She had a new guy with her; Stavros knew immediately that he was a badged trooper. He was not big or bulky; he just looked like he was supremely comfortable in his own skin, self-assured, and attuned to the environment. He looked straight at Stavros, but he was constantly scanning the periphery.

"This is Philip. He's one of our shooting instructors and will be checking you out."

Beyond the self-assured stance of a well-trained soldier, Philip showed no indication that he was one of the best close quarter battle instructors in the regiment.

They shook hands and headed for the car park where another instructor who went by the name of Reg waited by a Ford Transit. Climbing into the van, Stavros noted several cases of ammunition and kit bags in the back.

"I hope that ammo isn't all meant for me."

"Some of it, not all. We'll do some re-familiarization on pistols and SMGs and then shoot some exercises. Nothing too difficult as you won't be doing full-on ops over there. I understand you've done quite a bit of close quarter battle training?"

"We shoot a couple of hundred rounds several times a week when we're on alert status, sometimes more. But it's been a while for me." An unwanted image came to Stavros. A darkened house, a voice speaking English in an Iranian accent, a man staring wide-eyed as blood trickled from the bullet Stavros had just fired into his throat. Two others already lay dead on the floor. He shook his head to banish the picture.

"What weapons do you use?"

"Our small arms are all German—Walther and H&K. But I have a few of my own."

"We'll be using the PPK, the Hi-Power, the Ingram, all of which we carry in Ulster, and the Stirling, a weapon you might run into. No pressure, right?"

"Haven't felt any since I met Hunter." Stavros looked at her with a slight smile.

She shook her head and looked out the window. "You're trying too hard, Yank."

Philip caught the mood. "Right, no pressure."

Arriving at the Pontrilas range forty minutes later, Stavros lent a hand to unload and carry everything to the shooting stand and then listened as Philip gave instructions while Reg set up the targets.

They started with the easiest, a 7.65mm Browning PPK. Stavros owned one and knew it well, except his was a larger caliber: 9mm *Kurz*, what they call "three eighty" in America. With the right ammo, it was better than a brick through a plate-glass window. In either caliber, the PPK is an accurate self-protection and close quarters weapon. What it is not suited for is any situation where you might have to engage more than two bad guys at once because of its limited magazine capacity.

He went through about forty rounds single shot and double tap at short ranges of 15 meters and less before he changed over to the HP. The Browning was also very familiar, comparable to the Czech

CZ-75 in size and handling. He preferred the CZ but sometimes you can't choose.

He warmed up with the Browning on a single target. Slow fire, then double tap, then drawing it from his holster and engaging the target.

"Let's try some multiples," Philip suggested, and while Reg arranged the targets, he pushed a bit more.

"You're taking too much time on each round. Speed it up."

"I'm warming up, plus, I'm getting used to the Browning's action."

"Do I hear excuses?" Hunter chimed in for the first time. When Reg had cleared off the range, she picked up a Browning from the table, loaded it, and fired the full magazine into a target in about eight seconds. The thirteen holes could be covered by a small saucer.

"And I'm cold," she said.

Stavros knew he was under pressure. Philip looked at him with his head cocked to the side, waiting. Stavros replaced his empty magazine with a full one, let the slide chamber a round, and holstered it. He focused on the range in front of him.

Philip called a target number and Stavros drew and fired all his rounds into it as fast as he could. He pulled one of his rounds about an inch outside the otherwise tight group.

Crap, always when someone's watching ....

"Good, but do it again."

A second, third, and fourth run went better, or so Philip judged before moving Stavros on to multiple targets. Hunter loaded magazines without another word.

The afternoon progressed through several combinations of targets and shooting colored balloons on call before the pistol phase was declared finished. Then Reg brought out an Ingram MAC-10, a short little submachine gun with a very high rate of fire better suited for close combat in elevators than anything else, and a Stirling, a vintage bit of kit. He explained their simplicity quickly. Stavros, who had trained on the weapons at Bragg, listened politely and then managed to kill his assigned pieces of cardboard with both before Philip called it a day.

"We'll have some additional range time to practice later. For the next couple of days, we need to run a few short exercises to familiarize you with our field SOPs. We're going to head back and do some chalk talk."

They left the range and walked past the other empty lanes. Not many people were shooting that day, probably by design. At the far end of the stand was one last lane. Four troopers were standing together in a knot. One was aiming his pistol down range in a one-handed stance. He slowly squeezed off a round. The hoots and jeers from his mates seemed to indicate he had missed his target.

Stavros, Philip, and Hunter approached the group and were met with stares. One of the troopers greeted them. "How'd he do, Phil? Up to snuff?"

"Not bad, Goose. Needs a little practice."

"He sounded a bit slow."

Stavros had to interject: "All on target."

"Right, Yank." Goose turned away to face his mates. Stavros felt the hostility.

Hunter looked down range at the target. "What are you boys playing at here?" she asked.

"Shoot the cigarette out of the target's mouth and you get bragging rights and maybe a pint," said another. He turned to Stavros. "You up for a go at it?"

Stavros considered the challenge. He could see the man-sized silhouette 25 meters away. It was turned sideways with a cigarette dangling from a hole in the target's face. It was a pretty difficult shot.

"Yeah sure, why not?"

The trooper gestured at the Hi-Power lying on the table and Stavros picked it up. The slide was to the rear, the chamber empty, and no magazine in the well. He grabbed a magazine and tapped it sharply on the table to set the rounds and then slid it partly into the pistol. With the muzzle down range, he slapped the mag fully into place hard with the heel of his hand. The slide slammed forward, chambering a round. With the pistol in the ready, the hammer cocked and safety on, Stavros stepped into a shooting stance holding the pistol down at an angle and gazed momentarily at the sand of the range floor. The shot called for precision, not quick kill.

Goose chose that moment to speak. "So, you're looking to find your mate and get him out? He better hope we don't get him in our sights before you do because to us he's just another terrorist. I'll be happy to take him out. That's what I do."

Goose wants to rattle me, Stavros thought. He almost asked him how killing them all would sort out the problem, but he left it for another time. He took a deep breath and exhaled while still staring at the sand. He let the pistol's muzzle rest on the range table. In a measured voice he answered, "I don't think that would be a good idea."

"Why? He's made his decision."

"I've heard that before. First, he's an American soldier and therefore my brother. Second, Her Majesty's Government agreed to let us have him. That means, unless I'm dead, I get first shot at him."

"And if you're dead?"

"Then Hunter gets to bring him in."

Hunter's eyes widened a bit.

Stavros looked at the troopers while maintaining his stance. He breathed evenly and deeply and cleared his mind of distractions.

Goose tried again. "Ulster is a dangerous place. You might get killed or worse. You up for that?"

Stavros returned his gaze to the sand. "If there's a chance of making it right, it's worth it."

"I hope you're ready, Yank."

"I've been in worse places." He inhaled slowly, normally.

Goose was about to say something more but stopped when he saw the look in Stavros' eyes. Stavros looked up at the target and lifted the pistol smoothly from the ready position while clicking it off safe. He focused on the target, exhaled, leveled and aligned the sights, then focused on the front blade. He began a steady squeeze of the trigger. In the pause between his exhale and inhale, the hammer snapped forward. The primer exploded, igniting the powder which, in turn, propelled the bullet down the rifled barrel. He visualized the spinning projectile leaving the muzzle at a little over 375 meters per second and barely felt the recoil before letting the sights settle back onto the cigarette.

Or where it had been. Only a stub remained: his shot had cut it in two.

He paused for a moment, then cleared the pistol and set it onto the table. A tendril of smoke came out of the muzzle and wafted into nothingness. He smiled.

"Nice weapon. The first version was designed by an American." Stavros turned to his companions: "I guess we're finished here?"

Hunter grinned at Goose and his mates and followed Stavros and Philip toward the parking lot.

"You know Goose will be working with us, don't you?" Hunter said as she caught up.

"Great. He loves me a lot, I can tell."

"He's got a bit of an ego. Sort of like you, only brasher."

"Me? An ego? Hardly."

"Oh, yes you do, Yank. You just don't show it much, but I can see. Besides, anyone in this business has to believe they're good."

"Good, yes, but not better than anyone else."

"He'll get over it once you start working together. Unless you really prang something," Philip chimed in.

"If I do, I might be dead."

"Thus proving his point," said Hunter.

The van was headed back to the barracks, over the Wye River bridge and toward Hereford. Stavros watched the passing countryside and was struck by a feeling of being very much on his own, something he hadn't felt since Tehran. A sense of being an outsider in a strange place. For the most part, he had been welcomed by the officers, which was probably more political necessity than true acceptance. The "other ranks" came across as distrustful and standoffish, even resentful of his presence. He was not sure he would be able to mesh well with the team and thought he'd be under pressure to continually prove himself. The closer the van got to Hereford, the more things he recognized. He was beginning to know the neighborhood, not so much his "comrades."

16

It was a nice day on the farm and Neil was sitting outside the cottage contemplating one of his books when Rourke announced visitors would be coming. Not knowing what else to do, he kept reading. It was two days since the test and he had been left to his own devices. Rourke had disappeared a couple of times, driving off in an old Riley 1300 to parts unknown. He said simply, "Stay put, I'll be back in a while." Neil had nowhere to go, so he stayed.

The location, if not the accommodation, was idyllic. The house itself was a ramshackle stone cottage with a weather-worn slate roof, tended to by, as far as he could tell, a young lady who popped in and straightened things up occasionally. The surroundings were green and quiet; the house was ringed by woods that closed in on all sides. From where he sat in the back, Neil had a view of a small field backed by trees and the barn in which he had done his test. Birds and rabbits were the only visitors he could see. It was a good place for a safe house.

Food and drink showed up on the front steps early in the morning before Neil awoke. On the second day, he knew it had arrived only when Rourke carried the basket in and dropped it on the table while he drank his coffee. (He hated tea and after the shock of the first day's bad java, he insisted on making his own, filtering it through a Rube Goldberg contraption of a funnel and paper towel to screen out most of the dregs.) His morning breakfast, an "Ulster fry" Rourke had called it, was already made. Not as hot as he liked his food, but still warm. Bacon, sausage, baked beans, fried eggs with grilled tomatoes, and what appeared to be leftover potatoes and cabbage made into a hash he'd never had before. There was an acceptable soda bread, but he drew the line at the black pudding. The food weighed down the plate, so Neil knew he was being treated well. Rourke grumbled about it, but he knew he'd have to work off the grease or die of a heart attack if he kept up the diet for long.

It was several hours later as he sat reading, watching nature, and absentmindedly listening to the gasp of the breeze through the branches and the grass, that he heard the return of the Riley with its metalwork rattling down the lane and the crash of one of Rourke's mistimed downshifts. He found the piece of ripped newsprint that served as a bookmark, tucked it into place before closing the book, and waited. Footfalls came from the side of the cottage, not the hallway as he expected, and two men appeared from around the corner. It was Rourke followed by another familiar face, Danny Monahan. A third man came in last and stood back with his hands clasped together in front of him. Younger, tough looking, with long hair he kept brushing out of his eyes.

Security.

That said, in the daylight Monahan still looked like he was ready for a street fight. He wasn't that tall but he carried himself like a scrapper.

Neil stood and faced the three as they approached.

"Neil, my boy. Glad to see you're still with us," Monahan said.

"Why wouldn't I be?"

"Well, I was hoping that you wouldn't get put off by the tests. How do you like it out here in the countryside?"

"Not bad for a short while but I prefer the city."

"Won't be long now. We have some things to talk about."

Rourke went in the back door of the house, while Danny gestured for Neil to follow him in. Taking a seat at the kitchen table, Danny kicked another chair out and nodded for Neil to sit.

"It's time we talked about what you're here to do. But first, I'd like you to clarify a couple of things. The boys in the States said you were eager to help. Why?"

"My dad was chased out of Ireland after the war."

"Chased out? What for and by whom?" asked Danny.

"For defending the Republic. Chased out by the powers that be, he told me."

"The Brits, the occupiers, you mean?"

"Yes, that's what they are, aren't they?"

"They are indeed. So, when was this?"

"It should have been 1946 or 47. His naturalization papers were dated 1953, so I assumed he got those at least five years after he got to the States."

"Your ma didn't tell you?"

"She couldn't remember precisely. She was American by birth and only met him after he'd been in country for a while."

"Alright then. What did he do to 'defend the Republic' as you say?"

"He never said exactly, but he did say he carried a gun. I thought maybe he was in one of the armed cells or maybe intelligence, I don't know."

"Interesting. Because we've searched through our files and can't come up with anyone who worked with us and left the country under the family name Barry."

"I would imagine not, because he changed his name before he got to the States."

"Really? From what?"

"Ryan."

"Full name?"

"Liam Conner Ryan."

"We'll check it out," Danny said. He nodded at Rourke, who left the room. Neil assumed he'd be making some calls.

"Now then," Danny began again, "your job. What we need are two very efficient bombs. Small and deadly, not big, not 500 pounds of fertilizer. Can you build us something?"

"Depends, what's the target?"

"All I can say right now is it's buildings. Two isolated buildings."

"How big?"

"One is two stories, one three."

"Made of?"

"Stone."

"What effect do you want?"

"To kill the people inside."

"Can we get close?"

"One maybe, one probably not closer than 100 yards."

"Not easy. I assume these are hard targets or you wouldn't have come to me, so I need to see plans, maps, photos. I need to know where the people will be. What's the security? Can you get inside? Stuff like that."

"That'll take a bit of doing."

Neil wanted to tell him all the information he needed for a proper target analysis, but he wasn't sure Danny would have the patience to listen. Most people didn't. Their eyes would glaze over. But, for any attack to be effective, a good target study was required.

"You'll have to put together a good team to get the details. No cowboys who'll compromise the operation before we even get started. I'll make a list for them."

"I know what you'll be needing."

"I doubt that very much. This won't be like parking a van next to a pub and hoping for the best. I need exact info."

"You don't think we've done this before?"

"I know you've tried. This time, you'll be wanting precision, so I'll tell you what I need."

"You don't trust me or my men?"

"Frankly, no. God love ya, but you Irish could fuck up a two-car parade."

"You …!" Danny spluttered. "You just make the bombs, we're the ones that place them!"

"Listen, I grew up Irish and Catholic. I know how you operate. And you've done real well. Your bombs kill any housewives and kids who happen to be standing around. I was recruited to help you guys hit this target, whatever it is, so you better listen."

Danny was on his feet, face red, fists clenched, the muscles in his neck taut.

"Ours worked well enough on Mountbatten and at Warrenpoint."

"Warrenpoint was sheer luck. It was a fluke that a 2 Para convoy was on that road and Mountbatten was a soft target. If you want this to work, you need someone who knows not just how to build a bomb but how to make sure the attack is successful. That's me. I can show you what has to be done. Is that good enough?"

Danny looked like he was about to charge, so Neil glanced about and saw a cast iron frying pan close by. He picked it up and hefted the weight; it would do in a pinch. The pan was spinning in his hand at his side; light enough to swing easily and heavy enough to do damage.

The red-faced Irishman cocked his head. "You think that'll stop me?"

"Pretty sure it'll slow you down so I can kick the shit out of you."

"You're not worried about the afterwards?"

"Not really. You need me."

A creak came from the hallway beyond the kitchen, heavy footsteps. Two sets of eyes looked to the doorway as Rourke fumbled into the room. Rourke looked from Danny to Neil, to the frying pan, and back again and thought better of trying to say anything profound.

"The boss says they're checking on the name but to get on with it."

Danny stared hard at Neil.

"You're right, we need you," Danny said. "But don't push me or I might forget myself."

"I'll remember that."

Neil twirled the iron pan one more time, set it back on the counter, and sat down. Now that Danny had calmed down, he was ready to go to work.

17

To Stavros' thinking, the training days that followed weren't organized in any coherent fashion. He attributed part of that to the fact he was already well versed in most of the skills required, but also to the fact that the mission was unique: both in the target as well as its desired outcome.

Briefings and lectures gave him a sense of the people and the terrain of his target area, a few movies showed the aftermath of ambushes and bombings, and filmed interviews of downtrodden but still combative prisoners in an isolated gaol somewhere in the Kingdom gave him an idea of the nature of the men who carried them out. They were notable mostly for their evident hate of whomever was filming them.

He witnessed several practice Pagoda Troop takedowns of "terrorists" and participated in a forty-eight-hour surveillance tour, sitting in a close observation post watching the comings and goings of a farmer and his family through a high-powered spotting scope, taking meticulous notes on every conceivable bit of minutia in high-tech fashion—with a waterproof notebook and pencil, all the while taking care of bodily functions without moving more than a meter in any direction. When they withdrew, Stavros and his partner cleared their waste and camouflage from the area and backed out of their hide so slowly that even the animals didn't pick up on their presence. It had been a meticulous study in tedium, punctuated by moments when the sheep were amorous or the farmer, angry at his poverty, banged at things in the shed. He was glad that phase was finished and felt he was coming to the end of his train-up. It was more an operational familiarization of how his British allies did their job in the North than formalized training, but it ticked all the boxes of what an already-trained operative had to know. That was when the boys declared it was time for a bit of relaxation.

Stavros was lying on the bed in his small room when Philip, Reg, and another trooper named Tim walked in without knocking.

"That'll be the last time I leave my door unlocked."

"Come on, Yank, you're happy to see us now, aren't you?"

"Of course he is," said Tim.

Tim, the new guy, was talkative compared to the reserved Philip and close-mouthed Reg. That was probably why they were chosen to be his tutors of SAS procedures; they would never impart too many details or too many trade secrets to an outsider.

"Get your evening best on, mate. We're going downtown."

Stavros knew he couldn't back out of the offer, which was both a challenge and an opportunity.

"This isn't going to turn into an all-nighter is it? I have an RV with Hunter in the morning and I don't want to make her any angrier than she already is."

"Nah, this won't be a big piss-up, it's a weeknight for us too."

As they climbed into the car and even before he asked, Stavros was instructed on male-oriented English drinking traditions that left women mostly out of the equation and explained why Hunter was not there. He didn't think she was the type for such evenings anyway.

Tim was driving. Wearing a light nylon windbreaker that was about a size too small with the sleeves pulled up to his elbows, he was either ready for a bar fight or just wanted to look cool. For a trooper, his posturing surprised Stavros. With ginger hair and light green eyes, he could be taken for Irish, but he adamantly insisted he was a Caledonian from the north of Scotland although his accent seemed to lie elsewhere.

They drove across town to a place called the New Market Inn. Tim found a spot to park his Ford Consul in a well-lighted grass lot and they marched out of step down the street toward the pub. The night was young, the sky clear, and the air cool. It had rained a bit earlier and the puddles hadn't yet dried. If a car approached it was best to be far from the edge to avoid the spray. Some of the drivers appeared to take perverse pleasure in trying to drench the pedestrians, although they might have reconsidered if they knew who their intended targets were: four highly trained soldiers who wanted nothing more than to make it inside and drink beer with dry clothing.

Stavros thought the building looked turn of the century or older, maybe Georgian but, never having studied architectural history, he wasn't sure. It was a pale stone structure with two arched windows with a door and a couple of steps centered in the middle. They entered through the side entrance and found the place to be near capacity. It was clear it was one of the happening places in Hereford. There were a number of people Stavros had met or seen at the barracks, small clusters of fit men interspersed with frumpy civilians. He noted a pair of very attentive men sitting near the front entrance who were nursing pints and visually inspecting everyone and everything that came into the room. *They must be the designated intervention team.* The pub would be a lucrative target to any terrorist who wanted to score big on the Regiment's home turf because getting inside Bradbury Lines to conduct an attack would be near impossible.

Amazingly, Philip found a table and the four stuffed themselves into the chairs between two other tables filled with folks that were intent on drinking. The ambient noise was such that their table talk wasn't easily overheard. Reg went to get drinks. He didn't ask what anyone wanted; apparently there were standard procedures for drinking that had to be followed, Stavros thought. Four pints came back and they proceeded to put them away. They leaned in close to be heard over the din around them.

"Good people drink good beer," said Tim.

"Bad people drink bad beer," Stavros announced for no particular reason other than to be contrary. Looking around, he couldn't tell the difference between the good and the bad in the smoky environment. The dim yellow lights and cigarette smoke didn't help his powers of observation any.

"You have some amazing insight there, Paul," said Philip.

"It's not mine, but it seemed to be a good counterpoint."

Reg spoke for the first time that evening: "Well, I've drunk bad beer. Does that make me bad?"

"No, just means you have no taste," Tim said.

Stavros was still getting used to his Theakston's "Old Peculier." He turned the glass slowly as he held it up to the light, inspecting its color and the consistency of the head.

"Is this a good beer by your standards?" he asked.

"It's one of the best," Philip said. "Do you have good beer where you're at?"

"Nah, the beer in the city is bad. We have to get the good stuff from Bavaria or Czechoslovakia."

Stavros anticipated correctly that the conversation would be dominated by beer, the latest rugby standings, some discussion of football (European not American), and succinct, if ribald, observations of the pub clientele. So it was a surprise when Tim asked him a question. He was curious, not disparaging, but it was an area where Stavros knew he couldn't go, especially in public.

"Tell us about Iran. We heard you were on the mission."

"Sorry, I can't talk about it," Stavros said.

Tim was disappointed.

Stavros looked about. There wasn't a ripple of change in the room. No one noticed, no one cared. But Stavros did. The British soldiers who surrounded him were curious about "their American," the man they tended to and watched over. He hoped they didn't have any sort of expectations that he was supposed to fulfill.

He suddenly was very tired. Hunter had told him that the next day's exercises would start early. At 8 a.m., she had said, tapping her wristwatch. He didn't want to be late. To be late was to lose face with Hunter. Talking out of school was also to lose face.

"Listen, I have to be up early tomorrow," he began.

"So do we ... come on, have another," Reg said.

"No thanks, I can't. Can we call me a taxi or something so I can head back?"

"That's not how we do it here. I'll take you back," Tim said.

Stavros stood somewhat unsteadily, swaying a bit like a palm tree in a light breeze.

"Your 'Old Peculier' is some strong brew. I haven't had one in a while."

Reg and Philip exchanged glances and smirked a bit. Regaining his equilibrium, Stavros made for the front door with Tim close behind.

On the street again, the cool evening cleared his head a bit. He looked up into the sky and saw a blue-black bowl above him filled with thousands of tiny glittering lights.

"At least you can see the stars. In Berlin we can't see much of anything. Too much ambient light from the city."

"Listen, friend, I'm sorry if I made you uncomfortable back there. I was just interested in your mission. We could never have pulled off anything like that; we don't have the resources."

"I understand, but it's all still classified. What I will say is that, unfortunately, we had the means, but we didn't use what we needed."

"Why?"

"Politics, I think. Anyway, we have a new thing to worry about now."

They had entered the lot where Tim's car was parked. It was largely empty except for a few cars parked along the edge. Their car was in the middle of the lot underneath a big sodium-vapor light high atop a pole that threw down an intense umbrella of white light. It actually seemed warmer when he walked into the brightly lighted area. He was about to say something about it when Tim cut him off.

"Shit!"

He felt rather than saw the small van come flying out of the darkness behind them, the engine suddenly screaming as the driver accelerated. Its side door open, two figures dressed in black hung out the opening. By the time Stavros realized what was happening, he also saw the barrels of their weapons. Tim spun and pulled a pistol from under his jacket and went into a shooter's crouch. There was no chance to find cover. He fired twice, fully exposed.

"Run!" he yelled.

He saw yellow-white flashes as the submachine guns answered Tim's fire. Unarmed, Stavros turned and sprinted for the darkness.

He heard Tim yell something and turned briefly to see him fall. The van kept rolling, following him closely. He was sprinting fast when a blur came from the left out of the darkness. The man hit him like a lineman at full clip. Stavros felt like he had been slammed with a heavy punching bag; his head snapped to one side and legs went out from underneath him as his shoulder slammed hard onto the hard pitch. An electric shock coursed through his body. He tried to tense his neck muscles to keep his head from hitting the ground. He was only partially successful. Stunned, in pain, and pinned to the ground, he was unable to react. He sensed the van pull up beside them and felt hands grabbing him. A hood went over his head and cold, metal rings snapped around his hands held tightly at his back.

"The other one's dead. Put this one in the boot and go," said a voice.

Stavros heard another vehicle pull up and three, maybe four pairs of hands lifted him up. The next thing he felt was his head and legs dragging over a metallic edge and being released into some metal chamber. A clunk of a lid told him he was in the trunk. The car lurched forward and he slid to the rear. He struggled for a moment and then told himself to calm down. He inhaled deeply, and regularized his breathing. He must avoid panic, he told himself.

He knew he had to work quickly. The chances for escape went down fast the longer a prisoner was held. He couldn't give his captor more time to increase security.

He pulled his arms up behind his back until his hands were in line with his waist and began feeling the belt line of his pants until he felt what he was searching for. He stuck his fingers into a small recess inside the cloth band and carefully pulled out a tiny metallic tool. He savored the moment and then aligned the tool in his fingers tightly. He couldn't drop it. The car had slowed somewhat. It was moving quickly but not overly fast. He decided whoever was driving didn't want to attract attention. The tool found its target and he pushed it in and turned slowly until he felt one of the rings loosen and slide open. His hands freed, he reached up and loosened the cinch string and pulled the hood off. Now he had to wait.

It was ten minutes or so before he heard the crunch of gravel under the tires. Then the car came to a halt and the doors opened. He heard the voices.

"Get him out. I'll get someone from inside to help."

There was scratching on the lock and then the key slid into place. Stavros was curled up in a ball waiting for the moment when he heard the release. A shaft of light pierced the darkness as he kicked the lid upward with both legs. He felt a satisfying thunk of sheet metal on bone as the man outside tumbled back onto the ground. Stavros launched himself out of the car and onto the figure. Whoever he was, he wasn't going anywhere. Unconscious, out cold. Quickly he applied the handcuffs on the man and looked around. They were parked next to a small building, maybe a warehouse. The keys were in the boot lid. He grabbed them and started to move to the driver's seat on the left before he realized something was off.

Wrong side, you're in England, idiot.

He turned back and saw the man stir a bit. He patted the man down and pulled out his wallet and opened it.

Hot damn. An identity card stared back at him.

Alright mate, turnabout is fair play.

He drug the man up and shoved him into the boot, then hopped into the correct seat and started the engine.

Stavros cranked the wheel all the way to the left and stepped on the gas, throwing dust and rocks all across his tail as the car spun about. At the last second, he glanced in the mirror to see the door open and several figures tumble out of the building. He countersteered to straighten the car out and disappeared down the road.

Catch me if you can, assholes.

It took him several minutes to figure out where he was exactly. But several road signs helped and before too long he was in the small village of Burghill. It was dark and the roadway empty, so he stopped at an intersection and turned the motor off. He left the parking lights and emergency flashers on, just in case, and hopped out. After a stop at a letter box, he turned and walked determinedly off to the southwest. He knew the way home from here.

***

The next morning, after a hot shower and a second round of Tylenol C3s for the pain, Stavros came out of his billet and headed toward where he now knew Hunter would not be meeting him. Instead, as he approached the Element Headquarters building, he saw a cluster of people standing outside the front door in close and agitated conference. It was Rhys Brown who saw him first. Rhys broke into a smile and as he did, the others turned to look.

"Paul, you're late," Rhys said. "Where have you been?"

"I slept in a bit," said Stavros. "I might have had a bit to drink last night and I fell down."

The rest of the group stared at him, dumbfounded.

I see you, Tim! You've been resurrected! Stavros had to admit it had been realistic playacting, right down to the pain he still felt.

A big man with a bandage on his forehead came menacingly out of the scrum toward Stavros.

"What've you done with my wallet?"

Stavros recognized him, not from the pub or the ambush, but from his photo on the British Army ID card that had surprised him earlier.

"Your wallet? How would I know? But if it's gone missing, I imagine someone will post it to you soon enough."

***

It was a week before one of the groundskeepers discovered the large entryway mat lying in the tall grass near the southeastern corner of the barracks at Bradbury Lines. It had been discarded behind a warehouse building, its rubber backing well scarred by something sharp. A corresponding small piece of the mat was found hanging from the razor wire atop the perimeter fence about 15 meters away. It was brought to the attention of the commander who immediately realized the implications: someone knew how to enter a restricted area without being torn up by the barbed wire fence. But he doubted the American's fingerprints would show up on it. It was decided not to return the item to the hotel whence it came.

89

18

"Neil my boy, we have a new job to do," said Rourke.

"That would be?"

"We need to meet a shipment of goods and, since our expert is no longer available, it's your turn to inspect."

"Is that a good idea? Shouldn't you be worrying about compartmentation?"

"Compartmentation?"

"Need to know. I don't need to know how your logistics works."

"Ah, ordinarily I'd agree with you but the boss says this is a special case. Some stuff coming in and we need to look at it before we risk bringing it into country."

"How does that work? We're in country already."

"We are but the stuff isn't. We're going to meet it offshore."

"Offshore? Like on the water? I don't do very well on a boat. That's why I didn't join the navy."

"It'll be fine, lad. A short trip and I have sea sickness pills."

And so started the trip. Neil had one moment of "I didn't sign up for this kinda shit" but then relented and decided to put up with it. The trip from the farm to the port went smoothly aside from having to sit in the back of a van. He went from the van straight to the trawler at the dockside and didn't see much of the area other than a few lights. It was dark and he could only surmise they were in a small fishing village. He wasn't even certain which coast he was on although his sense of timing said it was most likely the east.

He descended belowdecks with Rourke and took up residence in a small sleeping compartment, somewhat well appointed and not lived in. Rourke grabbed the one chair, so Neil took over the bunk.

"Now we wait," Rourke announced.

A long vibration shuddered through the hull as the engines started, and before long, the ship began to sway as it moved away from the dock and into the harbor. Neil couldn't see any of the action; he could only imagine it and wish that he would soon have a horizon to look at before he got sick.

Neil was holding his own by staring with eyes closed at an imaginary fixed horizon when a hard rap brought him back to reality. Rourke opened the door and spoke a few words with the crewman before turning back to Neil. "We can go up now, we're clear of the coast."

They climbed up to the main deck and then higher to the wheel-house. The diesels thrummed as the ship sliced through smooth water, trailing a phosphorescent gleam in its wake.

The captain glanced at the intruders as the hatch closed and apparently made a quick assessment of the two landlubbers. "Don't lean on anything and don't touch nothing," he said before settling back in his chair to tend to more important matters.

Neil looked around the compartment with its impressively modern systems. Lots of lights and gauges—it looked nothing like any of the little fishing boats he'd been on as a child. The only thing he could compare it to was a Coast Guard cutter he'd suffered on during scout swimmer training. A brass plate screwed to the bulkhead caught his attention. He saw that he was on board the *Fredericka*, a Danish-built, Irish-flagged, mid-water trawler, 41 meters long, and displacing 600 tonnes.

"We're off the Skerries, in case you're wondering. We should make our RV with the other boat before long," the captain said.

Neil looked to Rourke for clarification.

"We'll meet the other boat and take a look at the stuff and then go home. If we approve the shipment, the other ship will put the stuff ashore with inflatable boats."

"Won't that look odd? A fishing trawler goes out and returns without a catch," said Neil.

The captain answered. "We found a problem with our gear. The main winch broke down. No winch, no fish, so we had to return to port for repair."

"That's an expensive inspection tour. Your folks could have inspected the stuff where it was shipped out from."

"Not really, it's coming from North Africa. No telling what might happen between there and here. There are pirates, and brigands, and cheats out there."

Neil stared into the night but couldn't see anything other than the light of the instrumentation reflected in the glass. He felt the ship running through the swells which were thankfully small and continued to hope his prophylaxis would keep his stomach in check.

To the southeast, the *Sonya* was running dark. Compared to the *Fredericka*, she was a ragtag hulk. Her hull was heavy with years of accumulated sea life, barnacles and weed, and she was streaked with rust—so much so that someone who thought her hull was painted railroad red could be forgiven. Underneath the oxidation, she had been yellow at one time. She hove to 25 miles off the coast and waited. Before long she was rewarded with the approach of *Fredericka*, which had taken care to make sure no government boats were nearby. The two ships met in a careful union of sorts, and two men transferred from the Irish to the Panamanian-flagged vessel without incident. Rourke and Neil were met on the deck by a short, evil-looking Russian guy who, without formality, led them below into the hold. A light was turned on and Neil saw what could only be described as any rebel's dream cargo. At least thirty crates of weapons, AK-47s mostly; one crate with four RPK light machine guns. Another with four RPGs. The ammunition was in another forty or so smaller, wooden boxes, except for five long, metal cases that contained RPG rockets. The last ten metal boxes were marked not with the Bulgarian Cyrillic of the others, but the Czech factory imprint "*Explosia a.s.*" He knew immediately what that batch contained.

Rourke handed him a screwdriver, which he used to snap the wire seal on one of the boxes. Inside and underneath sheets of wax paper were 25 kilos of off-yellow, clay-like bars layered in the box. It was the stuff Neil thought he might see in his test days ago. He tapped the packs with the handle of the screwdriver just to watch Rourke cringe backwards. He smiled inside. It would take much more than a tap to initiate a blast. It was Semtex, the real McCoy this time. It didn't smell like clay, or almonds, or oil; it didn't smell much at all. That's why it was considered good for sabotage—it was hard to detect. There were another couple of cartons for the electric blasting caps, all well sealed in aluminum foil, ten to a box.

Neil nodded at Rourke. The guns were good, the explosives were good. The ammunition would have to be tested. Couldn't really do that here.

"Good stuff," he said. "A gift from the Soviets?"

"Gaddafi, he thinks we're a stick to beat the West with."

Rourke passed a bundle to the Russian. "The rest you get after the stuff is well landed." It was the first installment for services rendered. The deal done, the cable transfer went flawlessly in reverse. It was apparent the crews were well versed in moving things back and forth at sea without getting them too wet. Then again, the waves weren't too big or high. Mentally, Neil wished the *Sonya* good travels and good luck in landing the cargo. He would be needing some of it soon enough for his own project, but both he and it had to get to dry land first. Then he went below to wait out their return back to the big green island and a solid footing that didn't continually try to move out from underneath him.

19

"Since you managed to cut the last training session short, the boss says you can go with us on a little trip. We're going down to the seashore," Hunter said.

"In this weather?" Stavros looked outside. It was an angry gray, wet, and cold day just like it had been for the previous four.

"You'll love it. Portsmouth is beautiful and we can get some decent food."

"Tired of Chinese?"

"You have to agree with me, Hereford doesn't have the best choices. It's either ultra posh or a chipper."

"Well then, by all means, let's go to Portsmouth. What are we doing there?"

"The eight of us are doing a short course at the Number One Training Establishment."

"Number One? Does that mean it's the best or just the first?"

"Both, actually. SIS runs the place. Just don't mention their name, they're easily upset."

"What do I call them then?"

"Maybe the 'Outfit.' Le Carré calls them the 'Circus' but I don't think they like that one much."

"Better than our 'Clowns in Action.'"

Stavros wasn't sure what to expect as they approached the place known as the Fort. What he saw in front of him looked very much like the obsolete American coastal defense sites ringing the Puget Sound that he'd visited as a teenager, then later as a scout swimmer doing a practice assault on Fort Adams in Narragansett Bay. This one was older in its layout with a moat and a ditch protecting the landward side and new buildings erected inside a very old and massive stone glacis. Its high security status was obvious from the double row of chain-link fence and pole-mounted CCTV cameras that surrounded the place.

"Not your run-of-the-mill seaside resort," he said.

"Maybe more fun, we'll see."

Stavros doubted that. The gray and the rain had been replaced by a foggy sky suffused with the light of a sun that just didn't seem to have the energy to burn off the tendrils of mist, which hung over the coastline like cannon smoke over a battlefield.

A little warmer at least.

They checked in at the gate post before driving through a tunnel and into the courtyard where a trio of blandly dressed Englishmen awaited them. As they piled out of the van and dumped their bags on the ground, Stavros watched the other people walking by who looked back with equal curiosity, if not disdain. He took it the others were the latest SIS student intake who all wanted to replace James Bond but would likely end up in a basement office somewhere filing reports. They looked to be recent graduates of Oxford and Cambridge and overwhelmingly white and male, much like the Agency. Comparatively, his group was well seasoned with two women and two whippet-lean brown-skinned guys of indeterminate, but probable South Asian extraction, and one big Black dude who sounded as if he came from Jamaica. They were rounded out with two very English guys who looked as if they came from the wrong side of the tracks and would beat the hell out of anyone who addressed them as "chaps"—and, of course, himself.

This will be interesting.

Hunter seemed to sense his thoughts.

"This is a pretty exclusive club."

"You probably feel like I did when I showed up at Hereford."

"Except these guys are all wankers. You'll see."

The housemaster, a wizened old gent who went by the name of Clive, parceled out eight spartan but comfortable rooms in a restricted area of the west wing and instructed them to take their dinner promptly at seven. The mess wasn't like Bradbury Lines. The food was better but they were met and fed in quarantine, isolated from the other students and the few instructors that remained late.

"I don't think they want us to contaminate anyone."

"God forbid they might actually have to speak with someone not of their station."

"Yob and toff," the girl named Helen said.

"Translate, please," said Stavros.

Helen pointed her thumb at her chest and said, "Yob, we're all hooligans to them," as she pointed at the other end of the room. "They're toff, our inbred elites."

"Buncha *skettel*," said Ade Campbell, the former Jamaican.

"What's that mean?" someone asked.

"Trash, man. They're all trash."

Looking at all the pasty, privileged faces of the Firm's current intake who peered back with a haughty cluelessness, Stavros decided he was happy on this team.

***

Classroom started at eight in the morning. Sharp. Which was a relief because his days had started much earlier at Hereford. It meant he could enjoy coffee and breakfast after stretching and a set of wind sprints on the long stretch of sand below the Fort's two oceanside bastions. He found his way there only after he inquired and was assured no overzealous guard would shoot him thinking he was an enemy frogman who'd flopped up on this not-so-secret beach.

When he was finished, Clive welcomed Stavros back through the heavy wooden portal that breached the seawall into the Fort. It was only when the old man pushed the door and secured the latches that Stavros noticed Clive's jacket obscured that he was missing his left arm. Stavros wondered if he hid his injury out of stubbornness or vanity. The door slammed to and the security system light went from green to red.

"Can never be too careful. We're all buttoned up now." Clive winked at Stavros.

In spite of his age and disability, Stavros had a feeling that Clive could handle himself. The tattoo of a skull with three small daggers on his surviving forearm was quickly covered when he put his jacket back on after closing the door. He knew each dagger indicated a successful op.

"Were you Special Boat Service, Clive?"

"Submariner, young man. But I did a lot of interesting things toting those SBS boys around. Not like the children upstairs, more like you and your crew. You're a Yank, right?"

"Pretty obvious, I think."

"True enough, I saw and heard a lot of you people in my navy days. Don't see many here though. In fact, you are only one I can remember in a long while."

"I don't imagine we normally have much call for training with you here. We have our own 'experts,' you know." Stavros did a set of air quotes to emphasize the word.

Clive's eyes crinkled as he suppressed a laugh.

"Yes, indeed. But watch out for these experts, lad. They can lead you astray."

Clive turned and nimbly disappeared down the corridor.

I'd love to hear some of your stories, Stavros thought as he watched the old salt walk away.

***

In the mess for breakfast, Stavros took time to look at the things his mind hadn't processed the evening before. Someone had said the Fort was originally built by Henry, which Henry he didn't have a clue, but that made it old. At least it would have been if the original fortress was still in existence, which it wasn't. It had been replaced, possibly moved in the late 1700s, maybe out of fear that Portsmouth would be sacked by the damned Yankee sea captain John Paul Jones and his crew of brigands.

A new history perhaps, but amusing nevertheless.

What now stood was a mix of nineteenth-century military fortification and twentieth-century adaptation. The mess hall was in a surviving portion of the original fort, inside the old officers' quarters. Exposed stone walls, a big fireplace at one end, and dark wood decorative work were graced with portraits of the Queen, the prince, and the royals as a couple. Along one wall, bracketed by the flags of the kingdom, were displayed images of men, dead heroes of the Empire it seemed. No names. No places. No dates.

The Great Game can be rough but someone has to play it.

That much had become very clear to Stavros, especially when it involved his comrades in arms.

The training was routine tradecraft stuff. The things Stavros had learned from Agency old timers, so-called annuitants, in Berlin. But the British instructors didn't cover some things, things he had learned from the older hands on his team along with a few tips and tricks from cops and criminals. Mostly, he had learned from an agency guy named Bradley who had shadowed him for a couple of weeks and taught tricks he had learned in places like Sofia, Riga, and

Leningrad. Bradley was an actor; he could be a diplomat, a street sweeper, a drunk, or a stevedore on the dock. All personas he had used fruitfully during his career.

But Stavros didn't mention the training or the experience he had gained from street-savvy acquaintances he met in bars and dark alleyways, or the things he had used in places he couldn't talk about. That was information he didn't intend to share with people he didn't know, people that could use it against him. Instead, he sat quietly and listened and absorbed what the gentlemen in tweed jackets said and drew on the chalkboard. They showed the students how to do their tradecraft the SIS way, the way that it had been done since Walsingham. It was the English way and therefore, the correct way.

When it came time to hit the streets, the students were separated and sent off on their assigned errands. They were given instructions to load and unload dead drops. Stavros was accused of not servicing his dead drop because the watchers didn't see him near the site. When he dropped the tiny capsule with the note inside on the table, the instructors were baffled. He didn't fill them in on what they missed.

Another instructor swore Stavros missed the brush-pass until she found the small package inside her shopping bag. She wasn't sure exactly when, where, or who had put it there.

Then came the surveillance exercise. Stavros strolled through the length and breadth of Portsmouth with an MI5 A4 team of watchers on his back, a team that swore they hadn't been seen. When he described the members of the team, their back-up vehicles, and costume changes, they thought he had inside help. A second team and a second run proved otherwise.

Then it was over, and the Hereford crew packed up to head back to base. Clive stopped by Stavros' room to say goodbye.

"Stay safe out there, Yank," he said, shaking his hand.

After he had left, Stavros looked at the small gold twin dolphins—a submariner badge—that Clive had pressed into his palm.

The course results weren't advertised but it was clear the instructors held Stavros with no small amount of regard. Hunter picked up on their deference and was curious.

"How did you do?" she said as they drove back.

"They said I did fine, no complaints," Stavros said. He leaned back in the seat and closed his eyes.

Hunter watched him for a minute as his breathing slowed and he fell asleep. A quiet man, she thought, wondering what his real story was.

20

Sarah had grown accustomed to her cover name and legend of Ruth Simon; the new job requirements not so much. Much of the tension of the previous weeks had disappeared, although, as several students discovered, not the reasons to fail. By the end of the first two weeks, the class had shrunk by two spots—a breach of elementary security protocols in one case, the failure to recognize an instructor's "recommendation" as sound advice in another. Arguing about it only hastened the removal.

As a graduate of the Agency's long course and with her personal experience, she had a leg up on her fellow students for the tradecraft training. For the most part, the men came from Special Forces and had the hard skills down pat. Some of them knew a bit about the soft skills, but not all. It was these hard men who could handle guns and knives who also provided comic relief. The task of trying to coax information out of a stunningly beautiful woman in a slinky red dress proved problematic for some. Of course, alcohol was involved, and generally the approaches went from awkward to stupid over the course of two or more drinks. The woman just happened to be a counterintelligence agent who drank iced tea out of a whiskey tumbler; if they got anywhere with her, they were able to move on. At the end of Week 8, student roster numbers 12 and 23 did not.

The women came from everywhere in the army. There were admin specialists and medical technicians as well as at least one violinist. The only thing that seemed to be common for the men or the women was that most were recent immigrants or first-generation Americans who spoke English as a second language. Beyond the physical and psychological aspects of passing assessment, they had all been vetted to the nth degree. A top-level security clearance was required of each before they were even considered for recruitment into the organization.

Sarah's background was unusual in the group, but only one of the unit cadre knew her full story and that was the man who recruited her, Hans Landau. He didn't share anything with the evaluators in order to maintain a level playing field. She'd have to make the cut based on her current performance alone. He even avoided talking with her in the assessment phase and he would continue to distance himself. Although he hoped she would make it through, he wanted no one to think there had been any influence on the selection process. Still, Sarah had much to learn as the mission of this unit was unlike that of her former signal intercept company, the Agency, or anything else that existed in the US military. It was a new endeavor altogether, a hoped-for solution to an issue that had only recently been recognized by the military following the Iran crisis. And that issue was simply, "How do we avoid having to rely on someone else's intelligence for our special operations, especially in faraway places where we don't have eyes and ears?"

21

Stavros looked out the car window and brooded. He thought the weather in Belfast was worse than Wales, and colder. The gray sky and rain hadn't broken for days and he hadn't seen blue sky since he left New York. The weather depressed him only slightly more than the briefings he had received before he departed.

He was in the zone at the moment, his thinking totally focused on the mission. Captain Rupert Hamish—late of Palace Barracks, Holywood, Northern Ireland—had given Stavros his last briefing in the UK before he left for the States to make a roundabout entry into Dublin and then to Belfast. His comments foreshadowed the words of the Agency people who briefed him a couple of days later in a safe house outside Washington. But there was always danger in accepting the word of an ally. Information from the enemy was always regarded with skepticism, not so much the word of a friend. Not one of the American analysts or operations officers he spoke with had ever visited the island. Their assessments relied on reporting from the embassy in London, from officers who were equally distant from the problem, and articles from the *Daily Telegraph*, which was not a neutral British newspaper. The reports were all prefaced with a caveat that read, "The source of the following information knew their remarks could reach the US government and may have intended to influence as well as inform." It seemed to confirm a British lean to the findings. He hadn't seen one report that discussed the motivations of the republican side of the issue in anything other than a negative light.

"It is the IRA's fault," they all declared in government-speak.

Hamish had put it more succinctly.

"It won't be over until they kill each other off and I, for one, am going to make sure it's the IRA and the republicans who are dead."

The sentiments of the master.

He knew the reasons underlying the Troubles belonged to both sides. It came down to turf: who controlled the land, the economy, the jobs, and who made the rules. The politics of power were almost as strong as the politics of religion and the two together amplified the problem.

The Catholics didn't control much of anything and that was a sore point, maybe *the* sore point. But when they tired of how things were and began to push for how things should be, the Protestants pushed back. Now it was like the Jets and the Sharks, only with professional league levels of violence carried out by groups cloaked with an array of initials for names. Some of the stuff was penny-ante like throwing rocks at soldiers; other times it was more like a bulldozer in a backyard garden, the pub bombings or kidnappings and murder. One side had the majority advantage and the army, the other had a really bad stubborn streak.

He shook his head.

Now, here he was sitting in a clapped-out-looking Ford Cortina. He knew this wasn't his war, but he was about to dive in.

At least he didn't have to pick a side.

Hunter shifted gears as she piloted the "Q" car effortlessly though the darkened streets. She was keeping up a pretty good pace despite the rough, rain-soaked pavement. When the car fish-tailed around corners, she brought it back into line with a smooth counter-steer.

Stavros watched the buildings slide past as the windshield wipers clapped and squeaked back and forth across the windscreen trying to keep it clear.

He called it a "Q" car because it looked like junk but hid a secret under its well-beaten exterior, much like the decoy "Q" boats used to fool the German submarines during both the World Wars. It was the product of good home-spun engineering, not by factory-trained mechanics, but wrench-turners that knew how to build cars for the streets and then make them look like they'd been beat to hell. He'd seen similar works of art in places like Tehran and he'd ridden with the Berlin police *Sondereinsatzkommando* in undercover cars that rivaled race-prepared BMW team vehicles, so the concept wasn't new. Engine, brakes, suspension were all reworked and then a hidden radio transceiver installed, along with lots of places to hide weapons. They ran light, no armor, as the heavy plate would just slow them down. It was better to outrun the guns if it came down to it.

"Where are the police?" Stavros asked. "I would have thought they'd be looking out for crazy women like you."

"That's a laugh. They're mostly bedded down this late. Plus Ulster Constabulary units don't often stray too far into this neighborhood; this is a no-go area."

"That's comforting. So anyone we meet out here will think we're daft or out for trouble."

Hunter didn't answer. She had an intensity about her when concentrating. He'd seen it before. It was focus, that time when the edges became blurry and the center super sharp and everything else became inconsequential. She had changed her appearance since he last saw her; her hair was now a disheveled dirty blond and her clothing looked well worn. Serious about her driving, she tossed the car about with hard precision. No room for error, or softness, or humor.

As they drove, Stavros reflected on the previous days and weeks, the training that had continued, the troopers—never really friendly—whom he had met, the clinical technicians giving briefings in darkened rooms from lighted stages. And now, the North seemed a cold and forbidding place. He felt like he didn't really belong.

That might be a good thing.

He saw enough negative on both sides to repel him from either.

It had started with a presentation some military engineers from Kent gave on the defensive measures that had been put into place. Barracks and police stations with high, chain-link fences and big wire mesh "umbrellas" to defeat the RPGs and homemade mortars. Saracens and armored Land Rovers running through the streets or standing at checkpoints. It seemed to be all about protecting the force and not the people. Those measures ended up separating the police and the soldiers from the community. Not the solution, but then he didn't have a ready answer for what measures would make a difference.

The intelligence analysts gave cold, factual assessments. He saw the photographs of the murders, the assassinations, and the bombings—most carried out by the IRA or INLA. Rarely were the loyalists mentioned, UDA or UVF or whatever alphabet soup of letters the opposing sides wanted to be known by. He knew both sides were there, both were guilty. But from his position sitting in the briefing room in England, it was obvious who was to be blamed. There seemed to be an implicit hostility against one side, the IRA, and an uneven morality about what happened on the streets.

Maybe it was because Northern Ireland was a royal inconvenience, like, "Why can't you take care of your own problems? Why must we be the ones to sort it out?" Or was it that Her Majesty's Government in London expected everyone to just know their place in the world and get on with it? There was no pure military solution to the Troubles; it was a problem that had to be won on the street with the people. Stavros also knew he couldn't take a side.

Prior to his insert into the North, he had spent many hours with Rhys talking about the approach he would take. He would be a freelancer trying to write about the effects of the Troubles on life for both sides, how it affected people and impacted living there. Everyone cautioned him to avoid being too direct in his approach. He already knew that. He needed to stay on the outside, to be far away, a foreigner, to remain neutral, never a threat to either side, open and above board, passive. He needed to talk to the locals about work, raising kids, playing football, shopping, anything but religion, violence, or the security forces, even though they influenced every aspect of life in the North.

How all this would help him find Neil, he was unsure. He had 1.5 million people to sort through in an area just slightly larger than Rhode Island, the smallest US state. When the question was asked, "Where do we start?", the answer was simple. "No problem, choose a town and look for inspiration," said the handlers. "He'll show up somewhere."

"So, this is a fishing expedition?" he asked.

"It's as good a shot as any. We have teams looking for outsiders coming in, but we can't do much more. We don't know what name he's using."

Not only a fishing trip, it's like trying to catch the one albino killer whale in the ocean. What are the odds?

Stavros made a suggestion: "Maybe you should offer up a target. Something not too dangerous but enough of a challenge that Neil would want to look at it."

As he expected, they said, "We'll handle such things from here. You just do the looking."

Neil could be anywhere from Belfast to Derry (the loyalists and English called it Londonderry) or between Banba's Crown and Cranfield Point, although he doubted he would ever set foot in the latter places. Or he could be just across the border in the Free State. No problem.

It was all on-the-job training, OJT, make it up as you go, because he doubted anyone had been stuck with this task before: looking for a special leprechaun, one who knew how to make a bomb from just about anything. His quarry had red hair, that much was true, but hadn't worn green since he left the army.

***

Belfast it was.

Stavros decided that Belfast made as much sense as any other place. Belfast was his port of arrival in the country and the place most Americans thought of once they stopped thinking of Dublin, Cork, or Tipperary. He really doubted Neil would show up in any of those cities. In actuality, Stavros thought Neil would be in the Republic, probably somewhere near the border outside Dublin or in the west in County Donegal. But any visits to the Republic would have to wait. He needed to see the true field of battle first.

So, it was off to the North and Belfast to start and, until Hunter picked him up that evening, he had been on his own. He was just about ready to begin questioning his approach to the problem.

He had cautiously stuck his head into a number of pubs, restaurants, and hotel bars, where he would sit and scribble in his notebook and open tentative conversations with anyone willing to speak with him. Once they found out he was an American, everyone wanted to know his ancestry and, upon finding out he wasn't Irish, wanted to know why he was there at all.

"I'm writing a piece on how the Troubles affect daily life in the North."

To which, he usually got an answer that went something like: "You can tell your readers that the [fill in with a choice of enemy plus an epithet] have ruined everything."

When he asked more questions, what he got was either a dismissive laugh or a furtive glance around the room as the subject was quickly changed. Not much came from anyone's mouth.

The graffiti on the walls—"whatever you say, say nothing"—was more than a security admonition like "loose lips sink ships." It was a warning. He knew what happened to traitors in the North. For that matter, even being suspected as a traitor might mark the termination of a life, or maybe the loss of a kneecap. No one wanted to share the time of day with a stranger, let alone the particulars of how bad their life was.

It also didn't matter how well he could shoot a gun or elude surveillance; Stavros was dealing with people who were either fanatical about their security or terrified of the consequences of talking out of school. There seemed to be little information he could glean from anyone that might be useful, even for his ostensible article on the Troubles. After eight days, he was no closer to finding his quarry than when he started.

Earlier in the evening, he had walked a route to make sure he was clean. The car pick-up had been planned and memorized in England before he went to the United States, and it was his first operational act since he arrived in the North.

He turned a corner and met the car on schedule.

"My name's Alice over here. What do I call you?" Hunter asked.

"I'm still Paul. Last name changed, it's Scalia now," Stavros said. "Kept the first name because who knows when someone I know might pop up. Now, I'm Italian-American from South Philly."

"That's more than I need to know, but as long as you're good with it."

"It's solid enough and my documents are all good. Made by the Pros."

Hunter stepped on a switch concealed on the floor of the car and released it. Paul Scalia, né Stavros, heard the crackle of noise from the hidden speakers as the radio signal bounced off one of the repeaters hidden somewhere high in the city and came back again. She keyed the mike a second time.

"Zero Mobile, this is Golf One."

"Golf One, Zero, go."

"Zero, we're coming in."

"Roger, standing by."

Hunter eyed Stavros as she drove on. "We're almost there."

"Golf One?" he asked.

"That's me, girl one. Zero Mobile is control. Clever, no?"

"Not really, but simple. What's my call-sign?"

"Your call-sign is Sierra One, but you have a codename too."

"What is it?"

"Goose wanted to call you 'COWBOY', but we nixed that as being too American."

"What did you come up with?"

"You're SEARCHER."

"Would that make Neil 'Debbie'?"

"I don't know what you're talking about."

He could see that Hunter had missed the reference completely. *Too obscure*, he thought.

"Forget it, it's a John Wayne thing. So what did you come up with for him?"

"He's VIPER."

"The only snake in Ireland. Will finding him make me a saint?"

A sideways look from Hunter.

"Doubtful. Your type usually don't make the grade."

"Just as well. I'm not Catholic."

"What are you?"

"A closed book. Religion isn't something that I talk about, especially here."

"Trying to stay out of it?" Hunter said.

"Trying to stay alive."

Stavros thought back to the arguments he'd heard back in Berlin between Neil and Ewen about Ireland. But he was a Protestant who didn't think much about the Troubles. It hadn't been his concern back then, but it had become one.

"You scared?" she asked.

"Of course. If I said I wasn't, I'd either be lying or crazy."

"You volunteered for this."

"I always volunteer."

"You didn't have to."

"Yes, I did. It's part of my job description."

"It was your choice. Besides, if you don't, who will?"

"No one. Back in the States, most people don't care unless it threatens their football and beer."

"You know the most important battles are fought in places no one gives a damn about. Showing up is half the struggle."

Stavros thought a moment before he spoke. "It's like being a sheep dog keeping the wolves at bay while the sheep eat their grass without a clue of what's happening around them. So few of us are willing to risk it all."

"That just means we have the greater share of the task."

He paused. "Saint Crispin's Day, right?"

"You got it."

"I know: the fewer men, the more honor. So I say to you, come, we have dragons to slay and maidens to save!"

"I don't remember Henry the Fifth mentioning dragons or maidens," she said.

"They were there. Dragons always be there, child."

"Are you Americans all so silly?"

Hunter killed the headlights and turned into a narrow, desolate street and finally into a fenced yard surrounded on three sides by what appeared to be abandoned warehouse buildings. The chain-link gate was quickly shut by two dark shadows as soon as the car passed over the threshold. Three other cars were already parked in apparent disarray except that they were pointed at the gate, poised for a quick exit. Several more human shadows could barely be seen, strategically placed to provide overwatch of the cars and the entrance to the center building. Hunter pulled her car around the yard in a wide arc and backed into position closest to the entrance without bothering to clear her route. She knew where she was going, and anyone stupid enough to be in the way probably deserved to be run over. Everything she had done this evening was tight, fast, and well executed.

Shutting off the motor, she opened the door and motioned for Stavros to follow. No interior light came on and the doors were left partially opened; they might have to leave quickly. There was also no need to lock up since five weapons were covering the yard.

Hunter made her way inside and up a steel staircase in the dark with Stavros close behind. The air smelled stale and trash was scattered across the floor. Crumpled paper and cardboard, old bottles once full, now discarded after their owners had drunk them empty. He shuffled along behind her through the detritus as she led him into a large abandoned hall. Stavros looked up to see old girders criss-crossing the roof high above him. The interior was what he imagined a Victorian workhouse might look like, and when the ancient wooden floor protested under his weight, he hoped it wouldn't give way and dump them in the cellar. Aside from the rush of water from an old millrace that ran along the back of the building it was quiet. The sound told him the windows were all open or had been broken by people who got satisfaction from destroying inanimate objects. In the cavernous room, he saw a tableau out of a crime movie: a table draped with a big Belfast city map stood near the center with four chairs arrayed about it. A lone, battery-powered lamp threw a weak circle of light onto the floor, a pattern that diminished at the edges and disappeared altogether in the gloom that shrouded them.

He recognized two faces immediately, two captains he had last seen in England: Rhys Brown and Rupert Hamish. Stavros had already categorized the two. Brown seemed to be a good officer, a leader. The other seemed aloof, distant. Actually, he didn't like Hamish at all. A little paunchy with dish-water blond hair, his attempt at a moustache was pathetic for a grown man and yet he affected the self-assured manner of an elite schooled officer that held everyone, especially the other ranks, with an unspoken disdain subtly delivered through manner and tone. In another era, he would have been a man born to rule the colonies ineptly.

In other words, he was a pompous ass.

Shadows moved in the background, gliding close to the light like moths, then fading away as they drifted off to another corner of the room: the protective security heavies. Well practiced, alert, unobtrusive, and very quiet.

Everyone, Brown, Hamish, and the others, were dressed in civilian clothing. Hamish, who again looked to be working on a different wavelength, was wearing a rather crisp and obviously new Barbour oilcloth coat, while the others wore well-worn clothes that blended with the locals. There were many Browning Hi Powers stuffed in waistbands evident along with a variety of submachine guns carried at the ready among the men. Hunter was the only woman present.

"Are we expecting visitors?" Stavros asked.

"We're in a no-go area, so anyone who shows up here is probably bad. We don't want to get caught with our knickers down, now do we?"

Stavros decided that Hamish liked to preach.

"Heaven forbid," Stavros answered.

"More importantly, we don't want anyone to see you with the likes of us. That would be bad for your health," said Brown. "But, let's get down to business. What have you been up to these last days?"

"I'm trying to break through a rock wall," said Stavros.

"Not getting much cooperation, are you?"

"Not getting any would be more accurate."

"Where have you been?" Hamish asked.

"Here and there, New Lodge, Duncairn, Shaftsbury, Falls, the port, the center of town mostly." Stavros pointed at the map to illustrate his travels. "I'm searching for inspiration but haven't found any yet."

"You probably need to shift west to the wards like Ardoyne, White Rock, Highfield. A good mix of loyalist and republican areas. It's a lot more residential out there. Just mind you don't get yourself shot."

"Have you gotten any intel on him? Maybe who he's working with?"

"No, not a whisper. We don't have any information on who or what part of the organization he's working with. We *think* it could be the same cell that took out Mountbatten and we'd like to confirm that," said Hamish.

"I imagine you would. You can't even check for his flight arrival information? That would be a start."

"We can't ask. Not only do we not have an identity, we can't tip off the authorities in the Republic who might give away our interest in him."

"Then what exactly do we need to discuss here?" asked Stavros.

"We wanted to get an idea of how you were holding up, a sense of how you were handling the pressure," said Hamish.

"Really? You risked bringing me here when you could have just asked Hunter to brief you?"

"Agent handlers have a tendency to be exceedingly positive about their assets."

Stavros looked over at Hunter who remained impassive. She'd heard it before.

"I'm not an asset."

"Well, she's not trained to do personality assessments."

"That's a basic skill for anyone trained to handle agents. Don't you trust Hunter's judgement, Captain Hamish?"

Hunter stared off into the darkness, sensing the tension. Stavros felt that inwardly she was cheering him on.

"It's not your place to be concerned with whom I trust, Sergeant," said Hamish. A touch of anger flared in his eyes.

At that moment, Stavros realized there was some sort of game going on that he wasn't privy to and that he wouldn't be able to decode that evening. Nor was he in the mood for games.

"Fine. In answer to your question, I'm in good shape. I just need to get on with it and see it through."

"'Sir', you forgot the 'sir'," said Hamish, his voice dripping with disdain. He was even more annoyed with the impertinence of the young man standing in front of him.

The hall was suddenly very quiet. The low rush of flowing water outside was the only sound. Stavros smiled but didn't feel it. He knew what Hamish was now. A controller. Not a controller of agents but a controller of people's emotions and initiatives. The emotions and initiatives of those who worked for him. Hamish stifled the independent action of his subordinates. He wondered why Brown didn't intervene. He looked at Brown's face. It said nothing except that he didn't want to be in the middle of the conversation. In the milliseconds elapsed, Stavros measured the distance between him and Hamish and Hamish and the windows behind, all while wondering if Hamish could swim. Fleeting thoughts.

Stavros looked straight at Hamish. Only a dickhead would demand to be called Sir.

"The word 'sir' is a term of respect," Stavros said. He paused to consider how much he wanted to push his luck.

Brown took a step forward and said,

"I think we're getting away from the subject at hand. What do you need?"

"I need intel on Neil, the arrival of any strangers, foreigners, anything at all. Don't you have any informants inside? Otherwise, I don't think I'll get a chance to spot him."

"Right," Brown said, "we'll get on it and try to pry something loose. We need to be careful though; we don't want to let on that we know he's about."

"Understood, but I can't ask about him directly either, you know," Stavros said.

"I know that. Just remember, whatever you do, if you see something or hear something strange, get out of there as fast as you can and let us know. You don't want to get picked up by the locals. As a stranger, they won't take time to question you and nobody will save your arse. They'll just assume you are part of it and then it's game over."

"Got it. Don't worry, I intend to avoid aggravating either side."

"One last thing. We can set you up with a clandestine radio so you can call for backup. It's concealable and has a hidden earpiece. Do you want one?"

"Not just no, but hell no. If anyone sees that, I'm instantly the enemy."

"I thought not, but I had to ask. Okay, Hunter, put our man back in place and get back to base safely," Brown said.

It was less a dismissal than a defusing of the situation. Hamish stood to the side, brooding. Stavros waited a moment to see if he would speak. When he didn't, he turned and headed at a brisk clip for the stairwell, this time with Hunter in tow. When they drove out of the lot Hunter finally spoke.

"Hamish isn't really army," she said.

"No? What is he then?"

"He's from Six."

"The Secret Intelligence Service? He's under cover as army intel?"

"Yes."

"So this mission is being run by SIS?"

"They have the executive authority. We're tasked to support them."

"They're working inside the UK?"

"I don't know about the decisions made in London, but it has something to do with your friend, VIPER, and his contacts in the South. But I didn't tell you that."

"That's great news. I thought this was just a search for my missing leprechaun. It's beginning to feel a bit more complicated."

22

His disagreement with Danny Monahan more or less resolved, Neil struggled with his targeting package. He was handicapped because no one would share what sites they intended to hit. He imagined they didn't trust him with the actual targets yet, so broad requirements would have to suffice. He hoped the reconnaissance teams would bring him enough detail that would be useful to build the bombs. He knew only that the targets were made of stone—that probably meant a castle or government building, maybe both—and the people inside would be government or, even better, a royal or two. He paged through his Baedeker and quickly decided on several possibilities around the province. There were several government buildings scattered around the periphery, but no one truly important would be there. Holywood's Palace Barracks, a nice fat army base, although it was nearly impossible to penetrate and there wasn't a stone structure he could find. Queen's University maybe? But all very large and difficult to blow up. He went through the castles one by one: Carrickfergus, Belfast, Bangor …. Each offered the same question—why would it be a suitable target for anything other than killing what few tourists there were in the North? That wouldn't be good for the cause. There were several other contenders though.

Parliament? That's stone, but too damn big. Belfast City Hall? Also too big. Maybe an army base or a customs house?

After his research, he was pretty sure he had the answers he needed and wrote his questions based on what he could see from the maps and pictures in his guidebook. Although he didn't name the locations specifically, he knew he would find out for sure when the recon came back or if Danny gave anything away. For the moment he was playing a game to get into his hosts' mindset. It was important to know exactly who he was trying to kill.

After several hours of contemplation, scribbling, rewriting, and condensing of notes, he had what he needed. He set down his pen and scooped up the wadded papers and dropped them into a metal trash bin. He picked up the bin and walked outside, placing it onto the grass. A wooden match scratched across the sole of his boot and was tossed in with the papers. There was a quick flare and then the papers curled and turned orange, then brown, then gray-black as the fire consumed them. As he stirred the burning notes, ash and sparks swirled up around him until nothing but a pile of glowing orange embers stared back at him.

He turned to see Monahan staring from the doorway. Neil walked back to the cottage, pulled a folded single page from his pocket, and handed it to the big Irishman.

"What's this?"

"The questions I need your people to answer."

"It looks like a survey for a landscaping company."

"That is so no one but the team will know what it's about. Their answers will tell me everything we need to know." Neil emphasized the "we."

"You're gonna have to tell them how to do that."

"I will. But you'll have to tell me which castle will be more important: Stormont or Hillsborough?"

Danny stared at Neil for a moment, then wheeled around and disappeared back into the house.

"Don't go anywhere, boy. You've still got work to do," Danny snorted, throwing the words over his shoulder.

Neil smiled to himself and decided he needed a beer.

23

Stavros decided he'd take Hamish's advice and try the pubs in the western part of Belfast. He would be a long way from where the tourists visited but maybe, just maybe, he might find an opening. He still felt a bit lost, like he was writing a novel while knowing little of the plot and only one character with an unknown motive. Everything else was a swirl of noise, most of it unimportant static. He knew somewhere in the country there had to be a clue; he just had to hold his breath, dive deep, and hope he was in the right part of the ocean.

He found a room for rent advertised in another pub. It turned out to be in a small home, a widow looking for some extra cash off the books. Her man had passed on several years before and she had no family to speak of, or she refused to speak of them. She was hoping for a long-term renter, but Stavros had offered her cash up front for two weeks and that sealed the deal.

After she cooked him breakfast the first morning, he told her he didn't expect any additional meals. The sausages were charred beyond what might be called jerky and the scrambled eggs would have sent Nero Wolfe back to his bedroom; twenty minutes of whisking were abbreviated to two minutes of a combination of stirring and searing until they had a consistency of congealed rubber and tasted worse. He told her he would be out most days and just needed a place to rest and catch up on his writing.

When he told her about his article, she looked at him askance and wondered aloud why anyone would be interested in their plight. She couldn't understand the words "human interest story" as anything more than a way to make people emotional or to profit off tragedy.

"What will it get for us?"

"It will call attention to the problem and might push people to change things."

"Not the people that matter, not the politicians who make their whole lives off of us. They'll never change," the woman said, an angry despair evident in her voice.

At least she listened, he thought. Maybe that was a point he could make, and he jotted it down in his notebook. Then he remembered he wasn't really writing an article and his conversations were more or less pointless in the long run. They served only one purpose, to find that one tiny clue that would tell him where to go next.

Shankill was unlike any area Stavros had yet encountered in Ireland. Granted the poorer inner city of Belfast was in sad shape, but here in West Belfast he felt like he was in a war zone. It wasn't quite the wasteland the analyst back in the UK had described without having seen it and it wasn't overt destruction that he saw. It was neglect coupled with passive or open hostility. Choking with rubbish, barbed wire strewn about and burnt-out buildings—it was a stark landscape. Soldiers and police in the streets, graffiti and murals on the walls, rats in the garbage.

Scratch that last, rats are in the garbage wherever you go.

Most of Shankill was oppressively deteriorated, the buildings crumbling, gray walls melded with the troubled, overcast skies to produce a monotone landscape, dotted with small trash fires and discarded, broken furniture. A banner was stretched haphazardly between two windows, its motto "No Surrender" crudely painted in white on the blood-red fabric.

The street had an unfriendly smell to it. The eyes of the people who lived, walked, or patrolled it reflected that sentiment, whether from distrust, anger, or despondence.

He was in loyalist territory. He knew from his briefings and he knew from his senses. Every prominent wall carried the inscription or image of their protectors, murals that were a warning to those who didn't belong and a thin shield of protection to those who did. It was incredible to think that the opposite faction was sequestered in an equally forlorn Falls district maybe half a mile distant.

He did his best to look uninteresting and uninterested at the same time. But as he walked up the street, he looked about, watching those he could see and for those he could not. He was violating rule number one of counter-surveillance: never look for surveillance. If you do, they will know it. But he knew the rules didn't count here. Normally, through the tricks of the trade, surveillance teams will eventually show themselves. But here, it would be too late. He didn't care about the rules because he wanted to see anything coming at him. He was a stranger in this land and there wasn't anything he could do about it.

He finally reached his goal at the top of the road, a small tavern called Harbour View. The name didn't make sense because there was no harbor for him to look at, but he accepted that there must have been an altogether reasonable answer of which he was unaware. He plunged into the pub after the gentleman at the front door checked his shoulder bag for weapons and explosives and, without a word, opened the squeaking metal gate to let him finally open the door.

Plunge was a good word, because it was if he had belly flopped into the local pool with a thunderclap of a splash. The place went dead silent for a good thirty seconds and, as he waited for his vision to adjust to the dark from the outside gray, he saw many pairs of eyes staring back. Some had a pint in hand midway to their mouths, others were turned away from the television screen, while only the bartender kept moving, diligently polishing a glass to a crystal clear shine. Perhaps too diligently. Stavros took off his fisherman's cap and walked up to a free space at the bar. After a moment the bartender relented and set down the glass and rested both his hands on the metal sink behind a well-scarred wooden bar front.

"What can I get you?" he said.

"A pint, please," Stavros said pointing at the Harp emblem on the tap.

The man stared at him for a moment, then grabbed a glass, not the one he been polishing, and pulled the handle, keeping an eye on Stavros while the golden beer flowed from the tap.

"You're not from around here, are ya? You're American?"

"Good call, I am. I'm from Philadelphia."

Stavros wanted his "Americanness" to be known to all those who might be interested.

"On vacation then, are you?"

"Not really, I'm a writer." He took the pint and set a £10 note on the bar. "Can you just run a tab with that?"

"Sure, mate," said the bartender. He scooped up the money and stuffed it in a drawer. "We'll settle up at the end." A half-smile flickered on his face.

Turning back to the open room, Stavros saw most of the patrons had gone back to what they had been doing. Only a few continued to eye him, mostly middle-aged men, as he moved to an unoccupied table near the front window. The table would be the last one to be occupied, he knew, closest to the door if a gunner came through it and to the shards of glass if a bomb went off outside. It was better not to think about it. He sat and pulled a small notebook out of his oilcloth shoulder bag along with a deck of cards. Flipping to a bookmarked page, he began to scratch a few notes about his walk and what he'd seen along the way and by the time he reached the bottom of his first glass, he'd filled several pages with his observations. He looked up to see the bartender set a new glass on his table and scoop up the old one.

"Thought you might be ready for another," he said. Again, with a half-smile that almost felt like a greeting, he was gone just as quickly. Stavros looked around him again and this time not a soul was interested in what he was doing. The pen went into the notebook as he closed it and he laid out a line of cards on the table, slowly dealing himself a hand of solitaire. He picked up the first and most obvious plays and placed the cards in their proper order before setting the deck down to take a sip of beer. He sat back contemplating the cards while watching the goings on in the background.

He didn't know much of the history of the neighborhood, but he did know this bar was a well-known loyalist hangout. It had been attacked by the IRA several years before when a three-man active service unit had burst into the place and opened fire while one of them planted a bomb just inside the entrance. Five local men had died.

What he hoped for today was that lightning didn't strike twice.

He went back to flipping the cards and making his way to getting rid of the entire deck when he felt a presence to his left rear. He knew it wasn't the bartender; he came from the front.

Stavros glanced up briefly and saw a young man roughly his own age, but lesser in physical stature and apparently not well off financially from the looks of his clothing. He was thin, sallow of face—*either too much smoking or too little Vitamin A*, Stavros thought—with an oily black mop of hair.

"Hi. What's up?" Stavros asked as he concentrated on the seven of hearts in his hand that had nowhere to go. He tossed it in the reject pile and flipped over a queen of spades. There was a red king waiting for her, but he held off dropping it into place and waited.

"Are you going to play it?" the young man asked.

"Getting there," said Stavros. "Waiting for an answer first."

"Just watching," he said. "Barman tells me you're American, a writer. What 'chu writing about?"

126

"I'm trying to understand a bit about the North." He placed the queen on the king.

"You mean Ulster."

"Yes, sorry. Ulster it is," Stavros said.

"That's an important distinction hereabouts."

"I understand, but I'm an American and I'm learning."

"Can I sit down?" the young man said.

"Sure."

Stavros shoved his little lines of cards into a pile, picked them up, and squared them back into a neat deck before he shoved them back in their box. He pulled his notebook close, opened it, and in a very precise script, he wrote the word "Ulster" at the top of the next blank page and dated it before closing it again.

"Now I will be sure to remember. I'm Paul, by the way," he said, extending his hand.

"William, William Graham," the other man said, shaking hands.

Weak grip, Stavros noted. He wasn't sure if that meant Graham was delicate or cautious.

"What's your family?" Graham said.

"Family? I'm Italian-American."

"Not that, your name. What is it?"

"Ah. It's Scalia," Stavros answered.

"Not Irish? Why would you be visiting Ireland then?"

"Like the barman said, I'm a writer."

"So then, Paul Scalia, what are you writing about?"

"You're a curious one, aren't you? I'm trying to put together an article on how the Troubles affect families."

"I imagine that's difficult. Not many here want to talk to strangers about their problems."

"Actually, I've noticed that. I haven't gotten anywhere, which is why I'm playing solitaire."

"Solitaire? We call it patience," said Graham.

"Patience. That's appropriate, especially for me right now."

"Well, good luck with your article then. I have to be going," William said, standing to go. He didn't offer his hand, he just stood, turned to the door, and walked out.

Curiouser and curiouser.

He drank his beer slowly and visually canvassed the crowd for their interest in him or William's departure. No one seemed to care. A couple more notes went into the book, none of which advanced his article, before he returned to his cards for one last round.

He could see it was getting dark and therefore time to go. He had no wish to return to his bed-down site when he couldn't see his surroundings. He stood and dropped his belongings into his bag and walked over to face the barman.

"Calling it an evening then?"

"Yes, I don't know the area well enough to stay out late," Stavros said.

The barman laid a £5 note on the bar. "You're good, son." *From mate to son.*

"What did the young man want of you?"

"I think he just wanted to know who I was. Asked me what I was writing about then took off," said Stavros.

"Strangers always attract interest around here. Take care of yourself."

"Thanks." Stavros replaced the fiver with a couple of £1 notes. "I'll be back."

He took one more look at the bar before he left. Minimal interest.

***

Outside, the sky was growing dark, but he figured he had plenty of time to reach his fish shop, the last checkpoint, to get some food before he did the last five minutes to his temporary home. Hat firmly in place, shoulder bag tucked under his arm, and hands deep in his coat pockets, he strode quickly back down the road.

It was only five minutes before he heard his name, an urgent call, more a whisper, but clearly spoken.

William Graham came out of a small alleyway, not much more than a footpath between houses but a good place to wait. He came alongside Stavros, who didn't slow down.

"Funny meeting you here," Stavros said.

"Not funny. Serious. Are you really writing about the Troubles?"

"Yes, just as I said. Why?"

"I want to talk with you."

"About?" Stavros looked about him involuntarily.

"I'm UVF. There are some things I need to talk about."

Stavros' heart skipped a beat or two.

Ulster Volunteer Force, damn. Not exactly who I need to be talking with, but still ....

"Okay, how?"

"Meet me tomorrow at the Waterworks. The north end of Swan Lake at 11 a.m."

And he was gone.

24

It had been a while since the survey team had been dispatched and Neil had almost depleted his personal reading material. Before long, he'd ask Rourke to get him some more books.

He had spent most of his days drawing schematics of devices and sketching diagrams of what he assumed would be the targets. Nothing had been confirmed to him, but Monahan's reaction had all but confirmed the two castles would figure prominently. Both were what he considered hard targets. There would be no stealthy approach and placement of a bomb where it could do its damage. There would be no repeat of what happened at the *Wolfsschanze* or the Vemork Heavy Water Plant. This time it would have to be a stand-off attack. No rocket propelled grenades, easily defeated by chain-link fence, or mortars that may, but probably wouldn't, hit the target they were aimed at. Precise and deadly was what he needed. The third requirement was also a limiting factor: size. An 800-pound ANFO charge would not work on a stone castle unless you placed it right next to the wall—and he suspected the teams would not be able to get close to the buildings.

He visualized the targets. Two old stone buildings, filled with people. Striking the buildings would be symbolic; striking the people would be devastating. MI5 officers, maybe a source or two, all the files … that would portend serious damage to their operations in the province. He ran the details and decided Monahan's bosses had chosen a good target. As to Hillsborough, that was another thing altogether. Mountbatten was just an over-the-hill personality.

A prince or a princess, a royal … now there's a target. The Queen …? That thought whirled around in his head like an impending cyclone. He might have to start looking for a new residence in South America or Antarctica.

When he finished, his options list was short, but doable. Now all he needed were the surveys, the recce of the target, to finalize his preparations.

25

The meeting should have gone off without a hitch. As the contact time approached, Stavros had a bad premonition, but then he often did. It was a primeval thing that most modern humans suppress but one that soldiers must reawaken in order to survive. When he was in the field, he felt closer to his environment than when he was in the barracks. His senses were more acute, his hearing attuned to unusual or out-of-place noises, his vision more focused. He used his best tradecraft and ran a long counter-surveillance route. He didn't see any slow-moving cars or people waiting in strange places; no coincidences, anomalies, or repetitions. There are no coincidences in this line of work—if you see one, you break off whatever it is you're trying to do and go for the alternate. Anomalies are a different thing. It might be a man standing in the wrong spot biding his time, trying not to look out of place, or a work crew that doesn't appear to be working on anything. Maybe a food stand that wasn't there before. Strange things that don't make sense. Repetitions were easier; see the same person or car twice and it was game over, time to quit for the day.

Early that morning, Stavros had left the house and followed the route he had planned out with his guidebook. He had stopped for a coffee in one place and breakfast in another, then he kept walking.

Now he was in position and thinking about the unknown factor that he had no command over, which was whether William had been smart that morning. Then again, he might not have a clue what he was doing or, worse, he might just be complacent. Someone can always unwittingly drag bad news to a meet. The previous evening, William had showed something, fear or wariness, Stavros didn't know which and he had no idea what to expect. So, he kept his eyes open for anything out of place. But nothing came, not William, not unwelcome intruders, nothing. After thirty minutes of wandering aimlessly while looking for what he didn't know, he turned and walked back toward his room. He decided he would visit the Harbour View in the evening and maybe William would show or meet him outside again.

When he finally turned onto his street, he saw why his antennae had lit up earlier. There was a gray Land Rover parked in front of his destination. He saw the Royal Ulster Constabulary markings and two policemen standing on the sidewalk talking.

No choice but to continue and no reason not to, he walked on until he was abreast of the men. They watched him approach warily, hands resting on their service weapons.

"Good day, officers."

"Are you Paul Scalia?" the shorter one with stripes on his shoulders said.

"Yes, how may I help you?" Stavros said.

"Do you know William Graham?" The look on the constable's face was grave.

"Yes, I mean, but only a little. We met yesterday evening."

"You'll be coming with us then, please."

"Why? What's up?"

"You're American, correct?" The two officers stared at him hard.

Stavros decided whatever they had in mind was serious and a smart-ass answer about being asked that a lot would be inappropriate.

"Yes. Would you like to see my passport?"

"Not here. Let's go downtown."

"May I ask why?"

A pause.

"Graham was found dead this morning. You were the last person seen with him."

26

The ride downtown was anything but silent, with the potholes rattling the Land Rover to pieces and chewing years off the car's life. Stavros decided it had seen better days, but then realized it had lived a short, hard life. They entered a closed street blocked by bollards and men with watchful eyes who carried their Stirling submachine guns and Ruger Mini-14s at the ready. After a quick check and a lifted gate, they were allowed into the courtyard sanctum of a police barracks.

Stavros had not been restrained. He assumed he was a person of interest but not a suspect in the demise of William Graham. He followed the lead constable into the well-protected building and up a set of worn granite stairs that had been polished to a shine by the passing of years and policemen's boots. They passed a reception desk where his escorts exchanged brief, cryptic messages of greeting that could have meant he was being taken out for execution for all he understood of the language.

First, they installed him in a small room. Small, but room enough for a table and three chairs. He was asked to sit in the chair facing the door, which was the only portal into the room. He saw there were no one-way, mirrored windows to observe and no overhead vents to asphyxiate him with *Zyklon-B*. It was simply a place to interview.

He sat for twenty minutes before a different constable came into the room. An officer rank apparently.

"I'm Inspector Flynn," he said.

Stavros stood. "Paul Scalia."

"We'd like to talk to you about your encounter with William Graham. We found him in an alley, shot dead. Three rounds to the head."

"I don't have a pistol."

The inspector was not amused. And so it went for twenty minutes, questions not only about William Graham, but why Stavros was in Ireland and even more pointedly, why he was in the Harbour View that day. Flynn seemed to have trouble fathoming why Stavros would want to be in Ireland, let alone write about it.

"So, you're not Irish and you have no connections to Ireland, right."

"None, other than studying the people of the conflict."

Flynn came back to the subject of Graham several times.

"Why do you think he wanted to talk with you?"

"No idea, other than he said he had some things to talk about."

"You said he told you he was UVF."

"He did."

"What did that tell you?"

"Nothing. Maybe he had something to say about what he had experienced, maybe he wanted to talk about football. He didn't say."

"What happened then?"

"Like I said, he told me where I should meet him and then he disappeared."

"What did you do after that?"

"I went back to my room and this morning I went to out to find him, but he never showed."

"After that?"

"I returned to the house where your officers met me, and they brought me here."

Inspector Flynn wrote a couple of notes and stood up.

"Stay here." Flynn left the room.

Stavros had no intention of moving, but he heard the lock turn and knew he wasn't going anywhere.

Minutes passed. *If they're trying to sweat the details of a crime out of me, they'll have a long wait.*

He waited.

The lock clicked and an exterior bolt slid free as the door opened.

It was another man, face half turned, hidden as he spoke to someone outside the room before he shut the door.

He turned and stood stock still for a moment.

"You're lucky that we were watching you last night," Hamish said.

"Why was I lucky?" Stavros said, only partly relieved to see someone he recognized.

"When I heard the Graham boy had been murdered, I thought you might have been involved since you were seen by the watchers in that pub. You know it's a UVF establishment, don't you?"

"I do now. Yesterday, I didn't know anything other than it was in a loyalist area."

"Remember I told you not to get caught up in anything or you'd get hurt?"

Actually, it was Rhys who told me that.

"Yes, but I didn't know anything about that until the policemen told me today."

"Yes, yes. Still, you're probably a bit too hot for Belfast right now. We're going to move you to a new area. It might actually be a better place for you to work."

"Where?"

"Armagh." Hamish said the word like it was a vacation spot.

"Great, that's bandit country," said Stavros.

"Maybe what happened here will work in your favor over there," Hamish said.

"I don't need help, I want to stay off everybody's radar. I need to be forgettable, so the best thing you can do is to keep me off the police blotters and out of the newspapers."

"Of course, that's all been taken care of."

"That's good. Apparently, the last thing I need is to be seen as anyone's confidant. That seems to get people killed."

"And we don't want anything to happen to you, do we? Your task is far too important."

"Important only as far as finding my teammate."

Stavros was wondering how similar British and American intelligence officers actually were. He was beginning to see parallels in how they spoke.

"You don't like me, do you?" Hamish was genuinely curious for once.

"That came out of the blue. Is it that obvious?"

"Since the other evening, yes. Why is that, do you suppose?"

"You remind me of some of our West Pointers. Officers that give orders and expect things to happen."

"That's what officers do."

"Some do. Some actually lead. I prefer leaders."

Stavros had reached a point of not caring what he said to Hamish. Perhaps it was the seeming fruitlessness of his search or perhaps he was just tired of the man, but his inner reserve was ebbing away. Hamish seemed not to realize he was up against a hard case.

"If it wasn't for me, you'd probably be on a plane home or worse yet, in a holding cell. The RUC seem to think you're to blame for Graham," Hamish said.

"First, am I supposed to thank you? Second, that's ridiculous. What motive do I have?"

"Your story about writing an article apparently doesn't ring true to the constables."

"Tell them to check it out with my embassy in Dublin. Being a good American citizen, I registered with them before I came to the North." Stavros was beyond worry; he was irritated with the process.

"They think it's a cover story. No matter, I told them you were a friend and they're prepared to let you go in my custody."

"That's very nice of them. And you too, I am very glad you are on top of everything."

"You don't sound very grateful."

Stavros was about to say, "Why should I be?" when the door creaked open and Rhys Brown stuck his head in the room.

"I heard you needed a ride," he said.

Hamish stared at two people now, clearly irritated by both. One for being insolent, the other for showing up at the wrong time.

***

After Rhys saved him from possible charges of assault on a superior officer in the RUC office, they travelled in an armored Humber Pig to a small military compound. Hamish had abandoned them at the RUC barracks, so it was Rhys and three soldiers in uniform, armed to the teeth, that rode with him. Once there, they switched to a small civilian sedan; Rhys sat in the front with a driver Stavros had not met, and Stavros was in the rear, a watch cap pulled down over much of his face. The car shot out a side exit covered by a couple of Bedfords and disappeared into the city.

It was twenty-five minutes before they arrived at the Element's small base buried deep inside what appeared on the outside to be a commercial facility. Only after they checked through a gate controlled by well-armed "civilian" guards did they enter the hidden enclave.

Their office space was a grouping of trailers inside the courtyard of a large, square building, in fact an empty warehouse without windows. Each section had a separate trailer, as did the soldiers assigned to the unit—*bashas* they called them.

Rhys guided Stavros into one of the shelters, the roof of which was festooned with an antenna farm connected to all the radios inside. There was a constant low roar of static noise until the radios were squelched to quiet their speakers. Large scale 1:12,500 maps were piled in a corner and several smaller-scale maps hung from the walls. It was a planning and command center from which the Element could run its operations and stay in close contact with other units both to make sure there were no friendly fire incidents, and also be close to support elements if required.

"Our brothers from the Regiment are close by, but we needed more space and, quite frankly, distance to make sure we can run our ops without any interference or danger to our cover," Rhys stated.

"Like senior officers who think you're in their jurisdiction?"

"Among others. Opinions are fine, telling us how to do our job is another."

"Well, he said I'm off to Armagh, which I gather is a pretty interesting area," Stavros said.

"Interesting as in, 'May you live in interesting times,' interesting?" Rhys said.

"Seems that way."

"It is. But I have to say, I agree with him on this. The loyalists around Shankill might have decided you're a threat after your meeting with Graham, so it's probably best if you move out for a while."

Rhys paused for a moment, looking very much like he was debating whether or not to continue. Shrugging off whatever it was, he said, "But before you move, we have an issue we need you to look at."

"What's the issue?" Stavros asked.

"We received information on an IRA safe site located in the Republic. It looks to be a bomb factory and it appears there are several young men there and one of them might be your VIPER.

We want to put surveillance on the place and determine what's up. And you will go with the team to positively identify him, that is, if he is your man."

"I thought crossing the border was out of bounds for you."

"Normally, yes. But with approval, very critical missions can be undertaken."

"Approval from London?"

"Yes."

"And this one?"

"We have approval and since you're attached to us, you're included."

"Will my folks be notified?"

"Hamish says the American defense attaché was informed."

"No pushback?"

"None that we've heard."

"Okay, if my guy is there, what happens?"

"We'll figure a way to get him out of there."

"And if I don't spot him?"

"You come back here and we continue to search on this side."

"Why not just do good photography and have me look at the pics here?"

"We want real-time intel. Then we can act before it's too late."

"I imagine I should leave my passport behind?"

"Right. We'll give you an identification card that shows you to be one of us."

"It's not permanent, I hope. I like being American."

"No worries, we'll let you be a Yank again when you return."

✳✳✳

Getting ready took the better part of the next morning. He had to scrounge some decent field clothing and boots, but with a quarter-master who Rhys instructed to "help him out as best you can," he got what he needed plus some. Although his Bergen looked as if it had seen better days, it was filled with good things, the needed things as Stavros saw them. He repacked everything later and memorized where each item was located so he could find it in the dark. It was a process he'd gone through many times. He had a Suunto compass, a small Streamlight flashlight, a pair of Zeiss 8×50 binoculars—the team would have the big optics—an aluminum mess kit and Esbit cooker (although he knew he wouldn't be cooking anything in the hide, he padded it well inside his extra clothing), a first aid kit, a smaller sterile compass in case he lost the first that went into his shirt pocket, a couple of plastic canteens with canvas covers that wouldn't make noise, two knives—one folding, one sheath—and then more socks and underwear. He brought a toothbrush but no toothpaste, nothing that gave off an odor, no hot sauce, no soap, nothing to give away his position to animal or man. The QM gave them some rations, enough for three days and wet, not dehydrated, because they could only carry so much water to the OP. He would not carry a firearm; he had no business shooting anything in the Republic and Rhys quickly acknowledged that point. The other members of the team would carry heavy stuff, but the mission was not about contact; it was about information collection. Who was at the site and what were they up to? These were the questions. Exploitation of the intelligence would either lead to extracting VIPER or they would break off and let someone else handle the "issue." That was his understanding.

Sufficiently kitted out, Stavros shouldered the ruck and walked with Rhys across the compound to another trailer. Rhys pulled the door open and they walked in. Stavros wasn't at all surprised to see Goose. Philip and Reg were also there, as was Hunter.

Goose appraised the newcomer for a moment and then said, "Welcome to our team house."

Not welcome to the "team."

For a fleeting moment Stavros wondered what Goose thought of having a Yank with him in the field, but Philip and Reg seemed to accept his presence amicably. Hunter … well, Hunter was Hunter, just as inscrutable as ever. Although she did deign to flick her hand in a wave hello.

"We're off soon. Got all you need?" Philip asked.

"I'm ready. Where are we going?"

Goose moved to the map and pointed at their present location. "We four will move by air to here—" He pointed at a spot near the border. Then tracing a land route, he said, "Where we'll be picked up and carried across the border at this crossing."

Stavros moved in closer to get the location.

"From there we'll move to a drop-off point, then we'll move by foot into position. It's about a 5k walk."

"Four of us? Who's not going?"

"Hunter will stay here to monitor our communications."

Hunter handed Stavros a copy of that section of the map, which he lined up with the big one to orient.

"Don't mark it," Goose said.

"Don't worry, I paid attention in school," Stavros said. He looked at Goose and both held the gaze for a moment. Finally Goose nodded and continued.

"We'll come out by more or less the same route the following night to our exfil point, which is here."

"How do we get over the border?"

"In the back of a milk truck," Philip said. "We stay inside. The border barrier gets moved, we cross. It's a closed road, no checkpoint, no *Gardaí*."

Stavros noted the position and transferred it mentally to his smaller map.

"What happens if we make contact or are discovered?"

"We run. We head for the border by whichever route is closest and least obvious. If we get broken up, we make our way back on our own."

"Kinda making it up as we go then?"

"Yes, we don't have any emergency evacuation on that side of the border."

"And no 'get out of jail free' card, either," Philip said.

"Could be worse," said Stavros.

"How so?"

"The East Germans aren't securing this frontier."

Stavros continued to study the map, making sure he could pinpoint the locations and knew the azimuths and distances without notes.

In and out, simple. But not really, he knew.

"Don't worry, we'll be with you," Goose said.

"I'm not worried. Anyway, all I need to do is run faster than the slowest one of you."

***

The trip to the airfield was relatively short and uncomfortable in the back of a van. They climbed out of the truck once it had stopped inside the protection of a hangar. The hangar opened up onto the field and their waiting ride, a Westland Lynx, sitting in the mid-afternoon sunlight that streamed down through the shards of clouds that seemed to have no place to go.

At least it's not raining. I hate flying in the rain.

Load up took all of two minutes as the rotor blades of the helicopter slowly churned through the air, their tips hanging down like wilted leaves without the airflow to support them. Hunter moved to slide the door shut from the outside, but hesitated long enough to say, "Good luck," to Stavros before securing it. She looked him directly in the eyes for once and seemed to mean what she said, and as she backed off from the door, Stavros gave her a thumbs up. Then the turbines shrieked as the pilot spooled up power for takeoff.

Stavros looked at Goose and the others as they gained altitude. They were all staring out the perspex portals, each seemingly lost in thought. Black Armalite AR-18 rifles stood like totems between the legs of each man, barrels pointed at the floor. It was better that way; bullets from accidental discharges generally did less damage going down than up in a helicopter. He settled back in the webbing and turned his gaze to the countryside, dark green, rushing by below. He was almost looking forward to the field again; at least he would have something specific to look for and wouldn't be flailing about seeking a needle in too many haystacks. But first they had to get into position.

The helo hit the ground with a bit of a bounce and settled into its new nest. The crew chief slid one door open as Philip pulled the opposite door open from the inside. The first thing Stavros noticed as he slid out of the troop compartment was the grass. It was flattened by the rotor wash and pointed outwards toward the edge of a circle away from the bird. He grabbed his ruck and followed the other three around the nose, hunched over, his head down just in case the blades somehow dipped too low. He cleared the edge of the circle and knelt as his comrades were doing and waited. The whine picked up again and the wind pressed him down further into the soft ground as the helo lifted off, pirouetted gracefully, and headed northeast back to its base at Bessbrook. A Bedford was waiting for them, along with a stick of soldiers in a spread-out defensive perimeter. There were many men, at least twenty that he could see. Regulars, the "Green Army" as the troopers called them, but he couldn't tell from what unit they came. They were looking away from them into the distance where any threat might emerge, standard issue British Army SLRs at the ready, just as a protective element should. The area had been cleared of locals and even the sheep seemed to have

145

disappeared from the fields. The helicopter's cargo was not meant to be seen by outsiders.

Stavros stood and trotted over to the truck. Throwing his bag into the back after the others, he climbed up the tailgate, into the bed and onto a seat. The tailgate clanged shut and was secured with chains and the rear tarp flapped down.

It was quiet. Momentarily.

The engine turned over and revved with a roar before they jerked off the field and onto a hard paved road.

"We're going to rendezvous with our transport. Wouldn't do to be seen here with a milk truck, now would it?" Philip smiled at the thought.

"You guys deliver 'milk' often?" Stavros asked.

"Not very. Takes a lot to get us approved for a border cross. I've only done it once before. Maybe Goose has been there more?" Philip glanced over at Goose who didn't respond. He sat with his eyes closed, trying to relax against the hard seat back.

It was another twenty minutes of driving before the truck slowed to a stop. The driver dropped the tailgate quietly, revealing they were stopped in a small lay-by on a quiet road. Goose swept the tarp up over the canvas top to reveal the yawning opening of another truck, a commercial van, and motioned for everyone to hop off. It was a simple transfer of conveyances. Everyone took the two steps between the trucks and hopped in the new vehicle. The doors closed with a solid whomp and they were in the dark—literally and figuratively. *At least I am*, Stavros thought.

Goose had an exchange with the two guys in the front cabin before he slid its door shut with a click and settled back with the rest of the team.

"About two hours to drop-off," he said. And that was all he said before he closed his eyes and again settled into a seeming trance.

Stavros noticed that there were no dairy products in the truck.

27

Stavros woke with a start as the truck came to a halt.

The brakes are quiet. Somebody actually takes care of the equipment.

The sun in the western sky had just set as they climbed out of the van. There was a thin orange-yellow crescent of light, just a minute slice, that Stavros could see through the trees which marked the edge of the earth. Before they had finished unloading their gear, the crescent disappeared finally, completely, and they were shrouded in the gray-black of dusk. The moon was not yet visible above the eastern horizon.

Goose spoke briefly with the men in the front of the truck, muted whispers confirming locations and pick-ups, before they drove off. The team were left standing on the road, hemmed in by trees that muted the sounds of the countryside.

"This is our RV point if things go to hell. If no one shows after sixty minutes, you're on your own to make it to the border," Goose said.

As planned, Reg led off. As "point man," he would bust brush, so to speak, moving quietly forward, finding the way, avoiding pitfalls and contact with anyone who shouldn't see the team, which was everyone. He was the big guy, not so much in height but brawn. He carried his rucksack like it was a school kid's book bag. But Stavros knew it was heavy, as carrying the radio and batteries was his job.

Goose followed, his blond hair invisible under a bush hat, the rest of him disappearing into the foliage, his DPM camouflage and netting worn as a neck scarf blending as well in the Irish Republic as it had at the landing pad in the province earlier that day. Stavros followed. Then came Philip. Stavros saw him at the beginning and then only knew he was walking behind him as he focused on following Goose. After a few minutes, his eyes grew accustomed to the dark and he could better see the silhouettes of the two men in front of him. He didn't want to fixate on the bobbing, yellow-green glow of the luminescent cat eyes on the back of Goose's hat. Stavros knew the man would not hesitate to leave his hat stuck in a tree just to fool him.

He could just hear the breathing of the others, rhythmic, unstrained. There were other sounds as well: the occasional scratch of a branch across the fabric of a Bergen, the crunch of dry leaves or the snap of a twig under a boot in the dark. They moved slowly. Walk ten minutes, pause for a couple. There was no enemy to expect, no danger of contact and a firefight, just caution. Didn't want to stumble on anyone.

Finally, a stream and a crossing. One man at a time. Reg went across first and scouted forward a bit, then came back to give the all clear. Goose crossed, then Stavros, feeling the water break the seal of his boots and the cold chill on his feet as it seeped in. No standing around, he waded across slowly, feeling his way forward to make sure each step was firmly placed before he shifted his weight. Then the bank and a scramble up and wait for Philip. All together they started out again, up a small incline to a ridge along which ran an old stone wall. Rocks dug from the fields were loosely placed to mark the limits of someone's property. The team stopped. Goose went forward and huddled with Reg. Whispers, then Reg came back to Stavros.

"We wait here," he said.

Philip closed in and they formed a little circle as Goose dropped his rucksack and moved away down the wall. When Goose had disappeared into the black, Reg whispered, "He's off to find our contact."

Stavros wondered at that revelation. No one had mentioned meeting a contact. Then, as if to answer an unspoken question, Reg said, "I tracked a bit left on purpose, so the guy should be to the right."

Philip said nothing. Stavros decided he would also remain mute and be the quiet American. He had nothing to bitch about. He was traipsing around Ireland and getting paid for it. Not the best scenery to be sure, but he was on full per diem for Belfast without the requirement to hand over receipts for his accounting.

Twenty minutes or so later, Stavros heard movement coming toward them from down the wall. He focused on the sound as did his companions, their rifles ready—not combat ready, but just to be sure ready. It was Goose. He knelt and shrugged his ruck back on.

"Almost there," he said. "We'll move to the support site and then go forward to the OP."

In unison, the team silently rose and moved into line. Goose led off, and again the dark forest to the front slid past them on the right and left as they walked the ridge until they were five. The fifth man, the contact, was sitting on the wall waiting. Another short conversation. Whispers.

Goose came back.

"This is the support site. Reg and Philip will set up here. Paul, for now stay here and I will go forward to get into position. Then when the second observer comes out, you'll follow after me."

"How do I find it?"

"Follow the string," the contact man said, grasping Stavros' arm and leading him to a line tied to a tree. Goose climbed quietly over the wall, took the cord in hand, and walked slowly forward. Stavros sat down to wait next to the contact, who he now understood to be a member of the first observation team.

After what seemed an eternity, another man, a new man, returned from the dark place that Goose had disappeared into.

"You next?"

"Yes, that's me," Stavros said.

"It's about 80 meters forward. When you hit three knots in the line, go to ground and crawl in the last 20 meters. The OP is about 200 meters from the target, but you still need to be quiet. There are at least four guys out there and they seem pretty alert. You'll see come morning."

Turning to his partner, he said, "Ready?" and then they disappeared, walking straight away from the wall somewhat in the direction the new team had come in from.

"We're on our own now, mate," said Philip. "We're your backup here. Goose has a handheld if you need anything and we'll report your findings back via HF to Base. So good luck."

"Thanks, but who were those two?"

"Our mates, same troop, different patrol. They've been here since we learned of the house."

The forest floor was covered with all manner of dead things shed from the trees and plants—leaves, bark, moss, and organisms slowly, silently decomposing into humus, damp and soft under his boots. As Stavros moved off through the darkness, he was again completely alone as he had been in Belfast, although now, in theory at least, he had cover from his comrades. Can I call them that? Comrades? Surrounded by the dark, he felt he was truly at the end of the string or, as some shit-head public relations fool called it, the tip of the spear.

The cavalry is far away. I am on my own again. He was getting used to the solitude and the frequent boredom that came with this sort of work. Even if he was with a team, he was still an outsider, not quite accepted, not quite friends. It was all part of his new job description.

His hand touched a tree trunk the cord was wrapped around. He felt around the gnarled surface carefully and found the other side. The cord started to slope down, and his hand slid along it; he felt one, two, then a third knot tied in close order. Time to drop. He knelt and felt the cold of the ground cover. It wasn't too damp, which was good, he thought. He began to move forward like a crab on his knees and elbows, the string now under his arm. He moved deliberately toward what he saw was the edge of the trees. The space beyond and the sky was slightly brighter than the black-green cocoon he was currently wrapped up in.

Slowly, quietly forward. Pause, listen. Move again. A swish of the grass as he pushed forward. The cord led to a dark shape on the ground in front of him and brought Stavros to a halt. He felt the object carefully. Manmade, nylon fabric. Goose's rucksack. Move around it. A boot. He tapped on it lightly. It moved.

"Come to my right." A whisper.

Stavros sidled up to the shape and quietly set his small Bergen down behind him. A ghillie net came out and he pulled it over himself and became one with the forest. Or so he hoped. Final adjustments to the camouflage would wait until the very early pre-daylight. Goose had already set up a variable Swift 15-60×60 spotting scope on a small tripod and was staring through it.

"It's quiet. The house is straight out there." He pointed with his arm and hand so Stavros could better orient on the target. The next bit of gear to come out of Stavros' bag was his monocular. At 15×50 magnification it was not as powerful as Goose's scope, but it was light and easy to work without a tripod. He scoped the area in front of him, the monocular braced in his hands, elbows firmly planted as a bipod on the ground. He could see a faint light to his front, but he didn't look at it directly. He swept from left to right in broad arcs, working across the field from near to far. He could see the forest bordered the field on three sides, one of which he was lying in. Although it was dark, the monocular amplified the ambient light enough that he could see the rough terrain to his front. The field was uncut, which he believed meant the farm was inactive and there were no animals or machinery to keep the grasses short. Finally, he came to a dark barn-like structure on the right at the far end next to the tree line. Sweeping left, he came to the house, more a cottage with light spilling dimly from a window. He couldn't make out much detail in the darkness, but he studied the even deeper shadows around the building. There wasn't any movement.

"Very quiet," Stavros whispered.

"Good things come to those that wait," Goose answered quietly. "Get some sleep. Your eyes will get a workout soon enough."

Stavros looked at the glowing arrow of his compass and marked the direction to the house with its rotating dial, closed the cover, and set it aside and then put the monocular back in its protective case and placed it in front of his head. If he woke disoriented, he wanted concrete points to orient himself. As a last resort, he knew the closest point on the border was 24 kilometers to his left rear on an approximate 50-degree azimuth. Once he closed his eyes, he wondered for a moment whether Goose would be there when he opened them again.

He felt pressure on his ribs, increasing, then a light punch.

"Wake up."

Stavros opened his eyes. It was still dark, but he could see a little better. He pulled back the elastic cuff of his jacket and saw that it was about an hour before sun-up. The end of night. The shadows had more detail, the trees more color. He looked across the field and could see sky gradually growing bright. He shivered a bit in the cold dawn.

Their lie-up was good. The previous team had set it up well, weaving branches and leaves together to block everything but two small holes for observation. Goose was behind one; he was perfectly placed behind the other. He didn't think he would have to add much to his camouflage netting. It was already studded with bits of coarse fabric in different hues and shades of green and brown that broke up his pattern. He pulled out the monocular and studied the terrain, adding new details to the ones already cataloged in his mind. He would continue to do so through the day. He came back to the house and saw a figure standing outside. Using the scope's stadia lines and the door as reference points, he quickly estimated the person's height to be around five feet five inches—too short to be Neil. The man went back inside.

"Got one," he said.

"Seen him," said Goose. "None of the others, yet."

Stavros itched at unseen things that had worked into his clothing, whether scraps of the forest or creepy crawlies, he couldn't tell. He pulled a small tuft of pine needles out of his waistband, flicked it away, and then settled down again.

"Fidgety are we?" said Goose. "You done this before?"

"Often enough, but usually with a bit more preparation."

"Where?"

"Germany. Either on the border or during exercises. Exercises sucked."

"Why?"

Stavros had been told the troopers of 22 SAS didn't do much long-range surveillance. That was mostly left to 21 SAS and maybe the 23rd, both reserve units. The 22nd seemed to prefer the direct action role, kicking doors, and blowing things up. That said, they did do surveillance in the North. Unfortunately, the American army wanted Special Forces to do it all. That meant doing the cool stuff along with practicing the not-so-sexy mission of watching Soviet road and rail traffic in case World War III began. Boring until it wasn't.

"Because I'm not really keen on sitting in a hole in the ground behind the lines counting trucks for weeks at a time."

"You have to do that?"

"Depends on where you're assigned, but yes."

"That would suck."

Stavros glanced over at Goose and saw him staring intently through the scope. He'd been at it for at least three hours.

"You should take a break. You're gonna burn a hole in the target."

Goose's head turned to him. Stavros could just see eyes looking at him through the small aperture in his ghillie suit. Appraising.

"Interesting camouflage. You look like an Indian."

"West or East?"

"American."

Stavros had used a burnt cork to darken his face. He didn't like the GI or the British camouflage sticks; both smelled intensely of insect repellent and burned if he got the stuff into his eyes.

"It's my war paint. Now, if I only had a tomahawk. Go to sleep."

"Right, but first take this." Goose handed over the spotting scope, which Stavros inserted into position.

"See you in a couple," said Goose and laid his head down on his mat.

Stavros watched Goose for a second. Until yesterday, he had not seen the man since England. He decided Goose must think he was stuck with a younger brother forced on him by his parents.

He turned back to the scope to fine tune the optics until the lines of the house became crisp and clear in the glass. At full power, the door to the cottage took up almost half the view so he dialed it back until he could see the entire house and some of the landscape around it. The sunlight was beginning to come over the trees. He could see it in a horizontal line across the field that moved slowly toward him like a curtain being drawn, turning the grasses lighter green as it progressed. It would soon be day and he was in a good position to watch the show.

He panned the scope as he had before, back and forth between the house and the barn, seeing and memorizing details, until he was satisfied he knew what everything was. He twisted the magnification back down to where he could see both buildings clearly from forest edge to forest edge and waited.

A sudden plume of gray smoke puffed out the chimney. Someone had thrown wood on the fire to warm the kitchen. Absent any cues to inform his thoughts, he wondered what the people in the house were doing. Were they drinking coffee and talking about their plans? Was Neil among them? What was he doing, and was he accepted into the group as a comrade, as an equal? Or was he tolerated only as necessary baggage, a means to an end?

Stavros realized he was projecting frustrations, but he didn't care. He was the only one listening to his own internal conversation so it didn't matter. It was somehow curious that both he and Neil were surrogates of a sort; mixed up in a war that wasn't really theirs. Stranger still was that although they had been brothers in arms, now they were on opposite sides.

He went back to staring though the scope, watching for anything. Soon he was rewarded. The man he'd seen before came outside and walked to the barn. He threw open one half of the big door and went inside but it was still too dark to see in. After about five minutes he came out, wiping his hands on a towel, and walked back to the cottage.

"That was exciting," Stavros murmured to himself.

A second man, about the same height as the first, came out and walked to the barn. Still no sign of VIPER, as Stavros was now thinking of his former friend. Yet, he couldn't quite make the mental transformation of Neil from friend to enemy.

Maybe adversary was a better word, less hostile. Sort of like Smiley's Karla, a worthy opponent but not someone you wanted to kill.

While he peered through the scope, Stavros munched on some of the granola he had brought along. It was a good food, required no cooking, didn't smell, and tasted better than C-Rations. It just crunched, which he didn't think would compromise their position at 200 meters.

Stavros picked up movement as the door to the cottage opened and out came a third man. Taller, skinny as a rail with a beak-like nose when Stavros saw it in profile. Black hair. Definitely not Neil. If he's there, he's still inside. "Skinny" joined "Short 2" in the barn where the interior was still in darkness. "Short 1" was the first guy they had seen. Stavros noted times and actions in a small notebook with a stubby pencil. Always pencil. Pencil works in the rain.

Agreeing on nicknames for people and objects was standard routine for surveillance teams. That included naming the parts of a building after colors and numbers to eliminate confusion among different observers. Saying "Subject appeared in window 3 on the blue side" was clearer than saying he appeared in the right-most window of the north side. One man's "right" might be another man's "left." Although they didn't have to worry about other teams, Goose would have to be briefed on the names once he woke up.

Which wasn't long in coming.

Stavros heard some rustling next him and glanced over to see Goose stretch a bit and roll about back and forth in one spot trying to loosen up. He went back to his eyepiece thinking Goose would come up with some pithy greeting.

"Bloody hell, I can't see," Goose said.

"What?"

"My eye is swollen shut."

Stavros looked over to see Goose leaning on one side feeling about his face gingerly.

"Yeah, my eye feels like a big fat peach."

Never having had the experience, Stavros leaned over to take a look, a difficult proposition between the early morning shadows and Goose's camouflage. What he did see told him enough.

"You've been bitten by something. Does it hurt?"

"Like hell, especially here," Goose said, pointing at a spot in the middle of his right eyelid.

"That's your dominant eye?" A statement as much as a question.

"Yeah, I can't use a scope worth a damn with my left."

"Do you have any drugs?" Stavros asked.

"Field dressings and morphine, that's it."

"You guys should come better prepared. I've got some stuff."

Stavros twisted around carefully after checking the field to his front to make sure no one was out in the open. He pulled a small pouch from his Bergen and extracted an even smaller bottle filled with little orange pills. He shook two out and reached them over to Goose.

"Take these with a bunch of water," he said.

"What is it?"

"Don't worry, it's not cyanide. It's Benadryl, an antihistamine. Good for bug bites and bee stings. Count yourself lucky that you don't have snakes here."

"You always carry this stuff?" Goose said as he gulped down the two pills.

"I'm also a medic. I like to be ready."

"Medic? You can change bedpans and stuff like that?"

"Yeah, that and a wee bit more, everything you can learn in forty weeks of training."

"Can you do brain surgery?"

"I can take one out, but I'm not sure how to get it back in. Rest your eye until the meds kick in. I'll tell you what's happening."

In whispers, Stavros brought Goose up to speed on the people and activity he had seen while he continued to watch the area to his front. A fourth man had appeared and disappeared into the barn. Now there were three inside the building and at least one in the house. The fourth was physically in between the two "Shorts" and "Skinny." He became "Larry." Still no sign of his old friend. He would not use VIPER's real name in the Republic, not verbally or written down where it could reveal anything if his notebook was somehow lost or captured. He did not intend to get captured by the *Gardaí*, but things happen. One SAS patrol had been caught inside the Republic several years before.

"An embarrassing map reading mistake," the team leader said at their trial. "Mea culpa."

Stavros didn't want to be part of a second mistake.

28

Hamish picked up the radio-telephone handset in the padded, secure office. The unit was connected to a large, cabinet-sized encoding device and then to a heavily insulated cable that pierced the wall through connectors impervious to manipulation or tapping and went directly into a radio relay system linked to a big antenna outside.

Sitting in a big comfy swivel chair, probably the only one in the building other than the commander's down the hall, he regarded the thick gray sound-proofed walls, decorated with sheets of instructions and timetables indicating when a new code was to be fed into the phone, and the proper procedures for firing the thing up. There was an armed forces calendar that showed the month with a happy photograph of soldiers being served a meal in some pleasant tropical spot, maybe Bermuda, but he wasn't sure. No pictures of Northern Ireland he could see after he flipped through the pages. The calendar was meant to lure gullible youths into the military, those who needed a way out of whatever bad circumstance they were in or maybe those who thought they could better themselves with a trade like medicine, or vehicle mechanic, or killer of men. It just depended on whatever tripped their trigger.

Hamish chuckled; he was above all that. Being a Harrow boy with connections, he knew he had arrived when he got into Her Majesty's Secret Service, a lifelong dream since he read his first Ian Fleming novel under the bedcovers after lights out. Everything he had done was oriented on that goal, from passing his A Levels in Classical Greek and Latin, to playing rugby, although he quit that after being knocked about a little in team scrimmages. He never even considered it possible that his Eton colleagues hated him or that his obscure foreign languages were not much use anywhere but in a library or museum; all he wanted now was a success, a big one at that, and he could pick and choose assignments. The op he was currently working fit that bill. Maybe he'd go to Paris or Vienna, somewhere upscale that fit his personality.

And certainly not Washington. It's probably still classed as a hardship assignment and, worse yet, it's filled with Americans.

He dialed the numbers for the office he wanted and waited for the buzzing to cease and the ringing to begin. After four rings, someone picked up.

"SUMMIT," the voice said.

"It's ARGON. I need to speak to SENTINEL."

"You have him. Go ahead."

"I have an initial operational report for you," Hamish said.

"Wait one."

A pause.

"Go ahead ARGON, we're recording."

"As approved by London and based on the intelligence that QUEST may be across the frontier, we launched OUTSIDER this evening with a small team to do a recce of the site. The team is in position now and will remain there for no more than twenty-four to thirty-six hours. I would like to reaffirm your instructions on disposition of the target if his presence is confirmed."

"I understand. If they find QUEST, the team is to bring him back if feasible."

"If they meet resistance?"

"Follow your rules of engagement. Avoid civilian casualties, but on no account should they risk any active intervention if there is a possibility of compromising the mission or the team itself. How many of ours are on the ground?"

"Two teams of four, eight men total. One in overwatch, one backup."

"Roger. Report when the mission is complete—before that if anything significant happens. Any questions?"

"Negative. Nothing further, ARGON is clear."

Hamish placed the handset back in its cradle and sat back, his fingertips steepled, eyes closed, in deep thought. There was one thing he had neglected to say, but he didn't think it was significant. It was always better to act first then ask for permission and, if anything came up, he would just use his best judgement.

29

Sarah's team had been on the target for a week, and even though the operation was taking place around Dallas, they were playing it real. The "target" of this final training scenario was ostensibly a drug kingpin that the "foreign" nation refused to arrest and extradite. One assumed that was because he owned a few politicians, or the government was afraid of his militias, or both.

The team's observation post was good, but the area was bad.

Oak Cliff was one of the most run-down and dangerous cities in the state and so it was chosen to test the skills and ingenuity of the team. "Kingpin's" safe house was placed in a dilapidated industrial park and the students were left to their own devices to get close and place a watch on all his activity. Their homework was to come up with an intelligence package that "Silver Bullet," the national special mission force, could use to find, capture, and extract the kingpin.

The surveillance team watched well. They came up with all the required information, complete with telephone numbers, security measures, maps and sketches, and recommendations on how to pull off the operation. The "Force" could take the info and do what they wanted. At least, that was the premise.

The team brought the evaluators into their OP surreptitiously to brief them on their work. They had survived the week without the police being called in on them or drug dealers trying to roust them, so they believed they were doing well. The evaluators were impressed. Smiles and handshakes went all around.

"There's just one problem," said the head evaluator.

"What's that?"

"The scenario has changed. NCA, the National Command Authority, has directed Silver Bullet elsewhere to a higher priority mission. You'll have to take down Kingpin on your own without backup."

30

Stavros avoided looking at his watch. He knew the hours passed slowly in the hide. It wasn't a bad place to be holed up except for the occasional bug under the clothing that required a well-placed, silent swat followed by a thorough search to ensure the creature's demise. The big centipedes were the ones that Stavros really didn't like. He watched warily as they mesmerizingly marched across the ground, their legs moving with a wavelike rhythm like oarsmen in a galley. He knew their bites could be a bit toxic but was happy that Ireland was nothing like Africa.

He could use a cup of coffee. He hated starting out a day without one, but there was no fire and he wasn't about to drink cold coffee, especially instant. Instead, he pulled out his canteen and took a swig of the lukewarm water. It tasted like plastic. It didn't matter if it was a US or British canteen, the water tasted just as bad. But it did what it needed to do. At least it wasn't laced with chlorine.

The sun filtered down through scattered clouds and it wasn't raining, which in Stavros' mind was a rare and good thing. It was also cool so there was no heat distortion, just a crisp, clear view of placid farmland.

Goose had taken the big scope back once the swelling around his eyes subsided and he could see again. Stavros kept watch on the bigger picture, the buildings and surrounding area, for surprises while Goose concentrated on the details.

By early afternoon, all four men were inside the barn but there was still no sign of VIPER. Goose was giving a running commentary on the action as it happened, which was sporadic. With the doors partly open, the interior of the building could be seen. It seemed fairly empty except for a small pile of off-white colored sacks, about 50-pound bag size, of what could have been grain, but the labels weren't visible. Whatever the men were doing was also unseen, hidden away from the opening, maybe in a corner of the barn. Artificial light seemed to come from one direction, so perhaps there was a work bench. Once in a while, one of the four men would pass the entrance with a tool, wire, or part of some kind. It seemed like they were occupied with something technical.

It seemed.

Nothing to write home about.

"Intel Report: Four unidentified men were puttering about in a barn doing things we couldn't see …."

Certainly not a report he would want to put his name on. But his mission was simple: confirm or deny VIPER's presence. And, at least on this day, he wasn't there. But there were hours to go.

The sun was beginning its arc toward the far horizon when Stavros saw a cloud of dust on the furthest tree line. It was making its way to the cottage.

"Vehicle approaching," he said before he saw it. It was moving too fast to be anything else.

"Got it."

It was a medium-sized van. Covered with dirt and painted-over company logos on the sides, it was unremarkable. It swung around in front of the barn and stopped in a sliding crunch of gravel that could be heard in the OP. A new man, henceforth to be known as "Driver," got out and walked into the barn. A few minutes passed before he came back out, Short 1 and 2 and Skinny in tow.

Driver pulled open the rear doors of the van.

Goose said, "Ah, delivery time. Let's see what they're getting."

The two Shorts pulled a bag out of the back. It looked similar to the ones in the barn.

"Can't see the label," said Stavros.

"Not yet."

Skinny and Driver pulled a second bag out. There was some hand switching as they tried to turn around, their footsteps tangling. Skinny missed the mark and tripped, losing his grip. The words were visible for a brief moment as the two fumbled with the bag on the ground.

"Thank you," said Goose.

"What is it?"

"Ammonium nitrate."

The bags went on the pile in the barn with the others.

"What do you think?" Goose said. It was the first time he had asked Stavros for his opinion on anything other than whether he was ready to go.

"It looks suspicious. No crops, no real farming going on."

It was conjecture, but what self-respecting farmer has fifteen bags of fertilizer delivered with no apparent means to put it in the ground? Then there were the four young men, and they didn't look like farmers.

Goose was silent for a moment. He pulled out his radio headset and turned a couple of knobs on the little VHF handheld he had. He spoke quietly into the whisper mike, quietly enough that Stavros couldn't hear what it was he said. Finally, he turned to Stavros.

"I agree. But are you sure none of them are your man VIPER?"

"I'm sure," Stavros said. "He's not there. Besides, that type of explosive isn't what I would expect him to use. ANFO is a low-order explosive that anyone can cobble together. It requires a lot of material and it's not very subtle. My impression was that he was called in for precision work."

"Then we've probably stumbled onto a different cell."

"Maybe. I'd go with that. What do we do now?"

"We wait until nightfall and report what we have. There's still a chance VIPER will show up."

Goose went back to his scope and watched as the off-loading was completed. There were maybe twenty-five bags total, around 1,250 pounds of fertilizer, enough to ruin several people's day if employed correctly. Stavros reflected that it just wasn't VIPER's style. He was a master of sabotage with small, crafty booby-traps. A phone booth wired to incinerate a target with a small propane gas bottle, a bathroom mirror set to administer a close shave of ball bearings to whomever threw the light switch. He was also very good with stand-off devices, and could remotely take out a transformer yard from 100 meters away.

Driver came back out to the vehicle and climbed in. Short 2 and Larry climbed in with him, and they took off down the road.

"We're down to two. Things may get quiet around here now."

"Get quiet? That was the most excitement we've seen all day."

Goose twisted the radio's knobs on, pressed the button, and spoke into his mike. Again, Stavros could not discern what he was saying. Then it did get quiet.

For the rest of the afternoon during the leisurely observation of the farm, Stavros thought about his current situation. It was usually both exhilarating and boring to be on a surveillance operation; this one met one of those expectations at least. It had the anxiety connected to the fear of discovery, in this case by either the people they were watching or the Irish authorities, as well as the thought that he was wasting his time. He'd spent a lot of time in the army, most of it worth the effort, and in some small way saving the world from menace. But this operation made him wonder if he might be in the wrong line of work. Not that he knew how to write a resumé that he could show anyone without a security clearance.

How do you describe nearly ten years of very secret work experience to a civilian without having to kill them when you're finished?

It was a conundrum most people didn't have. And now, after a day of trekking and lying about in the Irish Republic, he was actually looking forward to returning North and resuming his search for VIPER, the presumably deadly leprechaun.

But Stavros' thinking was about to be interrupted by a new reality. A couple of minutes before, he had seen a green light blink on Goose's radio: he was receiving a transmission. Goose didn't react but listened silently and spoke an audible, "Roger, standing by."

Stavros said, "What's up?"

"We wait a bit and then get ready to move."

Good, time to get out of here.

Nevertheless, he kept up his watch on the barn. He wanted to know where the two boys were at all times, especially before they pulled out of the OP.

He heard the crunch of leaves behind him and turned to see their two mates carefully making their way toward their position, Philip leading the way and Reg reeling in the guideline as he moved. A glance at Goose was met with a head shake. "Don't move yet."

Now they were four in the position, two up front, two holding down the rear.

He was back watching the barn when another trail of dust, then a car, a Cortina, appeared on the track. It passed the house and pulled up about 20 meters from the barn. Two men in leather jackets got out and walked slowly toward the barn. One had something small in his left hand; his right hand was perched on his hip under the jacket. The second walked about 5 meters to his side, a hand also on his hip. Skinny walked out of the barn and came to a quick halt when the first visitor held up his left hand and said something. It was too far to hear what, but it was obviously a command. Two pistols came out of their holsters and Skinny put up his hands.

"*Gardaí*," whispered Goose.

Strangely convenient.

The two *Gardaí* and Skinny walked back into the barn out of sight.

"Let's go," Goose said, breaking down the scope and stuffing it into his bag. Stavros followed suit as Philip and Reg moved past them and broke out into the field.

Stavros was alarmed for a moment, then the reality of what he was observing came to him.

Gardaí? Those guys weren't Gardaí. Christ, now what?

Stavros was in trail as the four men trotted across the field. The three troopers in front spread out into an arrowhead formation as they slowed to a walk and moved carefully to the door. Stavros followed them in. He saw that there was indeed a work space. It looked like his high school electrical shop class with all sorts of wiring and test equipment. Someone was either teaching or they were making several projects at the same time. Skinny was standing next to a pole, hands still raised, under the watch of one of the leather-jacketed "*Gardaí*" while his partner searched around the bench.

"Where's Short 1?" Goose said.

"He ran as we came in. No worries, we got him out back," said Leather Jacket 2.

Goose turned to Stavros. "Our teammates," he said.

Stavros kept his mouth shut. His accent would betray him.

Two more men, these in DPM camouflage and dragging something, came through a side door. As they cleared a fenced corral, two legs then a body appeared. They dragged it through the hay and let it drop next to the pile of fertilizer bags. The arms were over the head which lolled off to the side, a blank expression on the face. Stavros saw him close up for the first time. It was Short 1, his nose covered with blood.

"He ran straight into me and I cold-cocked him. He'll be out for a while," DPM Man 1 said.

Goose looked at Stavros with a visual shrug.

"Orders," he said.

Stavros turned, thoughts racing now. The door loomed before him and he took the escape route out, away from evidence, away from what he knew was to come. He strode away from the barn, stopped next to the car, and dropped his rucksack. He stood facing away and looked at the house. He waited.

After several minutes, Goose came out, Reg and Philip close behind.

"You squeamish, Yank?"

"No, but it's time to go. I can't be seeing this shit. Get me out of here now."

Goose looked at Stavros for a long second.

"We're leaving now. The pick-up is nearby. Philip, take him and go. I'll be joining you in a couple of minutes." Philip and Reg set off at a blistering pace through the woods, noise discipline be damned. It was turning dark when they got to the lay-by, where the truck was waiting with the doors open, two men standing outside watching the roadway. Stavros shed his rucksack, tossed it in after the others, and followed it to the rear of the truck as the doors clanged shut.

"We wait for Goose," said Philip.

About ten minutes later, the door creaked open, and Goose climbed in. The door slammed shut and he pounded on the wall twice. The truck lurched off.

"Mother of Jesus. Don't ever do that to me again," Stavros said.

"Do what?" said Goose.

"Take me along on a hit."

"Why, you don't think terrorists deserve what they get?"

"Were they terrorists?"

"Command thinks so. The stuff we found confirmed it."

"So, they're dead? Just like that."

"The Irish would never arrest them, and we can't have them hanging about making bombs to use against us. So exactly what should we do with them?"

"That's up to your government, but I can't be mixed up in that. If I was ever identified working with you inside the Republic, it would be really bad juju. I doubt my ambassador or commander would take it very well."

"They'd get over it. My orders say it's okay for you to be with us."

"On a hit? Really?"

"I didn't know it would be a hit before we got here, but we were given the sanction order to take them out and they knew you were with us, so yes."

"Sanction? I think we call it extrajudicial killing. I don't think my folks would be impressed with that. Nor would the Irish."

"They'd get over it eventually. But no one would find out it was us or know that you were even here."

"How's that supposed to work with two dead IRA back there?"

"It would all be put down to an accident, no witnesses, no evidence."

"I never thought I'd say this, but get me back to the North. It's safer there."

Stavros' mind careened back to Tehran for a moment. *No, that was different. Those men were all threats to us. These guys weren't even armed.*

3 1

Neil had not wanted to travel into the North but there was no other choice. His job should have been limited to putting the packages together and letting the boyos carry them to their destinations. But the target information the reconnaissance team brought back was incomplete and D-Day was approaching. Details were needed to make sure things would work as planned, as designed. One little anomaly missed in the recce could and probably would ruin everything. And that's how he explained the trip to Monahan.

"If you want this op done right ...."

He carried nothing that would compromise him. Only his well-thumbed Baedeker filled with notes about touristy things and restaurants, but mostly about pubs. He was an American searching for his ancestors, and visiting the North was just part of his voyage of discovery, while providing him a reasonably solid cover for action. He had no priors and with an assumed name he was pretty sure he wasn't on any Interpol Red Notice, so he didn't worry about anyone scrutinizing his passport when he crossed the frontier.

The problem was the act of surveillance itself. Getting too close was a risk. He didn't want to reveal himself to the security folks who looked for people like him. Monahan's team had already visited the sites and, although Monahan assured him they had been careful, a second or third pass might spook the police and be the undoing of everything.

Target reconnaissance could either be the most mundane thing in the world or very exciting depending on what value the owner of the object placed on it and how trigger-happy the guards were. And, although both Hillsborough and Stormont castles were not nuclear weapons storage sites, they qualified for more care than casing Harrods in London, although even that place was under fairly tight scrutiny of late. The castles were well protected and behind fences. It was possible to enter the gardens surrounding them but getting close to the buildings was a non-starter, especially at Hillsborough, which was the official residence for the royal family when they visited Northern Ireland. Granted those visits were rare events, but the castle was still used by the secretary of state as his residence. Security was therefore tight. Monahan did not tell him the "why" for each target, but the reasoning was readily apparent to Neil's sabotage-oriented mind. What he was trying to figure out was if and when one royal or another planned a visit. The event must be soon because Danny had told him everything needed to be in place within a fortnight.

As he walked down Dromore Road and into the Square, he visualized the strike. Where it would work, where it would fail. As he had already anticipated, unless they launched a full-scale military assault, he quickly confirmed that the plan could only work if it came from the east side of Hillsborough. It would be a stand-off attack.

He stood in front of the somber facade of Comber House, "Bonders of Irish and Scotch Whiskies." Looking at their display, he stared at the castle's mid-morning reflection in the west-facing window. He mentally calculated the distance and angles from the street to the entryway of the building, the height of the wrought-iron fences. It was roughly 115 meters from where he stood to the front door, almost too far for what he had in mind. He crossed the street, guide in hand, to the front of the Court House and walked around it slowly. He had one chance to do this right; he couldn't come back and pace around the place again. He watched a single government vehicle negotiate the entry and cruise up the drive to the entryway. A passenger got out, an official of some sort, and the vehicle wound its way back out of the compound. It would probably be the same for any official entourage. Seemingly paying closer attention to the Court House near at hand than the real object of his survey, he noted what he needed and then walked back across the square. This time he went into an old pub, the Coachman, and settled down for a cool pint and some lamb stew. He contemplated the Irish lass who brought the menu, delivered his drink and food, and then lingered too long for a waitress but long enough to encourage a handsome young man to talk with her. He was enticed at first but, put off by her language and tattoos (he preferred art on walls not on skin), eventually struck her from his wish list.

The pub's food was a different matter. Eating at the farm must have been an anomaly, since the food there was actually edible. He decided the pub proprietors were trying to drive away the tourists. The stew consisted of very mature, stringy mutton, boiled for at least a month and then mixed with last season's cabbage gone south and old potatoes turned to mush. The bread, also suspect, was hard and dry even after soaking in the juices, but at least no weevils that he could see. No wonder so many of his kin had left the island.

He pushed the dish to the far edge of the table and, unsated, went back to his mental field manual of demolitions and did his calculations until he was satisfied. Then, staring out the window, he cached the facts and numbers into his memory and thought about options. By the time he finished his early lunch, he had the concept and a plan.

Stormont would be a different kettle of fish. It was on the same grounds as Parliament but isolated. Isolated for several reasons, but the most important was that MI5 had offices in the building. Stormont was a harder target, a huge compound comprising many buildings, its biggest being Parliament itself. It was well protected but its public status, immense size, and the number of people working there made getting close easier. He didn't need to get close to Parliament though. His target, the smaller castle, was hidden away. Located within an exclusion zone, every road to the smaller compound was blocked by a fence and guarded by security. He knew from the team's report that he couldn't get close. Instead, he would content himself with checking the outside. For final planning, he'd rely on Monahan's vintage map that one of his minions had acquired long ago.

As he wandered through the once pristine, now ragged gardens, he got a sense of the size of the place and the level of security. There weren't as many policemen or patrols as he had expected. Like Hillsborough, it was apparent the Troubles had impacted funding: the buildings and grounds were slowly crumbling. HM Government's money was going elsewhere, if at all. Neil imagined London wasn't up to spending large sums of money during conflict. The big island itself was not in the best financial state.

He followed an unblocked road away from a roundabout in front of Parliament and saw the offshoots leading to the castle, each covered by a guard house and a gate. Soon, he realized he was a bit too far afield for a tourist and turned around. Heading back he saw a smaller road, almost a track, that led into the trees. The team hadn't mentioned it and they may have just missed it. After he checked to see that he wasn't being watched, he followed it around a bend. As the main road disappeared from view behind him, to his front he could see a parking lot filled with abandoned machinery and derelict cars. There was a thick hedge, beyond which lay a low building, its roof just visible above greenery. The castle's spired stone tower rose into the sky perhaps 80 meters away. He realized he had what was needed and quickly headed back out to the main road where he stood for a moment contemplating the tourist map he'd picked up in a shop. A police car cruising the road slowed down and stopped next to him. Neil dropped the map to his side and smiled one of his most disarming smiles as the window rolled down.

"Good day officers," and offense being better than defense, he said, "I wonder if you could help me out. I'm looking for the Somme Memorial. It should be near here, but I can't find it." He held up the map upside down and pointed vaguely at the site on the paper. "My great uncle was killed in the battle, and I should very much like to see the memorial." Obsequious was the word Neil thought of, trying to make himself very small.

One of the policemen unfolded out of the car and approached. *He's a big one.*

The cop was nearly as tall but weighed around thirty pounds more than Neil, a probable consequence of too much time on mobile patrols.

"I'm sorry sir, you're in a private area here. This area is all out of bounds. The place you're looking for is over there anyway," he said, pointing vaguely west. "You're all turned about."

"I apologize for the trouble, sergeant," Neil said, having deciphered the constable's insignia into an American rank. "I guess I'm not very good at following these things." He shook the map as if it were a bad child and turned as if to walk off in the proper direction.

"Wait a moment, sir," the policeman said. "Could I see your identification, please."

The blue passport came out and was handed to the man, its golden eagle logo face up and prominently visible.

"American?"

"Yes."

"I see," the policeman said, as if Neil's being American answered all his questions. Taking stock of the errant young man while flapping the passport back and forth on his palm, he finally handed it back to Neil.

"Yes, alright then. Cross over the main road there and you'll find the trail well marked. Please watch the signs next time or you could land yourself in serious trouble."

Neil turned for real this time and walked determinedly down the shadowed lane toward the long open artery in front of Parliament which marked the border about who belonged where in the policemen's minds. At the same, he wondered if he had updated his last will and testament recently. He blew the thought off; he had nothing to leave behind and no one to leave it to.

32

Stavros had no more friends in Armagh than he did in Belfast. In a tiny town of 14,000 news travels fast, and he was soon recognized as one of the few Americans that stayed in the town longer than what was required to visit Saint Patrick's Cathedral and get back on the bus. There wasn't a great deal of anything else to see and less reason to remain longer than one night. So his staying several days made him unusual.

Before he got there, he only knew of the town from the activity reports he'd been given, which were numerous and bloody. Reports written in terse militarese or intelligence-speak that told him nothing of the ground truth. He liked that description. "Ground truth" was what gave witness to what was actually happening, not disembodied intelligence reporting. Often it was just the little things, the things you don't see unless you're actually there, the feelings you can't sense unless they are right in front of your nose.

Once on the road, Stavros enjoyed the trip, uneventful as it was. He didn't have to do anything, which also suited his mood at the moment. It was an arranged taxi, a silent driver paid in advance, and time to watch the scenery. At least what he could see of it through the light rain that was falling. Under gray skies they slid by a verdant landscape that changed little as they drove. Small villages, lone farms; it didn't look like a conflict zone, save when they passed an armored personnel carrier sitting at a road junction, soldiers standing round it with their automatic rifles at the ready, or heard the clatter of a helicopter making its way across the countryside at low level. Whether the crew were looking for rebels or on a fool's errand, he didn't know. He knew only that he was glad not to be flying in such weather.

It was only when the car stopped in front of the hotel on Upper English Street that Stavros noticed something he should have noticed before. The driver had already been paid, Rhys said. Get a trusted man to drive; that made sense. What didn't make sense was the driver's Browning in a shoulder holster seen as he pulled Stavros' bag from the boot. The driver caught his glance, shrugged the coat closed, and smiled. "You're never alone, mate," was all he said as he slipped behind the wheel and disappeared away down the tarmac lane.

Stavros looked up and down the street, then up into the sky. He wasn't sure what the weather was doing. Wispy clouds sailed by and a light drizzle was still falling, so he decided he would wait to do his familiarization. But first things needing to be first, he decided to get into his room and found the entry to the hotel. The building had been standing awhile, that much was evident from its architecture and the structure itself: a plain gray stucco edifice, a door flanked by two puny reproductions of Corinthian columns. Definitely not Michelin starred, he thought as he pushed through the door. The interior was another matter. Victorian architectural details, dark wood paneling studded with gold-leaf framed scenes of hunting and horses, heavy carpets, leaded glass windows, and chandeliers throughout, showed a well-cared-for but dated establishment. The rooms weren't cheap, but he didn't have a limit on how much money he could spend. "Whatever is necessary to accomplish the mission," was what the finance man had said. His cover didn't support shelling out the bucks for the George V hotel, not that he would find a place like that anywhere nearby. Nevertheless, he decided the Caulfield Arms suited him well.

His first instinct was to settle in to his new, if temporary, home. He had no idea how long he would stay, but he had discovered early in his travels that making the room his own was key to a pleasant trip no matter what awaited him on the outside. He also checked the doors and windows to make sure they could be well secured. He hated surprises.

The room was newly appointed, as the hotel had done recent renovations: fresh paint—luckily well aired out—updated bathroom details. All "due to bomb damage" was what the receptionist had casually mentioned. No attribution, no blame, just a statement of fact as if it had been caused by just another everyday occurrence, which in some ways, it had been.

What happened to a people when violence was accepted as normal? Stavros had asked, "How do you cope?"

"You just learn how to live with it, but you can't let it get you down," the man answered.

The furniture was modern as was the artwork on the walls, a refreshing change from the darker, more conservatively decorated public area downstairs. When all was arranged to his liking, Stavros took a short nap, his refuge from the world for an hour, and then a shower before beginning a late-afternoon stroll.

As usual, it was an orientation stroll. He noted the places he had seen in his guidebook and walked the route he had surveyed on the map without having to refer to it. From the hotel, he walked south through the marketplace and along the edge of a large golf course. The course was another strange aspect of the North, a province under martial law but also a place where you could still knock a little ball around a huge well-manicured playing field. It was not a game Stavros liked. Granted it was single combat, one man trying to best himself, but it required little of the physical ability of other games and sports. Besides, it took too much time to play a single round, time he rarely had or would consider devoting to such a pastime.

Before long he found himself standing in front of a large building that he recognized from his guide. It was Saint Patrick's. As Stavros stood looking at the cathedral's details, he sensed a presence on the path behind him. He turned to find a priest, a young man not much older than he, but with a face full of worldly experience crowned by a smile. He would remember the smile because it appeared genuine from first sight and was complemented by sparkling eyes that said, "Welcome."

"Seeing our little church for the first time, are we?"

"You can recognize a tourist from a distance, I see," Stavros said.

"The locals rarely stop and stare like you were doing. You are an American?"

"I am. My accent gives me away, no doubt. My name is Paul."

"I am Father Michael. We don't see many Americans these days. Would you like to see the chapel?"

"Yes, I'd like that."

As they walked toward the main entrance, the priest explained the cathedral's history and the return of the Catholic Church to Northern Ireland, a history not mentioned in any of the reports he had read. Stavros told the priest of his family and background.

Although the sky was darkening behind them, they entered the church to a blaze of light and color.

"I must tell you, our recent restoration has been a disappointment for many. The new style has been called radical. Many of the original appointments were removed, unfortunately."

"To be honest, I have not been inside many Catholic churches and most of those were new anyway. I believe in God, but I just can't find my way into any one church."

"So, you're not Irish or Catholic, how is it that you are in Armagh visiting one of our oldest cathedrals?"

"I'm a writer," Stavros said, explaining his article, fully expecting the man to recoil from him as most did.

Michael didn't recoil. He thought for a moment and said, "A difficult subject to address, especially for the Church. Most of us don't adhere to any political party or support the violence. We have a moral obligation to try and stop the killing and help those who are suffering. But not all of us do. Some have crossed the line and I'm sad to say there are religious people on both sides who are involved."

"Not you though," Stavros said. He regretted it as soon as he said it. "Sorry, Father. It was reflex."

The eyes that looked at him were saddened somehow by the implication, perhaps. After a moment Michael said, "No, of course not. Perhaps we could all do more. Even you and your article can help change things."

He was smiling again as he led Stavros through the chapel and transepts to the altar, explaining the history and meanings of each along with the design changes. It was clear he was playing the role of teacher and not letting his emotions show whether he thought the new chapel was an improvement. Once the tour was finished, Michael walked Stavros to a side entrance.

"Where are you staying?" he asked.

"The Caulfield."

"Another historic building, even older than this one. I'll walk with you until English Street. No one will bother you if you're walking with a priest."

"Armagh is mostly Catholic?" Stavros asked what he already knew.

"The village and the surrounding countryside, yes. Very much so. We are also home to much of the violence. Belfast and Derry are the two other major hotspots."

"I came here from Belfast and I witnessed some of that violence. Of course, I also witnessed it in London several years ago. In 1975, I was near Selfridges when a bomb went off."

Wrapped in their conversation, they walked off the grounds of the cathedral toward the center of town, mostly ignoring the town that surrounded them. For once, Stavros felt there was some normalcy to Ireland.

"Violence has always been a part of life with us, unfortunately. It's hard for me to describe, let alone for you or any other outsider to understand how it impacts our daily life. Trust erodes, fear dominates, hatreds multiply, until it reaches a point where no one believes it can be turned around. That's what we in the Church must change, but we too have lost much of our credibility."

"How so?"

"Republican supporters want the Church to be more active in the struggle, and those on the other side, those who want peace, think we should denounce violence more. We priests are caught between Scylla and Charybdis."

"But at least one of the alternatives isn't bad."

"That much is true, but you risk being accused of disloyalty, of surrendering to the Protestants if you denounce the IRA. Sometimes even if you don't say a word. But I believe supporting the IRA is supporting an illusion and my loyalty is to a much higher authority."

"So, you must walk a fine line?"

"In my case, I try to remember that silence often equals consent, but it is true that I am careful. I shouldn't say this but some of my brothers don't heed that dictum."

They came to the edge of the campus near the main road and stood for a moment gazing at the yellow lights that spilled from windows onto the street. Finally, the priest reached out and grasped Stavros' arm, took his hand, and shook it firmly.

"Good luck with your article, Paul. I wish you luck but be careful."

"I will, Father. Thank you for being so open with me."

"I didn't realize there was another way," he smiled. "Oh, and try visiting Meehan's. There are usually some friendly people worth talking to in there."

He turned and was gone, disappearing into the dark. Stavros carefully scanned the area in a 360 before he walked off toward the city, wondering if any of his own watchers were about. It seemed quiet, and he didn't pick up anyone nearby. As he walked back toward his hotel, he thought about the conversation. It was the most meaningful talk he'd had in Ireland so far. He wondered what the priest would say if he knew what Stavros' real mission was all about.

It is for everyone's good, I hope.

The final 100 meters to the Caulfield Arms loomed ahead. But he could see there was an issue. A gauntlet of green guys with guns awaited him. The army was out and a brick of soldiers had set up a quick checkpoint. They were stopping cars on the street and people on the sidewalk. He had no concern other than the usual nervousness he felt when dealing with unknown authority figures with loaded weapons—he wasn't a criminal after all. He pulled his hands out of his pockets, held them away from his sides. It was a gesture meant to show he was not a threat but it was also a ready position if he had to react.

Stavros walked slowly up to the soldiers and stopped when they put up their hands in a universal sign that told him to step no further and demanded his identification. Slowly he pulled out the passport and handed it over. The soldier looked at the blue cover and embossed eagle for a moment then yelled over his shoulder.

"Corporal, here's one you should look at."

The corporal walked over and took the passport out of the much younger man's hand and opened it up. He flipped through the pages and returned to the one with his photograph and name. He asked the usual name and birthdate questions. He closed the passport and looked at Stavros closely. Stavros stared back.

"Paul Scalia, you're American?"

"That's me."

"What are you doing here?"

"Long story, but I'm a writer on assignment."

"Right. Do me a favor, Paul Scalia. Face the wall, put your hands up and spread your feet. We're going to do a search."

"No problem, Corporal, just be gentle, I'm ticklish."

"You Americans are always the jokers," the corporal said as he ran his hands over his jacket quickly, then inside and around his back. The soldier patted his pockets and then checked his pant legs, completing a cursory check.

"Turn around, Yank."

Stavros turned to a corporal that now looked vaguely familiar and who handed back his passport with a slight smile.

"If anyone asks, tell them we thought you might have stolen the passport. By the way, Golf One sent you a love note, mate. I put it in your passport. Now get along on your way."

That was a first.

Stavros headed for the hotel and dinner. He needed time and space to read the message and figure out what came next. He smiled to himself as he envisioned Hunter carving up the corporal who called her message "a love note" into cube steak.

***

Several hours later, after his meal and a map check, Stavros used the stairs to get to the ground floor and then found his way to the service entrance in the back of the hotel. He slipped outside and went into counter-surveillance mode to filter through the darkened streets until he was sure he was clean. Assured that no one was behind or in front of him, he continued on to the final approach and hit the pick-up point just as Hunter's car turned onto the short street. He was at the corner when she came alongside, and he jumped in as she rolled around the corner and accelerated out of the area.

"What's the emergency?" Stavros said.

"We got a hit. Your boy may have come across the border at Killea in County Donegal."

"Where's that?"

"Just outside Londonderry," said Hunter, tapping on the map lying between them. "Yesterday customs logged a lone American male coming across in a rental car. Unfortunately, whoever was on duty didn't bother to note the name or the vehicle registration number and we have no idea where he is now."

"I'd better get back out there and look around. Maybe he's got a room at my hotel."

"I doubt it. He'll be holed up somewhere safe."

"No, if he's here, he'll look like me: an American traveling with a cover story, able to move about easily. He won't be hiding. So, what's the plan?"

"We don't really have one. Without concrete information, we don't want to keep bouncing you all over the country looking for him. So you stay here but be ready to move quick. If we get anything, we'll move you to the location so you can ID him. I'll call your room or leave a message at reception. If you come up with anything, the accommodation telephone number still works; it's patched into our local safe house."

"Okay, that's a plan, but not really."

"You got anything better?"

"No, I want to talk with some locals tomorrow evening. Someone told me I might have some luck."

"Who?"

"A new friend. If it pans out, I'll let you know who it is, otherwise I'd rather keep my contacts close hold."

Hunter didn't appear pleased with not getting a name but evidently decided she would have to deal with it as best she could. But if she knew something of Stavros' plans at least she could try to provide cover.

"Where are you going?"

Stavros understood Hunter's query for what it was and gave up the information.

"A place called Meehan's. Apparently friendly people go there."

"For your sake, I hope so. Your record isn't so good."

"We'll see. Drop me up ahead. I know where I am and, by the way, the corporal who searched me called your message a love note."

Stavros could hear Hunter swearing as he hopped out of the car.

33

The windows of Meehan's gave off a smoky, citron yellow glow even at the early evening hour Stavros had chosen to visit. It lay down a cobblestone path too narrow for cars that was barred with bollards for good measure to ensure no one, drunk or terrorist, could negotiate it with anything wider than a wheelbarrow. Stavros did not have trouble with the bollards but the cobblestones were problematical: they were ancient, worn, and very slippery with the water someone had dashed on them earlier. With their rounded and polished tops, his feet would slither off their peaks and into the cracks between. They reminded him of his treks in Wales, little hills with deep valleys—treacherous if one did not pay attention. He didn't want to deal with them anymore so he migrated over to the flat plains of the sidewalk, which made progress significantly smoother.

He plunged ahead down the alley. He was wearing his best go-to-town clothes, which for Stavros meant loose wool trousers, a Shetland cable-knit sweater, and because the evening was cool, his best (and only) leather jacket, which had the shape and patina of those worn by the *Flying Tigers* pilots. Along with his hat, he might be mistaken for a crew member of a Mediterranean fishing trawler that somehow got beached in Ireland. Little did he know.

There were still signs of the times, a grated front door that required an attendant to unlock before entrance could be made—but only after the person had been fully scrutineered and declared trouble free. Aside from the accents and dress, he might have experienced similar caution on Hay Street in Fayetteville, where the most dangerous people were the drunken soldiers that caroused downtown. By contrast, however, the most dangerous things thrown into Fayetteville's bars were tear gas grenades. At least most of the time.

When Stavros finally did get in, he found the place to be quite pleasant, a far cry from most of the rather threadbare places he'd visited in Belfast. The ceiling was low but not so low he had to duck and it was darkened from eons of smoke. Heavy timber beams criss-crossed the ceiling, old and worn with character achieved through long years of aging. It was his idea of an old traditional pub. Only the bar was updated, with mirrors, rows of bottles and racks of glasses, fronted by a big counter that sprouted at least eight beer taps and stools for people who wished to get personal with the drink and the publican.

Not all the clientele were males; he spotted several obviously conjugal couples and several younger, more amorous—probably yet to be married—pairs. There were even tables free. But it was Friday, and when he saw there was a young female waiter, he took a seat at a small table near, but not too near, the big fireplace that was nursing a small fire, and waited. She came soon enough, said her name was Trish, and took his order for a pint and left with a nice smile and flip of her hair. He could get to like this place, he thought as he drew his notebook from the inner pocket of his coat. He looked again at what Michael had told him the previous evening, while the questions he should have asked came to him as he rethought the conversation. Trish came back with his beer and set it on the coaster and took his money. He considered saying something funny or interesting but looked at his watch, saw the time, and remembered who gave it to him. That was generally all it took and it worked again this time.

"You can look at the menu, but meals will be taken at home," Sarah had once said. He understood well enough as did she.

People looked at him curiously. With his olive complexion and his unruly hair they knew he was not from there, but they smiled nevertheless and nodded in his direction. The priest had said they were friendly, and it seemed to be true. Before long, all the tables were full and the bar stools occupied. A gaggle of men were arrayed around the dart board at the far end of the room cheering on a couple of guys tossing their missiles at a cork target illuminated with tiny searchlights. Then two older men walked up to his own table and asked to join him.

"Of course, I can't hold these chairs hostage," Stavros said.

The two sat and reached out their big rough hands to him. Peter and Conner they were and they joined him in a toast once Trish brought them their drinks. Guinness all round, it was. Stavros explained vaguely why an American of Italian background would be visiting Armagh but didn't mention his article. He wouldn't interview, he decided, he would listen and, if Father Michael had been a good example, he hoped they would just tell him the things he wanted to hear. He realized that his article often became the end not the means of his mission. Now it was something that could be set aside if it might mean finding Neil.

There are other tools in the drawer, don't get stuck on using just one of them.

So he listened as the level of the Guinness dropped and his new friends' banter increased.

"You're lucky you don't live hereabouts," said Conner.

"Why? It seems a nice enough place."

"It is except for all the violence."

"We have our own kind of violence in the States."

"Not like ours for sure," Peter countered.

"No, probably not. Ours is usually more personal. One guy shoots another and it's done."

"Oh, ours is quite personal. But it's one group against the other," said Peter.

"And sometimes the boys get confused and do their own kind in," said Conner.

"Never a good thing. Can I get you another couple of pints, gentlemen?" Stavros said, seeing the glasses were dangerously nearing empty.

"Don't mind if we do. Thank you, lad."

Trish was well occupied, so Stavros stood and walked up to the bar. He waited until the barman noticed him and ordered a round when he did. When the beers were poured, he took them on a tray back to the table, but not before noticing a couple of young men of barely the legal age sitting at the bar giving him the eye. Turning toward his table, he heard comments in Gaelic and laughter behind his back. The word "Dago" got his attention.

Not everyone here is friendly.

He did what he did best. He made himself small, seemingly unimportant, not a threat to anyone, but he knew it might not be enough. He knew he looked to be an outsider, a foreigner, unwelcome to some small-minded people. Hated more than the British by some because he was a potential threat; a threat to their livelihoods and to their women. He tried to ignore the comment and threaded his way carefully between tables and chairs.

"Paul!"

Hearing his name brought him to a halt. There was only one person the voice could belong to and he looked around to see Father Michael sitting at a table nearby. He was out enjoying himself with a beer and friends. The collar was obviously not going to spoil his evening.

"Hello, Father."

"I see you've fallen in with some of our folks. Be careful that they don't lay you low with the Guinness."

"I'm planning on ambushing them first."

Father Michael looked at him skeptically. "Good luck with that. I know those two and they'll be standing long after you've slid under the table."

"I'll take your counsel then. Hope to talk again soon," Stavros said and turned to reengage his new mates.

"You've met our young priest, have you?" said Conner.

"I have. Gave me a tour of the cathedral yesterday evening."

"Good man," Peter allowed before dropping back into his discussion of the latest football results.

At length he stopped and turned to Stavros. "We are not boring you with all this talk of football, are we? Do you have talks like this in America? Are you Americans fanatical about sports like we are?"

"Fanatical? I should say so, although we're more fanatical about some things than others. When I was a kid, one of our neighbors put up a sign that said 'Go Big Red.' He was a fan of a football team nicknamed 'Big Red.' Another neighbor got mad and ripped the sign down. He thought it was a sign supporting Communist China, the other 'Big Red.' It was just stupid politics."

"I don't think any of our teams get confused for communists but we do have our own stupid politics, I think you may have heard. And that can ruin the fun."

"That's not sportsmanlike," said Conner.

Shaking his head, he tossed back the last of his Guinness and stood up.

"We seem to be running low, my friends. I'll be back." He made a beeline for the bar.

Stavros watched Conner for a moment and said, "For us, the only subjects we have in the States to compare might be politics and race, but we shouldn't talk about that or anything like it."

"Or religion," said Peter.

"Or religion," said Stavros. He inclined his glass to Peter. "To sports without distractions."

"I can drink to that."

Conner came back to the table with three more brews. He glanced back at the bar where the young men sat, the same ones Stavros thought might be unfriendly.

"The boys at the bar wanted to know why we're sitting with you. They seem not to like you for some reason."

Stavros looked at Peter and sighed. "Speak of the devil. When I went for beers, I think they called me a 'Dago.'"

Conner said, "What did I miss?"

"We were just talking. Politics and race can ruin things and it seems those devils want to do just that," said Peter.

"They're harmless," Conner said. "And soon they'll be drunk."

"Young mean men are not harmless when they're drunk," Peter pointed out.

"Maybe I should go. I need to get some food in me anyway," said Stavros.

"Really? You shouldn't let some punks ruin your evening," Conner protested.

"I think it might ruin more than just my evening." Stavros drank largely and looked at the glass, which was still three-quarters full. "But then, I hate to waste a good beer. I'll be right back." He stood and walked over to Father Michael's table.

The priest held up his hand to his friends when he saw the look on Stavros' face.

"What's up?"

"I just wanted to ask if you knew the three boys sitting at the bar? Seems they've decided I'm an undesirable."

"No, I haven't seen them before. They could be from out of town."

"It's all right. I'm going to the loo and then I'll finish my beer and go. I don't want any trouble with them. But I hope we can talk again."

"I hope so too, Paul. Don't worry, we'll watch your back when you go."

Stavros avoided the bar as he moved towards the restrooms. He made short work of his business and pushed through the door back out into the narrow hallway just as one of the boys from the bar tried to walk in. He was shorter than Stavros. Face flushed, hair disheveled, he was moving too fast and almost stumbled before he caught himself on the door jamb.

"Slow down, mate," Stavros said. He smiled as if he really meant it.

"Feck off, Dago," the boy said and continued on into the bathroom, carried mostly by the momentum he couldn't control.

Stavros moved quickly and returned to his table and sat, watching tensely, waiting for the man to return to the bar.

"Had a bit of a run-in, did you?" Peter said. "I thought he might be going to try and jump you."

"He's definitely got a case of something against me." Stavros finished off his Guinness. Setting the glass down, he pulled a pair of thin leather gloves out of his pocket and worked his hands into them.

"Gentlemen, it's been a pleasure, but I think it's best I be going."

"A shame lad, but if you're about, drop by tomorrow. Me and Peter'll be here. Enjoyed talking."

Stavros stood and shook their hands. "Thanks for the beer, Conner. And Peter, I hope we get a chance to tip another brew."

He looked up at the bar and saw the third man rejoin his friends. They were staring and talking among themselves. *Time to put some distance between me and them*, thought Stavros.

He moved toward the door and waved a hand at Father Michael who was closely observing both Stavros and the bar. Then he turned and headed to the front door and out onto the path. It was cooler now; he looked up and saw a few vague stars. A good night for a brisk walk. Staying on the sidewalk, he strode toward the main road. He was almost there when he heard what he expected, footsteps of several men closing in on him.

Stavros turned. He was in shadow, a good place. Aside from the three men from the bar, he was alone. They were walking rapidly. One stopped. *Rear guard*, thought Stavros. Two kept coming, one a couple of meters in front of the other, his fists clenched, telegraphing intent.

"Fecking Dago, what are you doing in our country?" he said, the words spitting out at Stavros.

No time for talk.

Stavros took a step directly into the man's line of attack and punched straight forward at the bridge of his nose with the heel of his hand. Stavros' speed and the man's forward movement ended the fight before it started. The man's head jerked back, his back arched, and he fell backwards to the ground. The second man tried to get around his fallen partner and into the fight, but Stavros sidestepped and turned as his opponent tried to face him. Then Stavros took a step toward his new target, pivoted at the waist, and kicked, twisting his foot into a knife blade.

Focus. His energy focused on a point beyond the impact point. *Kick through it.*

From pure reflex and out of nowhere, he screamed, "*Kiai!*"

There was a dull thud and a crack as the side of the foot connected with the target's sternum. The man's body went horizontal and sailed back, landing on top of a pair of trash bins. The third man ran past him, avoiding the fight by hugging the opposite wall, toward the street.

Standing with his hands on his hips and breathing heavily, Stavros saw another man, Father Michael, walking quickly toward him. Stavros rubbed his right wrist; he'd overtaxed it a bit. It would be sore tomorrow. Punching hard skulls wasn't recommended, but then it was the best target at the time.

Michael reached him and looked at the two men lying on the ground.

"Are you alright?" he asked.

"I'm fine. They surprised me. What the hell was that all about?"

"Surprised you? I think it was the other way around." Father Michael looked at the second man who was whining softly amidst the garbage strewn about. "I think he'll survive."

Stavros knelt by the first man and leaned over to listen. His breath was ragged and smelled heavily of alcohol. Stavros rolled his wannabe nemesis onto his side.

"He's breathing, but he'll choke on his blood if he stays on his back."

Father Michael stared into Stavros' eyes for a moment.

"After you left, one of my parishioners told me they were troublemakers. I'm sorry you ran into them, they don't represent us. You had better get back to your hotel. I'll look after things with the police."

"I'll do that, Father. Thanks for being here."

Michael looked up the path behind Stavros.

"If I'm not mistaken, you have better backup than me around."

Stavros followed his gaze. Two figures silhouetted by the streetlights behind them, a man and a woman, stood watching. One slid an object back under his coat. The third young man was kneeling on the ground nearby, his arms pinioned behind his back.

Father Michael said, "Guardian angels, perhaps?"

You're never alone, mate. The words came back to Stavros.

"Perhaps. For what it's worth, Father, I'm a neutral party here."

"I think I understand," Michael said. He again grasped Stavros' arm and took his hand. "Whatever it is you're doing, son, I pray it is for good."

"I hope so too."

Stavros looked again. His watchers had disappeared, the young man nowhere to be seen.

34

On the outskirts of Dallas, Sarah's five-person team executed the drug kingpin's rendition well. After the fact, there was some argument about the blaze which engulfed the rear of the building and the small propane tank that exploded, but no one could (or would) say for sure who started the fire. When the rules of engagement were reviewed, the only definitive no-no had been that live ammunition was not to be used. Instead, blanks, simulators, and smoke provided the surprise and confusion that enabled the successful snatch. That and the "emergency vehicles" that blocked two of the escape routes. The fire department arrived shortly thereafter and quickly extinguished the conflagration and cleaned up the mess.

During the "hot wash" evaluation of the exercise, Sarah opined that a bit of urban renewal might have been a good outcome. No one actually lived in the area. The chief instructor believed the USG was saved paying for the damage because the buildings had already been condemned. Not a word of the event was reported in the news that evening. All the local drug dealers in the area of the takedown moved their businesses the same day. As far as they knew, the hit was real. The black helicopters that patrolled the sky for several hours afterwards seemed to reinforce that impression.

Back at Camp Jericho, the former students, now nineteen in number, moved to a new compound in a section of the post they had not visited before. Deeper in the woods and enclosed by double-fenced perimeter security, the facility wasn't even visible from its own entry gate. Warning signs declared that it was a US Forest Service Pest Control Laboratory and that highly toxic chemicals were in use. Most people chose to stay far away from the fence line.

The new unit members were to be assigned to one of six sections: global support, communications, or four regionals. But before that happened, Sarah found herself standing in front of the final board.

"You speak five languages," stated one of the members.

You know I do .... "Yes," she said.

"Which is your worst?"

"English."

"What other skills do you bring to us?"

"Besides languages, I suppose my knowledge of European fine art, international relations, or perhaps the travel industry. I learned a lot from my mother, she's an agent."

"For who?"

"For whom? She works with Thomas Cook."

"I thought you said English was your worst language?"

"It is, but that doesn't mean I speak it poorly."

The commander got the last word in.

"Miss Simon, you're a Farm-trained case officer; you could either work with Military Intelligence in nice places or you could get out and work for the Agency. They pay twice what we do. Why do you want to work with us?"

Sarah glanced at Landau sitting at the end of the table, seemingly occupied with his note-taking and studiously avoiding eye contact. She guessed the board members were cleared for most anything.

"Simple, I've seen how the Agency, Special Forces, and Military Intelligence work in the real world. The choice was easy."

***

The interviews over, the board members began closeted deliberations to determine where the newcomers would work in the unit. One by one, the candidates were called from the holding room to receive their verdict. As each departed, Sarah began to be concerned, and when she was the last person in the room, her stomach knotted up.

The door swung open and a man she hadn't seen before entered. Older, slightly portly, but with a confident look in his eyes and a nice smile, he carried himself like an experienced operative and leader.

"Sarah," the man said, returning her true name, and reached out to shake hands. "I'm Steve Elder, commander of Global Support. Welcome to Storm Azimuth."

35

As Neil made his way out of Belfast, he was glad to be done with it all. The atmosphere was oppressive; even its roads told the tale. In the South, the country roads were two-lane and barely maintained. In the occupied province of Northern Ireland, it was a different story. The roads were wide, military highways that allowed security forces high-speed access to any part of the province. It was as close as you could get to a war zone, but it wasn't a war between two armies. It was unconventional, a guerrilla war of terror and propaganda between the occupiers and the loyalists on one side and the rebel nationalists on the other. Most of the civilians were just caught in the middle.

He had crossed the border near Derry in the far northwest, stayed a night, and then proceeded cross-county at a leisurely pace, as he didn't want to appear in a rush. It required a bit more driving but was well worth the effort to get a sense of the opposition's security set-up.

Now, the job finished, he headed south, through Newry, down the Dublin Road, and across the frontier at the Killeen checkpoint. The British soldiers that trooped the line between the cars with their SLRs at hand paid less attention to the cars leaving Ulster than they did to those coming in from the Republic. Still, processing took time and he sat patiently in the line as the customs inspector checked the papers and identities of those in front of him against whatever possible offenses might have been committed over the past several days. He generally came up empty. People did not often commit offenses in the North and then escape to the South over the official border checkpoint. No, they usually stayed in the estates up North, well hidden from whichever side they weren't on, and hoped for the best. Neil also knew that being an American helped. Americans usually didn't commit offenses of the criminal kind. They might get drunk on Guinness and Irish coffees and throw up in the gutter, but generally they were just obnoxious tourists and by the time they crossed the frontier or got to the airport, they were sober again.

Neil hadn't been drunk in a long time. Not since that time years ago when he couldn't find any milk in his refrigerator and had Cheerios and gin for breakfast. It had been a long, rough night, and an even rougher morning had changed him. After that, he learned how to get to the ragged edge of the abyss and then step away.

In line with the other cars, he watched the wary armed men outside patrolling and inspecting in the drizzle before the scene became monotonous. He looked at the half wall that channelized the traffic into a single file. It was made of crumbling red brick topped with a tangle of barbed wire that was not at all intimidating to the black and white tabby that sat in its midst. The cat's tail flicked back and forth, bouncing off the razor wire as its eyes roamed over its territory. At least until they met Neil's and locked on. The tail froze and they stared at each other a long while. Finally, tired of the game, the cat looked away.

The inspector rapped on the window. Neil rolled it down and handed him his passport, international driver's license, and the rental papers. Wordlessly, the man in the dark blue raincoat with yellow reflective stripes perused the documents and handed them back with a curt, "Drive on."

Neil drove on.

On the edge of Dublin, he parked in a lay-by and gave up the keys to the young man who appeared from out of nowhere and took the car away. Then he walked over to an old Riley sitting nearby, threw his bag into the back seat, and climbed in. Rourke was driving and spoke little on the way back to the farm. Neil was okay with that.

As they drove through the countryside, he watched the storm clouds roiling up in front of them to the west and thought back to a day on Fort Bragg's auspiciously named Range 13. The students were training with demolitions, specifically firing systems, the things that make the explosives go bang. They fired electric and non-electric blasting caps and had seen how one could shred a steel helmet to pieces. Then they fired single blocks of explosives, both with a length of smoking time fuse and with an invisible electric pulse from a blasting machine through copper wires. Today, the students were making a ring main, a circle of detonating cord attached to twelve individual one-pound charges of C4 plastic explosive. With two electric blasting caps (for redundancy), they could fire all the charges at the same time from a central point. Ten students were watching from the bleachers at a distance while the other twelve, including Neil, were tying their charges into the ring. The instructor who was supervising the work grabbed for something in his bag and realized he'd left it elsewhere.

"Fitzpatrick, go get my test set from the range table," he said.

Neil quick-stepped up range toward the table and only knew something was wrong when the hair on the back of his neck suddenly stood on end. Static electricity. A thunder cloud high in the atmosphere miles away had sent it. A bad shunt in the firing circuit had taken it in. A mistake.

He didn't hear the blast; instead, the shock wave pummeled him forward into the sand. For a moment he lay stunned, flat on his face, until the rain of debris, some non-organic, most organic, stopped falling. When he was able to get up, he heard the others running to the scene and far away the sound of klaxons and sirens. When he turned to where his section had been working, he saw only black smoke and crumpled piles of what he knew too well to be death.

As Rourke drove on, Neil decided it might be a good idea to talk to the team about explosives safety when he got back to the farm.

36

From SUMMIT
Exclusive for ARGON

Lack of actionable information on QUEST prompts us to initiate additional deception measures to locate attack team planners as follows.

Contrived TV and radio press releases will indicate that Secretary State for NI to visit Londonderry for orientation and inspection of proposed Foyle River Bridge project. Possible travel of JEWEL to accompany SoSNI intimated.

ARGON is directed to orient its collection assets on Londonderry as soon as practicable.

Intent is to locate QUEST with the ultimate goal of identification and arrest or elimination of organizers with extreme prejudice if necessary.

Published ROE remain in effect.

Request daily situation summary and, as necessary, immediate updates for significant actions undertaken or incidents of a critical nature.

END
MOST SECRET

37

Philadelphia came to mind briefly when Stavros arrived in Londonderry. From the small hotel where he was staying, he could see the spans of the Craigavon bridge over the Foyle river to the eastern part of town. The houses reminded him a bit of the Old City district in his hometown, with its big bridges over the Delaware river that connected it to New Jersey. But that was about where the similarity ended. Yes, Philadelphia had divisions, South Philly with all its Italians, the northeast with the Blacks and the Irish, although the Irish were scattered everywhere. Philly was more accepting than say, New York or Boston, but there was still rivalry between groups, even fights, although none of it approached the violence and hatred he saw in Northern Ireland.

In Philly, the extreme violence, the murders, and assaults, if anything were focused. It was drug dealer on drug dealer, mafiosi on mafiosi, and very rarely was it one group like the Irish killing the Italians just because they were there. Stavros' real family lived in the northeast part of the city and growing up he'd dealt with more than one "ethnic" confrontation, none of which required gunplay or explosive devices. Perhaps the difference was that almost everyone he knew was either an immigrant or the offspring of one. The only people who could truly claim aboriginal rights had been forced out of the region long ago.

Derry, as the republicans called it, was harder to move around than Belfast or, for that matter, Armagh. Belfast was larger and the communities bigger, which provided large safe havens to disappear into, while Armagh was mostly Catholic. This northwestern Irish town was a different story, its streets and invisible sectarian divisions making it smaller than it truly was. A Protestant couldn't traverse a predominantly Catholic area, or vice versa, without worry. Its urban landscape was far more threatening than the surrounding countryside, especially for a stranger. Stavros knew too well that being a stranger held its own particular danger. It suddenly came to him that he was three for three: an incident in each place he had visited. He couldn't keep this up or he'd get a reputation.

***

"So, if VIPER disappeared, why all the fuss getting me to Derry?"

"Londonderry, you mean."

"I said Derry, that's good enough. Let's not get tied up in the politics of names."

Hunter glared at him. Then she decided he was an American who didn't understand or maybe he just didn't care.

"Tell me again why he's so important to you?"

"Who?"

"VIPER."

"He's my grail quest."

"No, really."

"He was on my team, he's a brother. We were friends, not terribly close, but friends still."

"What sort of bloke is he?"

"Now? I'm not sure. Before, he was a good soldier and teammate. Knew his job and did it well. Good sense of humor, bit of a rebellious soul. Drank a bit, actually he drank a lot, but then we all did. If he ever talked about Ireland, he'd complain about the British, but I never dreamed he was a hardcore IRA supporter. Something pushed him over the edge."

"What are you going to do if you run into him?"

"I'll say something inventive like, 'Fancy meeting you here. Would you like go back to the States with me this evening?' Or maybe just 'Let's grab a beer' and while we're drinking, you guys come in and arrest us both for being Yanks."

"I'm not sure either of those will work."

"Maybe not, but whatever we do, it'll probably be made up on the fly."

"Well then, Londonderry may be our best bet. It seems there will be a VIP visit soon and it would be a good target of opportunity for the IRA and your friend."

"When?"

"Within a fortnight. They haven't given us an exact date, but the Guildhall will be the main venue along with a brief stop at a river site where they plan on building a new bridge."

Hunter handed him a small map segment. "This is the location on the river, but it's also shown in the newspapers."

Stavros looked at the paper in the glow of the instrument panel and handed it back. "I've got the location and I don't need anything on me that someone might misunderstand."

"Are you getting nervous?"

"No, but I seem to attract attention."

"From what I've seen, you seem able to handle yourself well enough."

It was the closest thing to a compliment Hunter had ever given him. He chose to sidestep.

"So, this visit will take place before Belfast?"

"Yes, it's before the main trip."

"And they haven't said who is coming?"

"The secretary of state for Northern Ireland for sure and maybe a royal, but we don't know which one."

"So this is a good opportunity for them to strike. It's close to the Republic, a lot of hardcore IRA folks up here. What else?"

"Not much. We're concentrating our surveillance teams on known IRA supporters and the army is watching the border closely. The only thing you need to do is watch for VIPER."

"There's one thing I'm curious about, Hunter."

"What's that?"

"Why do you do this?"

"I want to stop the IRA from bombing our cities."

"That's it?"

Hunter looked at Stavros intently. "For the moment, that's enough."

Stavros knew he was pushing her, but he wasn't sure if he was pushing too hard. He saw then the anger in her eyes.

"Yeah, I understand. It's what we do," was all he said.

***

After Hunter had dropped Stavros to find his way back to his little hotel, he considered what he'd said to her. He wasn't just searching for a teammate, although that did play a small role. There was a bond that came from experiences shared on a different level, much more intense than drinking or training together. He remembered well the first time he'd worked with Neil, although he was sure his memory may have enhanced things. He first met Neil in the States, long before they shipped out for Berlin. They were on the same A-Team at Fort Devens, and theirs was selected along with two others to deploy to central Africa to a country that was in the process of falling apart ten years after ejecting their colonial overseers. It was the first time that he was deployed into the middle of someone else's mess but, he supposed, it was for a good cause. They were there to protect the American Embassy and help get all the non-combatants out of country before they fell into the hands of the guys with guns—either the soldiers or the rebels.

Their mission was almost finished, and the team prepared to exit the country. Only a skeleton crew of American diplomats remained in the embassy, the other forty-five having been evacuated home. And because the nearest large American force was ten hours away by air, it was thought totally prudent to only have a small force to protect those who stayed. The Marine Security Guard Detachment would be augmented with two Special Forces troopers. Those thirteen MSGs and soldiers would be all that remained on the ramparts once the three SF teams departed. More than enough, some intelligent staff officer had decided.

Stavros and Neil's team would not stay, but they had one more thing to do.

"What are we doing?"

"Exciting stuff. We're escorting the special envoy to the airport," said Jon DeFrehn, ODA-222's team sergeant.

Anywhere else, it would have been the most mundane tasking ever. Four unarmored Suburbans and three Peugeot 505s stood waiting in front of the ambassador's residence which was next to the embassy compound. The envoy had flown in three days before to negotiate an end to the uprising—actually an internecine squabble the president had instigated by forgetting to pay half the army, which prompted that half to become rebels, rip off their uniforms, and lay siege to the capital. They cut the road to the airport two days later. Negotiations had failed and the rebels still controlled a 5-kilometer stretch of the highway. But the envoy wanted to get out of this godforsaken country before his yellow fever vaccine wore off.

The highway was wide and hacked out of the palm forest, which meant a surprise ambush would be difficult, but firing on the convoy would not be hard. Another typical day.

209

The black Peugeots were standing at the head and tail of the convoy. Each car was manned by four rather mean-looking locals in cheap suits wearing sunglasses, not a long gun between them. Stavros had come to the realization that the only folks who wore sunglasses in this country were the ones you didn't want to mess with. Not because they were particularly tough but because they were the ones that had guns and no compunction about killing people. These dudes were the worst of the lot, the president's personal security, guys called *les Hiboux*—the Owls—because they usually only came out at night.

"The Big Man, the Grand Crocodile, the President for Life loaned us some of his best," DeFrehn said. The look on his face showed his disdain, but then he would know, having served in Africa with the Belgian Army before he emigrated to the States.

"Sounds like you don't like him or his boys," Stavros said.

"I don't. He's a thief and they're all stone-cold killers. I'm just here to keep the Americans safe."

The special envoy came out of the residence with Madam Ambassador at his side. That she was still in the city despite the events, as they were called, was testament to her dedication. She was a career diplomat, not a political appointee who had bought stock in the current president. But then, appointees usually didn't request an assignment to Third World countries as compensation for their contributions. The envoy was an older man, white hair, slightly stooped, with an expensive suit that had fit him better ten years earlier. Now in his seventies, he looked like the *éminence grise* he was, a man who pulled levers in many capitals around the world but on this day was tired and just wanted to go home.

The job would be simple. The locals would provide security fore and aft, while the center of the convoy would be made up of four Suburbans manned by the team armed with M-16s and a couple of M-203s. There might have been a sawed-off shotgun or two lying on the floorboards as well. There were also a lot of smoke grenades. Real grenades, the kind that exploded and threw nasty bits of metal in all directions, had been discouraged by the State Department in Washington for some reason. DeFrehn suspected the Foggy Bottom folks were scared that someone on his team would drop one in a bar. But everyone knew that only happened in Fayetteville. The fourth car in the queue, one of the Suburbans, was reserved for the special envoy and the embassy's political officer—the "politico"—with the assistant regional security officer riding shotgun, and a local driver.

Tom, the assistant RSO, was quite the card. He refused to bend to the new ways of doing things even if some were not so new. For one, he refused to use a typewriter, preferring to write his reports out long hand, and he carried a long-barrel Colt .357 revolver in a shoulder holster, instead of his issue Smith & Wesson .38 Special, not that either one would be much help after six rounds. But he looked good with his handlebar mustache and alligator-skin cowboy boots. Unlike his boss, he was willing to put his butt on the line.

Good-byes completed, the envoy was bundled into his vehicle and the fun began. *Les Hiboux* climbed into the first two cars and began to roll with the lead Suburban following. The envoy came next, fourth in the convoy. Two more Suburbans and the final Peugeot followed out the gate, onto the wide avenue that fronted the embassy, and southeast toward the airport.

Fourteen kilometers to do and the first five got them to the line of demarcation where the forces loyal to the president hunkered down behind brick walls and several rusted Cadillac Gage V100 armored cars. There was a short slow-down as the blockade was moved and the convoy plunged forward into no-man's land. Inexplicably, a short while after they no longer had the cover of the army, the Peugeots peeled off. Stavros, back in the third embassy vehicle, saw the lead Suburban slow and stop to speak with the *Hiboux* who stood next to his idling car. A crackle came over the radio.

"He says the car is broke and they can't abandon their guys. Actually, I think they don't want to be out here."

Tom said, "Keep moving. We're on our own; our brave escorts just abandoned us."

"They're not afraid when they're the big men in town, but put them up against soldiers and it's a whole 'nother story. Chicken shits," came a voice from one of the other cars.

"Maintain proper radio procedure."

"Like anyone listening gives a damn."

At speed, the temperature was bearable. It felt like 80 degrees instead of the 90 with 110 percent humidity. The rainy season was almost on them and the afternoon deluges would begin soon, you could see it in the ominous clouds overhead. As they moved, the flags on the front fenders of the envoy's car, the Stars and Stripes on the left and the blue State Department flag on the right, snapped and crackled in the wind. The flags were the only protection the convoy had besides the men and guns looking out in all directions. Armored vehicles often weren't provided to Third World embassies in those days; they were only given to ambassadors of First World countries where the threat was negligible but status all important. Besides, everyone knew the rebels respected flags.

The Peugeots became specks in the rearview mirror, then disappeared altogether as the convoy rounded a bend. The Suburbans picked up speed, 60 mph on the concrete road, one of the only good roads left in the country, the rest having been neglected so long that they had turned back into jungle tracks. The convoy formed a wedge, lead vehicle with the envoy's running close behind, the last two security vehicles to the rear but close enough that they could jump ahead to provide cover on either side. The lead car varied his speed, slower, then faster, but always reserving the last bit of power for a surge. Eight kilometers down, six to go—sixty football fields of wide open road.

An incredibly fast streak of brilliant white followed by a smoke trail shot over the first Suburban, followed by a yellow-orange explosion of flame in the trees on the other side of the road.

"Christ! RPG," Neil yelled.

"Action left!"

"Stand on it!"

The men in the lead vehicle didn't see or hear the rocket, but when they heard the radio call, reflex took over and the car surged forward, its big four-barrel carb howling as it gulped in air. A second, better aimed rocket hit the edge of the road just behind and threw shrapnel and debris into the envoy's vehicle.

A distant chatter of automatic rifle fire could be heard as figures danced out of the tree line shooting haphazardly at the vehicles. They must not have expected much resistance, but the convoy wasn't about to stop. From the windows four M-16s opened up, ripping off thirty rounds each, mags dropped and new ones slammed in. More automatic fire.

Another RPG fired, the third, this time accurate. A flash at the front of the envoy's vehicle. Staggered, enveloped in gray smoke, it rolled on, slower now. The driver was slumped forward, hands fallen from the steering, blood streaming down his face. The side window was shattered, the car beginning to wander on the road. Tom dropped his pistol to the floor and reached over, grasping the driver, wrenching the body out of the way. He stuck his left leg across the transmission onto the gas pedal while grabbing the wheel, taking control and standing on the gas once again. The vehicle was on its last legs. The engine was shrieking, clanking, and protesting while the steering was pulling hard left. The politico was in the back screaming something unintelligible into his ears.

From the third car, Stavros could see that the front wheel of the envoy's was toast.

Then it was gliding. No power.

"We're down and out," Tom said, yelling in his mike over the noise to his rear and outside. He was trying to guide the car to the right away from most of the gunfire, but he could hear the pings and thumps of rounds hitting the car. Luckily there were three other vehicles for the rebels to aim at. Tom piloted the car to a stop, smashed the gear lever into park, and threw his door open.

They had passed through the worst of the kill zone and their return fire had dissuaded many of the rebels, but some kept coming. The lead vehicle slammed on its brakes and backed up to protect the front of the car while the two follow cars provided a shield on the left and to the rear. Everyone but the drivers piled out and were laying down covering fire while Tom pulled the envoy out of the car and pushed him to the third vehicle and onto the back seat.

The politico was still screaming, "Get us out of here!"

"Shut up. You're making us nervous," said Tom, adding a slap to the politico's face for emphasis. He pushed the man toward the safety of the fourth Suburban.

Stavros was outside his car, protected by the engine compartment to a degree. His M203 fired, its buckshot load sundering the leaves of the brush and any person caught standing. A second 40mm round fired, this time followed by the crump of a high explosive warhead. Then a third. The rebels' fire stopped for a second. It seemed they might be reconsidering their odds. Stavros reloaded and checked behind him.

Grenades were thrown and noxious clouds of white smoke began to obscure the road from the forest.

"Get the driver!" Tom yelled. He was still getting the envoy into the car.

"Leave him, get us out of here," the politico whined.

Neil slapped him hard in the head and pushed him into the rear cargo bay of the Suburban.

"Tom told you to shut up," said Neil.

Two men grabbed the driver and placed him on the back seat of the lead vehicle and hopped in after.

"Mount up!" DeFrehn was in command. Doors slammed and the envoy's car roared off, followed by the others in a reverse wedge, the rebels' sporadic fire being answered with bursts from the M-16s.

DeFrehn turned to Stavros, his weapons sergeant. "Where did you get the HE rounds?"

"The defense attaché had a few lying around his office. After he was evac'd, I thought I should secure them," said Stavros.

"Good initiative."

The politico said, "I'm going to write you all up when we get home. You risked our lives for that driver."

The envoy turned around in his seat and addressed the politico with disdain. "Where I come from, we would have done the same thing, so I suggest you keep your mouth shut or this might reflect badly on your career."

The envoy had dropped his crisp Foggy Bottom accent and reverted to the twang of his native Mississippi.

DeFrehn spoke: "Where *do* you come from, sir?"

"Tarawa and Saipan. 2nd Marines. Your men did good today, Top."

***

As they approached the airport perimeter, a phalanx of V100s followed by troop carriers was rolling down the highway toward them. The vehicles slowed and made an opening to let the convoy pass through and then continued on toward town.

"Looks like we might have started something," said Neil.

"Hopefully, they'll finish the job before we have to go back," said DeFrehn.

***

That evening, after helping write the after-action report at the embassy compound, Stavros and Neil walked across the wide, empty boulevard and had a couple Tembo beers at the Safari, one of the few bars still open in the city. The place served European-style dishes, logical because it was owned by an expat and run by his wife, a local girl who looked mean and was ready to kick the butt of any lazy employee or customer that got out of hand. The beer was drunk straight from the bottle; clean water was too precious to wash glasses.

They ordered dinner. Mussels were out because the month didn't end in an "R" and, anyway, Sabena wasn't flying them in for the expats because of the rebellion. Instead, they had hamburgers and *frites*. The *frites* were on the menu because the owner was Belgian; the hamburgers were there because his wife knew how to do business with the Americans from across the street. The burgers were well done, because eating beef in Africa was always an adventure, the cheese came from a laughing cow, and they were slathered in Dijon. You really didn't want to try the ketchup.

"Do you think it's really beef?" Neil asked.

"Didn't taste like elephant," said Stavros.

"Never had elephant."

"Not very tasty. It's fatty."

"Good to know. I'll skip it if it's offered."

"Now, crocodile … that's a different story."

"I know, it tastes just like chicken. I ate alligator in Florida."

"With enough Tabasco, almost anything is edible, except elephant."

"I'm glad this place is still open," Neil said.

"Have you ever noticed that breweries and bars are the last things to go out of business in a war zone?"

"I guess they don't want the soldiers more pissed off than they already are."

"If there wasn't beer out here, we'd have to drink at the Marine House."

"That's a depressing thought; they can't go out on the town and I don't want to see any of their old war movies."

"You could play pool."

"I'm lousy at geometry. I prefer darts anyway."

"This is a better way to end the day."

After they had eaten, they sat together silently, listening to the night buzzing of the cicadas, the rhythmic strains of *soukous* dancing across the rooftops from the bars in the *Cité*, and the occasional angry crack of gunfire in the far background; two Americans—one very Irish, one very Greek—sipping their barely cool beers on the dark patio, deep in the warm heart of Africa.

38

"What do you think?" said Danny Monahan.

"They're difficult but doable targets," Neil answered.

"How so?"

"They are both hard targets with good security. You'll need some reason to get close to Stormont Castle, some cover like a delivery company. Once you can get in close, it'll be relatively easy. The other one will be dicey. There's no way to get real close to Hillsborough, so we'll do a standoff attack. But in both cases, we'll be using the same method."

"Pray tell," said Rourke.

Danny looked at Rourke like he'd spoken out of turn but let the transgression slide.

"What's your plan?"

Neil grinned; this was one of his favorite toys. A technique he'd learned at a special training camp called Site 29, a very esoteric school for saboteurs. The courses were taught by the experts, mostly retired demolitions specialists along with a few engineers and chemists but they were all alike in that they loved to work with explosives. And with an unconstrained budget and a hidden location to experiment, they had plenty to do.

"I'm gonna use something called a platter charge."

"Explain," said Danny.

It was the day after Neil's return and once again they were sitting in the kitchen, the fire warming a perpetually cool stone cottage. Neil picked up a small plate and held it by the edge vertically, turning it side to side.

"This is a platter. Now imagine the same thing but made from metal and about 10 inches in diameter. On the back side is plastic explosive, wired with an electric fuse and a timer. Got it?"

"So far. What do we do with it?"

"Not it, them. Six of these inside a vehicle aimed at the target all timed to go off simultaneously."

"What does that get us?"

"A big bang with six super-heated projectiles traveling at 6,500 feet per second."

"Holy Jesus, Mary, and Joseph. That's over a mile a second."

"It'll punch a hole through steel plate and, at the distance we're talking about, it's the best bet for a stone building. No guarantees though."

"Why not?"

"Stone absorbs shock better than metal, so penetration is hard to calculate. That said, anyone in front of the building will be toast and anyone directly inside is going to be really messed up from the spalling—the shrapnel and stuff that comes off the inside wall. And, if we get one through a door or a window, then we'll have a goal."

"So, we nail the bastards when they arrive at the house."

"If you can. We'll have to get the delivery vehicle in position and then walk away. That is, unless you have a *Kamikaze* among your boys."

"I don't think so."

"So, we plan on a timer or, better yet, a remote control."

"What else do we need?"

"Plastic explosive, 120 pounds total, twenty-four blasting caps, twelve plates, 10 inches in diameter and three quarters of an inch thick, and about 200 feet of duplex electric wire, like 18 or 20 gauge." Neil handed Danny a list.

"You sure you got the numbers right?" Danny said, his tone sarcastic.

Neil ignored him. "And the plates need to be copper."

"Where are we going to get something like that?" Rourke asked. He was out of his depth.

"There's got to be someone in Ireland who uses copper plate."

"There is. I know someone who worked with Irish Electrification. He can help," said Danny.

"And the delivery?"

"Already thought of that. If we don't need to get inside the buildings, it's even easier. You put the things together when we get the stuff."

Rourke had picked up the saucer and was contemplating it while spinning it on the table. "We need a codename. Can we call it a layer cake?" Rourke said.

"Nah, we'll call it a boxty," said Danny.

"What's a boxty?" Neil said.

"A potato pancake. We're going to serve them English bastards a hot breakfast."

39

Stavros sat on a bench where he had a good view of the event's proposed location. The authorities had done him the favor of marking the site with some signs and tape in preparation and he imagined that some sort of circus tent or tarpaulin would be raised. Thus far, nothing had been done. He could see the northern part of Waterside, a mostly Protestant enclave on the other side of the river. A wide expanse of open land on the river's edge backed by Ebrington Barracks stared back at him ominously. That spot would have been better protected for the event, which made him question the logic of the authorities. The only thing this side had going for it was its proximity to the Guildhall. Some local bureaucrat chose this site for its ease of access, not for security. To his mind, it didn't make sense. It wasn't consistent with the understandably paranoid British security practices he'd seen so far. That said, this side was easier for him to watch without being totally obvious. There was enough foot traffic to hide in and plenty of places he could set up his stakeout and not be arrested by some suspicious cop.

The bench was good. Out of the wind, backed by a wall, he could use the monocular he had forgotten to return to the supply folks to scan the area. If he was careful. He kept a well-thumbed Collins

Birds of Britain in his lap, the explanation for staring at the river so intently.

He fished around in his pocket and found a package of *Gummi* bears he had been saving since Germany. After his walk in Wales, he'd decided to bring along extra sustenance and now he was down to his last pouch. He grabbed three of the squishy sweets and pulled them out. It was actually four, but he ate them all anyway because life was uncertain. You could never tell what might happen.

He practiced his BS cover conversation. *I'm looking for a redshank—elusive little buggers ....*

Of course, he'd already seen several but no one else knew that. He'd go back to listening to people in the bars later in the day, but for the moment, he was just an observer watching birds and people. Occasionally, he would close his eyes when the routine became too routine. He fell into a trance a couple of times, only to pop open his eyes with a start when a door would slam or squeaky brakes disturbed him. He'd spent a bit too much time in a pub the previous evening and would visit another tonight. He looked at his watch and planned the day ahead; he would have to include some nap-time later if he was going to keep up with this grueling way of boring himself to death. *Boredom is a hazard of the occupation. Time becomes molasses and surveillance takes the word excitement to a new low point.*

A pigeon strutted by on the ground and for a talking-to-himself moment he wondered about Sarah. Where might she be and how would they make things work? When she was a "regular soldier," there were never complications. Now she was one of the elite like him—although he scoffed at the idea of eliteness—and how would that affect them? The pigeon flapped its wings, startled by a sound, and flew off. Stavros came back to the job.

This is not the time or place .... Why not? When will be the right time to think about it?

It was late morning, but the sun hadn't broken the hold of the wall's shadow, so it was still cool. His Norwegian army anorak tightly wrapped around him, he would have liked to move to a warmer spot but this one had choice viewing. There was no better place to observe, and he'd already walked around several times. Staying put was also a sound idea, since the last thing he wanted was to be in the middle of the target area if Neil should appear. He imagined the conversation would be awkward.

Seemingly hundreds of herring gulls soared over the river, screeching in a language that must have made sense to the birds but was an annoying cacophony to the humans on the ground. He watched as one pivoted sharply on its wing and made a tumbling attack on an overfilled wastebasket that had dumped its contents on the ground. Derry's bounty turned into people's rubbish had changed the birds' diet. As for the garbage, the maintenance crews must be on strike or slowdown or maybe there just weren't any workers. He had no clue about the local labor situation and made a mental note to bring it up in one of his bar conversations later. He wrote some more of his article in his mind as he watched a more interesting bird, a lone kestrel, contemptuously sailing alone on the winds high above all the other birds, hunting for its meal. Stavros thought the sleek raptor was looking in the wrong place; the rats on this side of the river were too big, too well fed. He should be hunting the grasslands; that would be the best place to find food. He thought it was not unlike his own hunt: set out the bait and wait for the predator to show up.

Bait? Who's baiting who?

40

Neil was in the barn cobbling together wires for the firing system when Danny walked in, to be met by loud complaints. The American was frustrated. He didn't have everything he needed. He was still short the copper plates and without those he couldn't begin to work the plastic explosive. The only thing he'd been able to do was supervise two relatively clueless mechanics working inside the two delivery vans. The six platters would be mounted inside the cargo compartment of each van, two rows of three on one side. The skin of the van had been removed from a three- by two-foot section and replaced with a fiberboard advertising sign. With that in front of them instead of metal, the metal platters would not have anything significant impeding their trajectory when the charges fired. Weight had been added to the opposite side wall to counter any lean in the trucks' suspension, something a sharp-eyed security man might notice and want to inspect. Once the platter charges were mounted, light panels would be fixed inside to hide the modifications. Then at the last minute, the truck would be loaded with cargo to make close scrutiny difficult. The cargo had a secondary role to act as tamping for the explosive.

It will be a glorious little thing, thought Neil. *Too bad I won't get to see it go off.*

"Okay, my boy, time to get your traveling shoes on," Danny announced.

Neil turned to Danny. "What's up now?"

"It looks like we might have another chance to hit them even before the others. I need you to check it out and tell me what you think." He handed Neil the newspaper page that described the new bridge and the secretary's visit.

"Derry then."

"It's an easy trip. You can pop over and back or take your time. The other visits have been delayed a week so we have nearly two weeks."

"It shouldn't take long, maybe one overnight."

"I have a helper for you over there. Knows you're coming. And there are some places for you to stay if you want."

"I usually find my own spot. But give me the person's contacts just in case I need something."

"You don't trust us, do you?"

"No, not at this stage of the game. Besides, no one knows me, and I shouldn't need help. By the way, when will the plates arrive? They're holding up final assembly and you need to get these vans over the border a couple of days in advance."

"No worries. They'll be here when you get back. My contacts were able to shape them with a bit of a curve like you wanted."

"How did they do that without machining them?"

"They put the plates over a hollow form and dropped a wrecking ball on them dead center. They said it worked like a charm."

"Lucky Charms," Neil said.

"What's that?"

"I was thinking that if we are lucky, we'll find gold at the end of the rainbow."

"You Yanks believe in all that nonsense, don't you?"

"Not really, I don't anyway. In the States, it's just a way to sell breakfast cereal to kids."

"Whatever, we've set you up with a car to go over this evening," Danny said, handing him a notecard. "This is your contact's address and telephone number in Derry. Use it if you need it. Just say Stewart sent you."

"This person is trustworthy?"

"Quite, been providing us information for a while now and has no close contact with the boys on the front line."

"If there was such a thing as a front line; this is a war of the shadows. How does his information get to you anyway?"

"It just does, my boy."

41

"Good morning, Ralph. It's day three of Operation *Birdwatch*," Stavros said to his new friend, the pigeon. He had been at this so long he'd taken to naming each bird. At least the ones he thought he could recognize. He thought he might be turning into a crazy person, talking to them as he was. Luckily, no one heard him, although one little old lady looked at him longingly like she wanted to adopt him. He shivered involuntarily and gazed through his monocular at the circling gulls, hoping she would move along.

But he wasn't thinking of the birds or even about his friend, the errant leprechaun called VIPER. He even tried not to think about Sarah except when he checked the watch she gave him, her knowing reminder of what he had at home whenever he got back there. It was still morning, just as it had been the last five times he looked at his watch. He shook his wrist and watched the sweep hand. It was still running but maybe the minute hand was stuck.

Why do you do this?

He remembered his schoolboy excitement of playing soldier, which eventually turned into a patriotic fervor to fight the communist menace. It was simple: us versus them. Then that commitment changed as he grew into the job. Many thoughts ran through his mind, too many for a guy trying to watch the crowd, but they were there nevertheless.

Duty? I have my Boy Scout duty to God and Country, a soldier's duty to the Constitution, what else is there? But I am not defending my country, the Constitution, or, for that matter, God, as far as I can see.

It came to him slowly because thinking about duty was not a daily or even a weekly event for him. But he knew that interspersed with his normal day-to-day life were the real things that made a difference. His experiences in Africa, East Germany, and Iran had showed him what it was and it was different from the oaths he had sworn to; it was more personal.

It's for my brothers.

The only way Stavros could help Neil was to find him. Derry seemed to be the event that might bring Neil back to the North, if he had ever left. He abandoned his customary perch on the bench to do a walking circuit of the neighborhood. A working public telephone beckoned him over. It was time to check in with his handler. Coins inserted, number dialed, Hamish answered, who after saying that Hunter was out, gave him the news that things looked good for the visit. Stavros spent several minutes trying to figure out what Hamish was telling him, but the details were fuzzy. It seemed a source knew someone's cousin that heard from his uncle or some such nonsense. Stavros was about to give the "double naught Six spook," the lowest grade for intelligence reporting, when Hamish finally blurted out that VIPER was coming across the border. So much for communications security, but he didn't think the IRA had taps on the British Army's telephones. At least, he hoped they didn't. Hamish also gave the code word to execute a car pick-up with Hunter later that evening. In the meantime, he would stay in the area and observe.

He started on the embankment and headed around the hall toward the open plaza. Or he would have if the patrolling RUC

228

constable hadn't positioned himself on the path. His back was turned but Stavros could see enough of his face to recognize him as the same man he'd already seen twice in two days. He didn't care if the RUC were supposed to be the good guys; at this point in the game he didn't need the attention. It would be prudent to wander a bit further away from what would be ground zero.

He headed for the Tower Museum and the city wall. Entering from Magazine Street he found the stairs that would have permitted him access to the roof of the tower. But the roof was closed because of the security measures. A shame because it offered a good view of the plaza and the looming Guildhall. This wouldn't do, he decided, so he reversed course back out of the building and wandered Magazine Street until he found an unguarded ramp up to the ramparts of the city wall. He slipped up the path quickly and found a secluded corner of the Water Bastion to disappear into. With an excellent view of the terrain from above, he was able to get close to the wall so he wasn't obvious. He scanned the area quickly with his monocular, like a lifeguard on the beach looking for a black fin to break the water. He was in the game again, but it was a game that required at least two players.

Where are you, buddy?

42

Neil thought the crossing from the Republic into the province was a cakewalk compared to any of the checkpoints into or out of Berlin. Neither the Irish nor the British possessed the pathologically deadly technical sophistication of the East German Border Guard Command. The isolated cross-over Rourke used was more like stumbling across the US–Canada border between Montana and Saskatchewan. Nary a Mountie nor a State Trooper in sight.

He noted that it would have been a good place for tourists because there was no wait, especially tourists who might want to witness the Irish smuggling trade, but then the authorities might have objected. Neil didn't mention his observations to Rourke who had no sense of humor. Odd for an Irishman.

It had been fairly early in the evening when Rourke dropped him off near Bogside. The district didn't look terribly threatening, but then no one was about. He began to wonder if it was a holiday because even the military and the police seemed far away. But he was okay with that since he didn't want to get stopped again. His story was a bit murky and he imagined the conversation wouldn't go well.

A friend from the Republic gave you a lift over the border and dropped you off to do some sightseeing? You forgot his name did you? Really, now?

He worked his way to the city center, making sure he was clean of any surveillance, whatever their affiliation, before he stopped to make a telephone call. Instructions received, he followed them until he came to the back stairs of a set of flats and climbed the stairs to a certain door on the fourth floor. He knocked twice and waited until the door opened, then slipped inside, unseen by the other residents.

***

The next morning, he headed for a certain cafe to meet his new friend. The girl from the previous evening had told him to expect a woman carrying a blue shopping bag, the kind people use to buy a few things from the deli or the bakery, the kind with long shoulder straps.

He was nursing a coffee when she walked in and came straight to his table and took off her big sunglasses. To say Neil was stunned was a bit much: she looked radically different than when he had left her bed hours before. He was even more appreciative of her looks now: sparkling dark eyes, nice smile, clothes that fit her curves well but not too well. Attractive. He wouldn't throw her out of bed for eating crackers, he thought, which was good because he hadn't. But her hair color was totally off the wall, raging punk, reddish purple. It was … well, striking. Luckily she had a hat.

"Hi Neil!" she said and sat down without an invitation. "Call me Branna, that's my real name."

"Branna? That's also a nice name. You look different."

"Just on the outside. I'm your arm candy while you're here."

"Are you now? And what's our story, where was it that we met?"

"Last night. The Grand Central."

"I take it we had a good time?"

"I think you know we did. That's why I'm here. Like what you see?"

"You're a forward lass, I can say that. Not bad on the eyes either."

"Then you won't mind me being with you."

"You can be my guidebook. I left mine in the Republic."

Branna ordered a pastry and tea and finished them both almost as soon as they hit the table. Seeing Neil staring at her, she became a bit shy, but only a bit.

"I was famished. You're picking up the bill today." No question.

Neil didn't answer. Instead, he said, "What did they tell you about me?"

"Your name and what you looked like. Oh, and that I was to hang around you all day until you get tired of me. You're not tired of me, are you?"

Neil smiled. "Not yet." *But we'll see.*

The work day began with a circumnavigation of the city center. Gradually the circles became smaller until they were at the focal point of his visit. The Guildhall Plaza. He looked at it from the Shipquay Gate then the steps of the hall itself and marveled at how open it was but also how easy it would be to seal it off. They strolled along the river and saw the orange cones and tape where the event would happen, and he noted possible places from where he might launch an attack. If Branna was wondering what he was doing, she didn't let on and she didn't ask. Neil for his part didn't tell. They walked on and took one more circuit of the plaza. In its middle he stopped and did a slow turn to take it all in. Branna did the same, taking off the hat and spinning about, her brilliantly purple hair flying about her. As she danced, Neil evaluated the target from the open air to the east, to the red sandstone beaux-arts facade of the hall, to the weathered gray of the city wall. The only disconcerting thing he saw were the modern watchtowers, their upper decks protected by chain-link fencing hung from poles to defeat any rockets that might be fired at them. After four hundred years, the city was again under siege.

He looked up at the ramparts and watched a couple of soldiers standing over the Shipquay Gate.

"Is the city wall closed to tourists?" he said.

"Mostly. I think some small organized groups can get up there but we can't."

Then who would that be? Neil thought. His sharp eyes had picked out a motionless figure in civilian clothing near the southeast bastion of the wall, seemingly watching him, holding something up to his face. The man's arm came down and their stare continued. Then he turned and moved and was soon lost from view. Uneasy, Neil knew it was time to go.

43

Stavros told Hunter about his "sighting" a few hours later when she picked him up. She had acquired a different "Q" car, a banged-up Opel that looked as clapped-out as the Cortina she'd had in Belfast but was just as deceptive. It was also a runner. Hunter got them out of town quickly and soon they were on a nice straight stretch of road, a seeming rarity in Ireland or, for that matter, much of the UK. She powered up through the gears and Stavros kept silent, listening instead to the sharp crackle and roar of the exhaust as it trailed out behind them. The windows were open and the cold wind grabbed at anything loose in the car, so he kept his hands close to his body and resisted the impulse to fly them outside. He glanced at the speedometer and saw it was cresting 90 mph as the telephone poles zipped by on both sides. Hunter was smiling, her eyes fixed ahead, looking for the next possible hazard. It was still relatively safe to be on the road in the late afternoon, the orange sun low on the horizon behind them. The car hit the peaks at speed, lifting off the crest of each and setting down in the trough beyond without complaint. Or at least only once, when the tail bottomed out after a particularly long leap. Ahead, the first buildings of a village appeared and she backed off the throttle, a tap of the brakes, and double-clutched the downshift just for fun, and then another as the engine howled down its deceleration. Hunter loosened her concentration and came back to the relatively mundane world of tradecraft.

"You were saying?" said Hunter.

"I saw him today," Stavros said.

"Why didn't you call?"

"I did. I talked with Hamish this afternoon."

"He told me you called this morning but he didn't say anything about a second call."

"He should have said something. I told Hamish that I lost him. He was with a woman. I'm sure it was him. Right size, build. Hair. Walked the same way. He's got a beard now, a big red one. He looks like a Viking."

"Where exactly did you see him?"

"In the middle of Guildhall Plaza. I was on top of the old wall, but by the time I got down, he disappeared."

"How did you get up there? It's an exclusion zone."

"A ramp was open. Nobody seemed to care."

"You have all the luck."

"Maybe, but I still lost him. He was gone when I got back to ground level."

"What did the woman look like?"

"About five feet six with long hair, although it was a color not found in nature. That's all I could see. She was wearing big sunglasses and a hat."

"Did he see you?"

"I don't think so. I was pretty far away and using my birdwatching monocular."

"Birdwatching?"

"Long story."

"Never mind. Do you think they'll try to hit the event here?"

"I don't see why they would. Both the plaza and the river sites are really bad."

"How so?"

"They can't get close enough to do damage unless they just want to kill civilians. It would be like blowing up a county fair. Only a small chance of hitting anybody significant."

"Why would he come over then?"

"Because an opportunity is an opportunity. Someone needed to check it out and he may be the best target analysis guy they have. I doubt if they'll bite though."

"Why?"

"If they were already going to strike one target, why would they change their plans at the last minute to hit Derry?"

"So, we're back to square one."

"Maybe, maybe not. They might want to try something, so your folks will wanna be ready for an attack. But we still need to look for him. I'm going to troll some bars tonight. He may not have left town yet."

"Which ones?"

"The River Inn, the Black Gibbon, maybe some more. I think he'll pop in for a beer if he's still hanging about."

"Don't confront him. He'll have backup."

"Won't I?"

"You might, but if anything happens, we'd like to avoid another shootout at the OK Corral."

"And here I didn't think you cared about our history."

"Only the bloody parts; the rest is too weird."

"I'm beginning to think you don't like us Americans."

"You're all a bit brash for me and you want everyone to be your friend."

"Maybe we're too trusting."

"Or maybe you think we should all believe in America the beautiful, the land that can save the world."

44

The Black Gibbon—an allusion to some long-forgotten military expedition to China? Or maybe a pirate ship on the Red River Delta? Or just a name that the owner never explained. Probably the latter, Stavros decided. Everyone tries to find a most unusual name for their establishment, partially to build customer recognition but also to hide the sameness. Still, it was a cool name.

Once inside, Stavros saw nothing nautical, nothing alluding to marauding pirates in the South China Sea; it was a pub like every other pub in the UK. Low ceilings, lots of wood, big beer glasses, blue-gray smoke clouds hanging low, and regulation dart boards. And Stavros, now almost a fixture in the bar, had been here three nights running, along with visits to several other places, but the Gibbon kept drawing him back. Perhaps it was because he felt accepted if not fully integrated into the pub's society. He'd learned to appreciate that in other places where he was the odd man out, the one of a kind, the only white guy in an African bar. The divisions were here, he thought. Just not as visible in the people, maybe in the graffiti.

He wasn't even sure what section of town he was in, Protestant or Catholic. It wasn't far from Bogside, so maybe Catholic. But then, this side of town used to be more Protestant. There weren't any orange or green flags, so maybe it was neutral territory. That is if such a thing existed up here. The last two times he'd visited, no one had talked religion or government and he wasn't going to be the one to bring it up.

He didn't feel like isolating at a table, so he wedged himself in at the bar and watched the clientele. From behind his wood parapet, the barman startled Stavros by calling him by name. "What'll you be having tonight, Paul?" he said, a broad smile on his face.

Stavros furiously tried to remember. Luckily, it came to him.

"A pint of Guinness, Ted, thanks."

Ted held a glass at the ready and went to work pouring the brew. The requisite 119.5 seconds to pour ticked by, then Ted set the glass down on the bar. They passed a solemn moment together as they waited for the beer to settle and finish.

"There ya go," Ted said, proudly presenting his latest work of art: a perfectly poured pint.

Stavros sipped off some of the dense foam on top to get at the liquid black gold deeper in the glass and said, "Well poured, Ted. You've made me a happy man."

Ted grinned, inordinately happy with the compliment.

Standing at the bar, Stavros eventually scored a stool from its previous occupant, a man who was challenged away to toss feathered missiles at a colorful cork target. Settling in, Stavros sat half facing the bar, half facing the dart board to watch the match. His senses were shrouded by the activity around him. The second pint started to warm him up but he could also feel it dull his edge. But it came back to him quickly.

"You're not English are you?"

Stavros looked for the voice and found it came from the woman standing close to his back. An assessment was in order. She was an attractive girl. She had a coquettish, fresh smile, black hair, greenish eyes, and a darker complexion, not pink and ruddy like he always envisioned a local lass should look. But even from the short sentence she spoke he knew she had to be Irish. If she'd been an assassin, he'd be dead.

Luckily, I'm not on anybody's kill list yet.

"I'm American. Why?"

"I had to make sure, I don't like English. Ted told me you're a writer. Are you a Shaw or a Joyce?"

"Neither. I'm a journalist trying to research an article."

"Wanna tell me about it?"

"Maybe, but you're standing and I'm sitting."

"Follow me, I've a table over there," she said, pointing vaguely at the back of the room.

It suited him better anyway. The place was crammed full, and people crowded around the beer taps as part of the "I need to get a beer now" scrum, understandable but annoying if you're the one constantly being elbowed.

And, in following her, he noticed the back side of her was attractive as well. She moved surely through the crowd, displacing an offending obstacle of a man or two as she went. She had curves but wasn't soft; athletic was the word he finally found for her. She was wearing a long wool skirt and a sweater with a leather jacket that accentuated her figure rather than hid it. He noted her ankles, well turned and not at all the indicators of a beefier body to come. Before she sat down, he checked the time and realized he hadn't worn his watch. He had left it and his passport in his room. With a bit of guilt, he wondered momentarily if it was a sign, but thought it better not to think about it; Sarah would be upset.

Stavros had visited the Gibbon twice before. The first time was a short in and out; it didn't seem the sort of place he would want to spend much time in. The second visit was better, partly because of Ted's convivial personality, partly because he started to feel attached. Maybe it reminded him of his favorite *Kneipe* in Berlin; it was just damn comfortable. Now, with the girl walking in front of him, he was thinking he could get used to the place.

The pub stood just off Queen Street not far from an oral surgery office. It was an odd thing he'd noticed about Derry: the proliferation of dentists. Maybe there was a tax benefit or perhaps it was the Republic's proximity that made it lucrative. Lots of pubs and dentists. The pubs he understood, but he had no clue if there was a connection between the two.

Stavros put that thought from his mind and reoccupied himself with matters at hand, specifically the woman. And the more Guinness he drank the better she looked. He wouldn't admit that to anyone, especially Sarah, but it was true, at least for the moment. He chided himself at the same time. He didn't even know the woman; she could be an idiot or a basket-case which in his experience was often the case with girls that picked up men in bars. But he didn't know that for sure yet and he felt he owed himself the opportunity to find out.

She called herself Branna.

Once suitably introduced, he settled in and leaned close to hear her, as the noise was making the translation from Irish English into American English difficult for his brain. He wasn't so acclimatized to the language that it was automatic.

"What is it about?" she asked of his writing.

"It was going to be about the people, what they see and feel, what they have to endure."

"But?"

"No one would share with me, so I decided to make it into a story."

"No one wants to talk about it in a bar. We're in a war, after all."

"You call this a war?"

"What would you call it?"

"An insurgency," said Stavros.

"What's an insurgency?"

"It's a street fight, a rebellion, not a big thing like a war."

"It feels like a war."

"Maybe if you haven't been in the real thing."

"Have you?" she asked.

"No, but I have experienced a rebellion."

"What's the difference?"

"Intensity. Rebellions start out small and grow. They're violent but very much off and on things. Most importantly, a successful one needs the people's support. I'm not sure the people support this one."

"Some do."

"Some is not enough. Besides, the Catholics are the minority, aren't they?"

"Yes," she confirmed.

"That makes it even more difficult. An insurgency can't survive without people. Che found that out."

"Who's Che?"

"Che Guevara, a false prophet," he said.

Stavros put his thumb into the head of his third beer and inspected the imprint it left. He counted to ten; the imprint remained. He decided the beer was fresh based on a rumor he'd heard once long ago.

"What happened to him?" she asked.

"He's dead. He thought he could start a rebellion without people behind him."

"That was rather arrogant."

"I think that's the way of the world. Political leaders hold the world in contempt and see the people as prey to be lived off. He was one of those and paid the price."

"Is that how you see the IRA?"

"I can't say because I don't know them. But I think it might apply to everybody in this mess: the IRA, the UVA, the British."

"Who's the worst then?" Branna asked.

"How should I know? I'm an outsider. All I can say is the group that resorts to violence against innocent civilians has the biggest chance of losing popular support."

"That would be all of them then."

The evening devolved into a conversation that left few openings for silence. Branna talked about her childhood and the breakdown of her family. She had a mom to support and little opportunity to do so.

Stavros pried: "What do you do?"

"I make myself useful. I'm a secretary, a waitress, whatever you need me to be."

Her comment opened an interesting line of conversation which Stavros declined to take.

45

"Why Storm Azimuth?" Sarah asked.

"You mean why are we called Storm Azimuth? It's the unit's codename for message traffic. We're actually called Foreign Operations Group, but no one ever uses that designation. The codename is supposed to protect us," said Elder.

"Supposed to?"

"Hopefully. We change the codename every so often because someone compromises it. I think it confuses everyone, which is fine with me."

"I'm confused. So, what do I tell people that I do?"

"Around here, tell anyone interested that you work for the Forest Service. You can be a tree hugger, a smoke jumper, a biologist, whatever, and you'll have a civilian ID in your true name soon. What your overseas cover will be depends on your talents, which we'll develop as we go. For the moment, we have a tasking, a training mission in Europe. You're going because you're one of the few qualified women."

"Chosen because I'm a woman or in spite of that?"

"Both. You know your stuff and we need to mix up our teams. Ten knuckle draggers look out of place in the city. Five men and two women, not so much."

"That means two women can replace five men?"

"You didn't hear that from me, but in some cases, yes."

"In that case, I'm all in. Where we going?"

"You actually don't have a choice in this, but anyway we're going to Germany first. Then we'll get instructions, but it sounds like Beirut. We'll have a team meeting this afternoon and I'll introduce you to the others."

"Beirut? For a training exercise?"

"Yeah, you're in the big leagues now, kid."

"When?"

"We leave in eight days. The coordination paperwork is in. Passports are processing—for the exercise you'll reuse your training alias and docs. Make sure you're packed for three weeks. If you need anything, talk to supply. Special equipment will be shipped over by diplomatic pouch and we'll meet the courier somewhere; that's all being planned out."

"Okay, I can do that, but what is our mission?"

"So far, all we have been told is that we're going to put surveillance on a target and then do a hand-off to the National Force."

"*In Beirut?*"

"In Beirut."

"*Hay Zeus.*"

46

Before the disturbance began, Stavros returned from his appointment in the Gents' room made for him by three pints of Guinness and an overworked bladder. He made it in and out of the toilet in record time, driven as much by the rancid smell of piss as the overpowering scent of chemically replicated gardenias. Back in the main room, he rejoined Branna whose complexion had taken on a healthy glow, no doubt fueled by the Harp she was drinking compounded by a shot of Bushmills that she tossed back like a pro. Stavros' own shot added to his declining blood to alcohol ratio and, as he attacked the fourth Guinness, he vowed to slow down. He needed to get home and he'd done very little watching of the crowd for his quest. He'd spent his time more or less captive and listening to the woman across from him instead of doing his job. He didn't want to put himself out of commission for anything that might happen later. If he kept up his current pace, he might spend the rest of the evening sitting under the table and regretting it the following morning.

It was probably at this moment that everything went to hell and the operation took a different turn for Stavros. It could have happened earlier, when he went to the bathroom, he wouldn't know for sure. In either case, he wouldn't recognize it until much later.

A sharp crack, the report of a pistol, broke the normal clamor and silenced the crowd. Years of gray dust fell from the rafters and quickly mixed with smoke. A command was screamed.

"What'd he say?" someone said.

"What the bloody hell?" another asked.

Confusion for most. Some knew what the sound was and were scared.

"Loyalist bastards," Branna said. Her eyes were wide open—with fear, Stavros thought.

Suddenly, people were shoving themselves away from the commotion; some went down onto the floor, intentionally or falling off their chairs. A table crashed over, glassware exploding on the tile floor. A yell. A scream. A shout. And more again. The noises all merged into nothing intelligible. Just panic.

A second shot, a pause, a third.

Branna stood up.

"Get down," Stavros said.

"No, I've got to get out of here." Frantic, she turned towards the back of the bar. Stavros stood and grabbed her arm. She pulled, tugged it away.

"Come with me!" She pushed, head down, purse snatched up against her chest, and plunged through the crowd and into a hallway. Branna turned into a human battering ram as several people went down in front of her or were pushed to the side. Stavros was doing his best to keep up. She wasn't determined, she was instinctive, heading for safety and security.

Stavros considered, if only momentarily, rushing toward the gunfire, a reaction he thought appropriate for a soldier. Then he remembered one of Murphy's Laws of War: Don't ever be the first. So, he consented to be led away by the woman. *She's from here, she knows what not to do.* Not more than ten seconds had passed.

He applied himself to the task and put both hands on Branna's shoulders. He wasn't pushing her, she was pulling him. Moving fast,

246

they headed down the hall, the noise following them, still loud, still chaotic. A slight corner, a hidden door, the latch turned, and a rush out into the night with the cacophony inside, pouring out behind them. Branna paused and then pushed on.

"This way," she said. Now she was a horse running for its stable.

Away from the noise, they moved down the dark alley. The smell of rotting trash and old urine filled the air and turned the stomach, while the brick and stone walls absorbed the sound of the tumult behind them.

"What was that?" Stavros asked. The cool air was not making his head feel any better. If anything, he felt worse.

"I don't know. Maybe they wanted to rob the place or shoot someone. Damn Proddies!"

"That means you're Catholic?" The words came out a bit slurred.

"I am. At least, I was born that way," she said.

They walked on toward a light where the alley intersected a street. Stavros was feeling nauseous. He staggered, caught his shoe on a crack and stumbled a bit.

"Are you alright?"

"Not feeling so good." He saw the ground swimming around his feet. The streetlight stabbed at his eyes.

"Come on, I'll take you to my place. It's not far. You can lie down there."

He started to say "My place isn't far" but couldn't. Instead, he followed passively as she steered him to the end of the alley and leaned him against a building. Everything was blurred, the woman fuzzy. He closed his eyes and started to deep breathe.

If only ....

He opened his eyes. She was gone.

Gone. A set-up.

He tried to move, needed to move, but couldn't. Two indistinct shadows moved around him like hyenas sniffing and circling a wounded buffalo. He felt his arms pinned hard to his side. Something rough went over his head. His breathing was labored, his muscles felt useless.

"I can't ..." he said.

The lights went out.

47

The team was gathered in the ops *basha*. It was time to decide and act.

"What happened?" Rhys asked.

"It was a total balls-up. We lost him," Goose said.

"What a cock-up! Where were you?"

"Outside. We were all outside. The Gibbon is a Catholic hangout. None of us can hold our own for long in there."

"How can you cover him if you're outside?" asked Hamish.

"One of our ferrets was in there."

"Who?"

"SOUP SPOON."

"I don't know that name," Hamish said.

"His details are in my operational notes."

"You know I don't read those. How long have you been working with him?"

"A week maybe," Goose said.

"Who recruited him? You aren't supposed to be recruiting informants."

"I didn't, a friend from MI5 loaned him to us."

"You had a local watching our asset? What did you tell him?"

"That he was watching a possible bad guy."

"We're getting off the subject. What happened?" said Rhys.

"From what the RUC reported, some rowdies lit off a bunch of fireworks inside the bar and caused a panic—SOUP SPOON said it was pistol fire."

"Where did SEARCHER go?"

"SOUP SPOON thinks he saw him go out the back with a woman. He's not clear on the details as he was face down on the floor."

"A frightened ferret," said Hamish to no one, obviously pleased with himself.

"Did you check the back?"

"Yes, but it was ten minutes or so later. Nobody there," Goose said.

"The RUC had a report that might help. Someone saw a guy being helped into a van by two other men at the end of the alley," Hunter noted.

"Helped?" Rhys asked.

"That was my question. The witness said she couldn't see for sure but thought he might have had a hood over his head."

"Vehicle description? Registration?"

"Ford Transit, light colored, maybe white. Nothing more."

Rhys stood and stretched his back, arms over his head. Something he did when anxious.

"Bloody Hell. Have the liaison office get a report out to all on the van, including the RUC and especially the border. Tell them to stop and search for a possible kidnapping victim," Rhys said.

"Do we tell anyone he's an American?" Goose asked, making his way out the door to the commo center.

"No. There's no need to give the cousins any bad news just yet."

"Time enough for that later? Right?" said Hamish.

"Are you enjoying this? We could very well have lost an operator," said Rhys.

"It will teach them that this is no cakewalk."

"Teach the Americans or our Paul?"

"Both. They know nothing of small wars; the only way they know how to fight is with bombs and artillery," Hamish said, dismissive. "Look what a cock-up of things they made in Vietnam."

"Wonderful, so if he has been kidnapped, the Yanks will come in guns blazing and everyone will get killed. That'll be fun to watch," said Rhys.

48

When Stavros woke, it was still dark. Through the heavy hood it was very quiet and cold, and the air still smelled of damp wood and rotted potatoes. Smoke from a peat fire, acrid, stinging, assailed his nose but did not warm. In addition to being cold, he was also pissed. Branna: he would remember that name. But he directed most of his anger toward himself. He'd let himself down, sucked into allowing the woman to distract him, to cripple his senses, to set him up.

His sleep, short or long? He wasn't sure, but the thumping pain in his head had eased. He breathed deep, slowly, and exhaled. All seemed normal there: the anxiety was gone. He hated the attacks; they made him feel weak, if only in the moment, but nonetheless ….

Again, he tried to stretch. The bonds on his hands and feet were still tight, but he could fidget some. He tried to create some space to work his wrists back and forth, but he didn't want rope burns. Slowly ….

Footsteps across the floor above his head again. *Just one person? No, maybe two.*

A door creaked, hinges squeaked, the air pressure in the room changed. He felt the breeze of a temperature shift.

It was the moment he had thought about, the one he dreaded and the one he wanted over with. It was the moment that the instructors had played out for them in every SERE training: the prisoner's introduction to the zookeepers, the person or persons who would ask questions, intimidate, and determine your fate. That is, if one hadn't already been determined for you.

Showtime.

A switch clicked and light filtered through a thousand tiny spaces between the threads of the hood's fabric. *So, they do have electricity here.*

The heavy tread of boots came down wooden stairs, shuffling and clunking with each step, a pause at the bottom, then quieter across the floor—probably hard-packed dirt. Whoever they were, they moved about him. One of them grunted and Stavros heard the rustle of cloth, then a small bundle hit him in the chest and fell into his lap. He felt the cold steel of a belt buckle on his leg.

"Put on your trousers."

"I can't, my hands are tied."

"Wait."

He could feel the man's breath on his back, smell the boiled cabbage he had eaten the night before, the cigarette he'd smoked minutes ago, the sweat which was probably perennial. Stavros' hands were undone, the bonds re-tied in front. Then his legs were freed.

"Now put them on."

Wearing the hood, it was like having to dress in the middle of night. He shook his pants out and carefully slid them on.

"Stand up."

The hands spun him around twice or three times and walked him to the stairs. He thought they were trying to confuse his sense of direction, but it made no difference; he didn't know where he was anyway. With no shoes or shirt, he was cold and wary about stepping on something.

"Step up."

He did. Slowly. He lifted his foot and felt forward for the step. One at a time. One of the two was leading, he knew. The other had a hand on his shoulder, forcing him forward. He felt the doorframe, the door hinged on the left. It became even lighter outside his hood.

He was turned to the right and pushed forward again. He walked forward five steps, then eight, and was jerked back to a halt. A chair scraped the floor. He felt it slide in behind his calves.

"Sit." The hands pressed down. He sat.

It was quiet for a moment. He felt the presence of several people. Breathing. Something on a table being moved. A shift in another chair.

"Take it off." A new voice.

The hood came off. He blinked and his vision came back to him. He rubbed his eyes with the backs of his hands. He stared at the big man sitting across the table from him. The man stared back with a hard intensity won by years of distrust.

Stavros looked around him briefly. He saw a small, rough room. Windows on the right, the drawn, dirty curtains edged with light. A plain wall with no decoration on the left, the same to his front but with a wood door. A plain wood table in front of him, empty but for what looked like his wallet. A bare hanging light glowing above him. A small house or cottage somewhere. Not an office, not a warehouse.

"Don't look around," the voice commanded.

"Why am I here? Why have you brought me here?" Stavros said. He knew it was better to insist on his innocence up front.

"Who are you?" said the man.

"Who are *you*?" Stavros asked back.

"Answer my question."

"Paul Scalia, I'm an American." His voice was even, a hint of indignity.

"Sure you are. What's your birthday?" The man held a card in his hand.

My driver's license.

Stavros gave his birthday.

"What's your address?"

Stavros gave an address, his first girlfriend's, the one on the license.

"Where's your passport?"

"At my hotel."

"Why?"

"I don't carry it when I go out at night."

"Why?"

"Because I might lose it or get robbed," Stavros said, trying to keep the anger and anxiety out of his voice.

Silence. Somewhere a wall clock ticked away, second by second by second.

"You secret service or something? Who do you work for?"

"I don't work for anyone, I'm freelance. A writer."

"Army?"

"I did serve four years, but I got out."

"Why?"

"School. I wanted to do something else with my life than carry a gun."

"Education is overrated. If there aren't any jobs, who cares what you know about English history."

"I can't argue with that," Stavros replied.

"Why are you here?"

"How should I know? You brought me here."

"Why are you in Ireland, I mean?"

"Am I in Ireland? I thought I was in the North."

"Don't get smart. Why are you here?"

"Seems like everyone wants to know that. They wonder because I'm not Irish and I'm not on vacation. Apparently, the only Americans who are supposed to come to Ireland are Irish emigrants or distant cousins of someone. Why do you care what I'm doing?"

"You didn't answer my question. Why are you here?"

"I'm writing an article about the Troubles."

"Why? Because we heard you're looking for someone."

"We? Who are *we*? And couldn't you have just asked me in the bar?"

"What would you have told me?"

"The same thing I tell everyone, I'm writing an article about the Troubles."

"Who do you support?"

"Support? I don't follow you."

"You like the loyalists?"

"Not particularly."

"The republicans then?"

"I voted for Reagan, yes," Stavros said. He realized too late it was the wrong moment to be smart.

Silence for a moment then a nod to the men behind him. They stood him up. A swift punch to Stavros' right kidney brought an electric shock, a convulsion, his muscles tightened in pain. More shots to the abdomen; the pain surged. Two hands kept him upright. Stavros breathed deep and tried to will the agony away. It refused to go.

"We're not playing games here, boy."

Stavros' words spluttered out. "Fine, I don't support nobody."

"What are you doing here?"

"I'm a writer, I told you …."

How long do I need? The Navy pilots who spoke in SERE training, the ones who survived the Hanoi Hilton, said they tried to make it forty-eight hours before saying anything. That gave their comrades time to change code words, plans of attack, everything—they just assumed it would be compromised. Many made it longer. Then he realized that rule didn't apply here. He could never admit to anything; he could only maintain his innocence or escape. Unless his comrades rescued his butt first.

Otherwise.

Otherwise what?

Otherwise, maybe you die.

49

Rourke was intrigued but somewhat baffled by Neil's set-up in spite of the diagrams and the explanations. Neil pointed out the hidden arming switches and wiring and, of course, the copper platters arranged like stadium lights in a grid on the inside wall of the cargo area the two trucks. That was before fiberboard panels were screwed over the framework to hide the explosives. The vehicles were clean and ready for action. The next step was to load them up with cargo, and then Neil would make the final connections before the drivers took the vehicles to the isolated border crossing where they would enter Northern Ireland and begin their separate treks to the targets. Timing was crucial; the trucks would spend no more than two days in the province, all in concert with the timing of the visit. Watchers would be in place to monitor the security situation before the trucks made their approach and were positioned for the attack. Simple but nerve wracking.

"When is the visit?" Neil asked.

"Five days," said Rourke.

"So they cross the frontier in three days?"

"Unless something changes."

"When do the drivers get the word to position and arm the devices?"

"They have the go-ahead when they leave here. The Hillsborough team will abort only if the visit is cancelled. Stormont goes ahead no matter what and with it Box 500 will cease to exist."

"Box 500?"

"The postal address for MI5 at the castle."

50

Hamish pondered over his words for a couple of minutes. He thought he would say that it wasn't completely clear what had happened to the American—one minute he was in the pub and the next he was gone. He decided it was better to let London know as little as possible under the circumstances and he began to type his message on the transmission form. He had to refer to the instructions several times to ensure he had the heading and addresses properly formatted. The last thing he needed was for some communications technician to critique his work and actually read his message. Letter by letter, he carefully hunted and pecked at the machine with his most uncontroversial word choices.

Finished, he carefully pulled the form out of the machine and looked it over. Satisfied with his handiwork, he placed it in an envelope and carried it down the hall to the commo shed. He handed it to a bespectacled sergeant who glanced at the heading and allowed Hamish to enter his domain. It was a maze of machines and wires which meant little to Hamish, but he did manage to keep his form under surveillance to ensure the sergeant didn't read it before he fed the paper into the optical reader. The machine swallowed the form and spit it out the other side, its contents having been read and transmuted into an indecipherable code for transmission. A yellow light came on, followed by a green. The commo sergeant picked up the form from the tray and handed it to Hamish. "It's been sent," he said.

Hamish fed it directly into the shredder as the sergeant watched, slightly amused and slightly bewildered by the strange officer before him.

Hamish stared back. "If you read any of that, forget it now or you'll be shoveling snow in Antarctica soon." His ego thus sated, Hamish wheeled about and strode back to his office.

51

"Sentinel," the operations director, handed "C" the message across the wide expanse of his mahogany desk. "C" regarded his subordinate, one hand on his pipe as he puffed, the other taking the paper with a snap of the wrist. The OpsDir was an experienced man, a man that might one day be sitting in this chair. But not yet, he thought. Not yet. He read the message.

MOST SECRET // IMMEDIATE

From ARGON
Exclusive for SUMMIT

Contact with OUTSIDER lost circa 2400 hours yesterday.

Believe OUTSIDER to be victim of an abduction carried out by as yet unknown perpetrators. Incident took place inside a known Catholic-biased establishment near Bogside. OUTSIDER was last seen by a local source exiting rear of location and has not been seen since.

All provincial security elements have been alerted. ELEMENT continues search.

Station fears OUTSIDER may REPEAT may have been transported beyond the limits of our jurisdiction.

END
MOST SECRET

"C" looked up again, his pose reflective as much for thinking as presenting the image of a thinker.

"I thought this might happen and, indeed, it has."

"Instructions for ARGON, sir?"

"Tell them to monitor the situation and under no circumstances are they to cross the border in pursuit."

"Understood. Anything else?"

"Let the Americans know their man is missing. They wanted into this and now they'll find out what it's all about."

"Yes sir, I'll handle that through the home secretary."

"Right, now go ahead and get the message off. I don't want our man to do anything silly. Who is he again?"

"Hamish, Rupert Hamish."

"Ah, yes, the one with the unfortunate name. Who calls their child Rupert, anyway?"

"His parents were wealthy missionaries in Africa."

"That would explain it."

52

Stavros' blurred vision was beginning to mess with his brain. He was still suffering from whatever drug he had been given and his mouth was drier than a wad of cotton. He needed a drink, but it was obvious he wasn't going to get one. Rapid-fire questions continued to assault him, but he couldn't understand half of them; whoever was talking kept dropping into a heavy brogue that seemed like gibberish and his confusion seemed to enrage the interrogator even more. He looked at his wrists and in the dim light saw the raw skin, fluid weeping slowly from the wound, infusing the manila rope with its red tint. It was just the first of the wounds that he imagined he would suffer; the pain in his head had slowly been supplanted by the pain in his back. His bruised kidney throbbed, and his shoulders ached from being wrenched back by the restraints.

The pain he had suffered in the SERE course had been academic compared to what he now expected. Being confined in a hot box or sprayed with ice-cold water was nothing compared to the physical stuff he knew was coming. It was all a matter of endurance and he knew he must resist. They would not get his secret, the truth behind his presence, but he wasn't sure if that even mattered to whoever these people were. They had him as their captive, maybe that was all they wanted—a chip in some game to be played. Or maybe he was a threat they just wanted out of the way. In either of those cases, truth wasn't what they would be looking for.

He looked at the table, keeping his eyes down. He kept his mind on his story; he became his story again. He wanted to show he wasn't a threat, he was nothing, a writer who couldn't hurt their cause, a nothing.

The questions came again and he stuck to his story. Over and over again.

"Stand him up," said the man.

"Look at me," he said. "My name is Colin. I can either be your friend or your enemy. Just answer my questions. Understand?"

Stavros nodded.

"I said, understand?" Colin said. "Answer me."

"I understand. And I have been answering you. You just don't want to believe me."

"That's because I know you're lying."

"I'm not. I've told you …."

A nod from Colin to one of the goons behind him. A sharp thwack of a wooden rod against the back of his thigh. And again, against the other. The pain seared up to his lower back. It wasn't that bad, he thought. His lower leg reminded him that he'd felt worse.

He repeated his story. He looked down and to the right when he told it as he'd been taught. Whether the gimmick was true or not, it was an indicator.

But how would he know? He's not a pro.

His hands were re-tied behind his back. His stomach in the open, unprotected.

The questions came again. The goon stood to his side now, the rod raised and waiting, watching Colin (if that was his real name) for a sign. It came and the wood whirred through the air to slap his abdomen. It felt like a burning rod.

I am Staff Sergeant Paul Stavros, 729-76-6614. Name, rank, and serial number. I could tell them that. It would be simple. And it would be over.

He wouldn't. Never.

The cane came again. Across the back of his arms, the front of his thighs, and then his groin. Burning, searing pain. He wanted to scream and yell, let off the pressure. He didn't. Maybe his comrades had found him. Maybe the Irish police would come. He was sure there must be a dragnet, looking for him. Somebody must have seen something. Maybe someone saw the vehicle they drove him away in. Ted at the bar must have described the girl to the police. She's probably in custody being asked all the right questions.

The cane swatted again. A new target: his shins. Not too hard, he prayed. No more breaks. He inhaled sharply and breathed quickly. He looked at the goon with the rod. He wanted to know who was hitting him as much as who was asking the questions. The man had a determined smile on his face. Stavros kept his face a blank mask; he would save what he was feeling for later.

To hell with that, I will dwell on it.

His tormentors turned into his targets. He had read something somewhere: "Bitter bastards with guns."

He looked at Colin, memorizing the face since the clothing would change. A mole on his chin, the thinning reddish-brown hair, the intense gray eyes. He would remember them like points on a compass. The skinny guy with the rod became "Rat-face." A pencil-thin moustache unlike anything he'd seen in Ireland, matted brown hair, beady black eyes, and a long, thin nose on a long, thin face. Still, he had some power behind his swings. Must have played stick ball or whatever it was kids play up here. A brief glance at the other goon was all he had managed. It was enough for the man to become "Dumbo." He would remember.

"Who are you looking for?" The questions started again, although they were focused on his mission.

How did they find out? He questioned his tradecraft. *Did VIPER see me? Did the priest say something?*

At this point, Stavros wasn't sure of anything. But he persisted. His story would stand, there could be no wavering. The beatings continued. So did the pain.

Colin didn't try to catch Stavros in a lie; he was straightforward, anything but subtle. He knew one direction and took it. No switchbacks, no curves, no U-turns.

"Don't you care if you alienate Americans?" Stavros said.

"They won't know," Colin said.

Stavros understood that his interrogator's mind was made up. Colin had the solution if not the confirmation he wanted. *Why? The game must be big if they risked kidnapping an American.*

"Take him outside and take care of it," Colin said as he stood up, shoving the chair out of the way. The hood went back on and the hands grabbed his shoulders and forced Stavros forward, guiding him toward the door. Stavros' toe caught on something, he stumbled and cursed. His foot hurt more than the beatings. He felt the breeze as he went through the door, the fresh outdoor air unsullied by sweat, smoke, or sodden, rotted potatoes.

Stavros breathed in deeply. Even with the hood, he tasted the outdoors. He sensed the grass and the pines, heard birds screeching as they flew off alarmed by the sudden intrusion of humans into their realm. Pushed again, Stavros paced slowly forward, carefully feeling his way with his bare feet. There were two of them, he knew, but with the hood over his head and his hands tied behind his back, there was little he could do. The hands stopped him and he felt a boot behind his knees. His legs buckled and he went to the ground. The hands kept him upright, stable, on his knees. He knew the position; he'd felt it played out before. That was training. This was real.

Bastards.

The hood came off. He was staring into the woods.

"Don't move. Keep your eyes where they are."

No answer. Nothing to say.

He heard the rack of a pistol slide as it chinked back then slammed forward.

"Goodbye, Yank."

"Wait!"

"Wait what?"

"You just going to shoot me? For what?"

"That's the idea, Yank. Because you're a problem. Now make peace with your god."

"Fuck you."

A moment. Silence. He felt a presence behind his head. *Christ* ....

Click.

He fell forward onto his face. Pushed by a boot. Heard the laughing, both of them.

Bastards.

"That was funny, Yank. I wish I had a camera. The look on your face."

Rat-face, grinning wildly with the pistol in hand, was standing in front of him now. Dumbo was just laughing maniacally, doubled over, holding his belly.

Back on his knees, Stavros raged inside. He didn't think. He pushed up, a steel spring let loose, propelled himself forward like a running torpedo and head-butted straight into Rat-face's abdomen. Rat-face's eyes bulged and he went down backwards, hard. His head thumped solidly on a tree root and he lay still. Stavros rolled off and went at Dumbo, standing, hands at his side, frozen in place. He attacked again but aimed at Dumbo's head, hitting him with his forehead between Dumbo's eyes and hearing the crunch of his nose. Dumbo went down. Stavros staggered a moment and spun around.

Rat-face was still on the ground. He looked back at the cottage. The door was closed. His head hurt now, more than the beatings, his eyes watered, his vision was blurred.

Fuck it. His obligation to resist was over.

He sprinted into the brush.

He'd seen a movie that came back to him now. A rebel soldier to be hung was dropped from the gibbet. The rope broke and he ran, escaping into the brush. He ran, on and on, until he saw his wife standing, waiting for him on the grass in front of his home. On he ran, into her arms, to her embrace. She wrapped her arms around him. And then the rope snapped tight around his neck as he hung twisting below the gallows. A dream.

On he ran, and on, even deeper into the forest.

53

Their documents had been thoroughly vetted. Granted, the cover identities for some of the team members were shallow. Having been created for training scenarios, they were not back-stopped very deeply. But there was enough there for a short training operation overseas. Credit card histories were reviewed to make sure nothing could be attributed to government expenditures; everything had to look businesslike. Telephone numbers were covered by "secretaries" who knew their "employees" and could field questions appropriately or by answering machines that would frustrate any caller. Sarah's passport in the name of Ruth Simon was not American, it was South African, and although she didn't speak Afrikaans, her practiced English accent was enough to confound listeners into believing her story.

Besides, the Huguenots made their way to the Cape as well.

"Don't get into personal details when you talk," the Agency instructors had said. "Stick to business. Know your story backwards and forwards, so you can say it normally without thinking. Avoid going into your imaginary closets that make you remember where each piece of clothing is hung, when you bought it, and what color it is." Anyone who got too deep in the weeds about their family history would be admonished, especially when they couldn't carry the story from one day to the next. Candidates unable to follow those simple rules were no longer with the program.

That was eons ago. Her professional and personal life had gone through major changes in the last months, starting in Berlin. From her job as a voice intercept operator, interpreting Warsaw Pact military and diplomatic communications, to working in the East on a couple of clandestine operations, she had moved on to complete training as an intelligence case officer before joining Storm Azimuth. Then there was her Paul. She wondered for a moment where he might be ….

Hans Landau stuck his head into the room, startling Sarah a bit. "All alone?"

"Yes, the others are all out shopping for the last-minute stuff they forgot. I'm just contemplating the trip."

"That means you're ready."

"As I'll ever be. Are you deploying forward?"

"From here? No. It seems things are in flux."

Landau grabbed a chair, turned its back to Sarah, and sat down facing her. The room was well lit but small and hidden deep inside the basement of a building somewhere in Germany that had been leased to an American corporation with well-hidden links to the US government. Several tables were covered with maps and papers that would go into safes when it was time to go. When the team moved forward, the papers would go into diplomatic bags and be taken back to the States.

"Originally, I was going to Crete to provide backup for you guys. But we just got a message saying to hold tight, we're going to redeploy elsewhere."

"The team? So, all the prep was for nothing?"

"I wouldn't say that. We're supposed to be ready for a change in plans. A new target."

"Any clue to what's up?"

"No, but whatever it is, it's not an exercise."

54

The branches slapped and lashed at him, biting his face and body as he ran. He was soaked but wasn't sure if it was blood or water. But he wasn't listening or feeling, he was running, concentrating on keeping his balance with his hands behind his back. He crashed on. A root grabbed at his foot and he went down headfirst into the moss. He got up again and continued on, his breath searing his lungs, his thighs burning. He stopped. Chest heaving, he listened to the forest. He heard shouts but no one crashing through the brush behind him. He had some time, he thought. He sat on a fallen log and pulled his legs up and his arms down under his butt to around his calves. The last time they had tied him up, he had maneuvered his arms to gain some room. He hoped it would be enough. He made himself small and got the rope down to his Achilles, then pulled hard, his chest between his legs, and pulled more. His foot slipped in the loose dirt, he rolled over and lost his balance. Then he was on his side on the ground, still pulling, struggling, grunting, cursing. One hand slipped under his heel and he pulled his right leg through his arms. Stop, take a breath. Breathe slowly. Halfway there. He bent his left leg and pulled his hands around to the front, the second time easier than the first. He pulled himself back up on the log and looked at the knot.

Boy Scouts they weren't.

He bit the rope and pulled with his teeth, worrying the knot. Slowly, back and forth between sections, he pulled and spit out the bits of manila twine that came loose. The rope moved. He began again, back and forth, grinding his teeth into the coarse rope, pulling. Then he had a bit free. He twisted his wrists and one side came loose. His wrist snaked through the gap, his hand followed.

Free at last. He smiled to himself grimly. The rest of the rope came undone and he tossed it on the ground. Then he picked it up and coiled it. You could never tell when rope might come in handy. He stood up, stretched, and moved on.

He went as fast as he could, doing the best he could. He talked to himself every once in a while. *How are your feet?* They were numb, luckily. He saw they were dirty, but he also saw the scrapes and cuts, blood mixed with mud. He kept moving. He had to, although he had no clue where he was. Or even if he was in the North or the Republic. He thought it was the Republic, he didn't know why, just an inkling. *That's where I would have taken me ....*

He wasn't sure how fast he was moving. He was running light, no Bergen, no weapon, nothing to slow him down other than no shoes and socks. Minor issue. He crashed on through the brush. Up a little embankment and down the other side. A small stream flowing to the right. He looked up into the cloudy sky to find the sun and couldn't. It was too gray and dark, the forest too thick. He sensed that if he was going west, the stream would be going north. He knelt at the edge, took two fistfuls of water and swallowed them.

Sheep-shit dysentery be damned.

He stepped into the water, trying to walk on the silty bed, stepping over branches and big rocks. The water was cold and after a while he climbed onto the bank and rubbed his feet warm, then continued on dry ground. He had to keep up the pace, get some distance from the cottage and his tormentors, to survive.

He could have stayed, tried to bluff them more. He didn't break, even with the threat of execution; he could handle more. They might have let him go. He saw himself walking through Shannon Airport to the Pan Am gate for New York. Sarah would be there when he arrived to throw her arms around him. But he wasn't there, not yet. He had to go on. *Half a league, half a league, half a league onward.*

The stream petered out and tinkled into a small pool. He saw the water tumble over a log and onto some rocks. The pond stretched out in front of him and he saw why it was there. A pipe in a low berm that ran across his front slowed the flow. There was a low metal guard rail atop the berm. A road, beyond it an open field. He knew it was a danger zone—there wasn't even an emergency exfiltration point waiting for him—but there was no choice. He was hungry, cold, and exhausted, mentally and physically, in that order. He couldn't go back. He stumbled on out of the brush into low bracken that bordered the road and half scrambled, half knee-walked up the berm. He pulled himself up on the guard rail and his eyes searched left for the best way out. Then he shifted his eyes in the other direction and felt his stomach drop.

Across the road, an older man who had been seated on the stump of an old tree stood up. He smoothed out his well-worn Mackintosh and cradled the double-barreled shotgun into a casual port arms as he walked toward the half-naked man who had appeared from nowhere out of the marsh forest.

"You had a nice run of it, my boy, but we'll be returning back to the house now," said Colin.

Stavros' head sank to his chest. The rain began to fall.

55

"Now what?" said Hunter.

"You tell me, he's your boyfriend," Goose whined.

"*My* boyfriend? I thought he was yours."

"Come off it, he's a Yank."

"Otherwise you'd be alright with him?" she said.

"Shut up."

"How about liaison?"

"What about him?"

"Has he gotten any info? SEARCHER was taken away in a van; has anyone seen anything?"

"There was one interesting sighting. An army patrol saw a white van on Orchard Road south of Drumconnell near the border. They reported it because it was driving across a field."

"Where did it go?"

"They don't know, but there are unofficial crossing points all along the frontier around there."

"So maybe he's in the Republic?"

"That'd be my guess."

"And we can't go across."

"That's what Hamish said."

"Why?"

"London's orders," said Goose.

"Fuck London. When has that ever made a difference? He's one of ours."

"Is he?"

"Yes, even if he's a Yank. He's a mate and a cousin. We've worked with him for how long now? We can't just leave him to the rats, can we?"

"You sound like him."

"I understand him a little. I wouldn't leave you either."

"That's good to hear."

"You're supposed to say you wouldn't leave me."

"Oh yeah, that too."

"Leave who where?" came the voice from behind.

Goose and Hunter both swiveled in their chairs to see Rhys standing in the doorway.

"What do you two have up your sleeves?"

"Nothing, Boss. Just chatting."

"Right, and I think I just saw a pig fly by. Tell me what's up."

"He's probably in the Republic. Why can't we try to find him?"

"Our orders are pretty clear …."

"Orders. If it was one of us, what would we do? Shouldn't we at least try?"

"How would you go about it? The Republic is a big place."

Goose stood and looked at the wall map and pointed with a pencil. "We think he may have been taken over the border around here."

"How do we know?"

"Liaison said there was a report of a suspicious white van there about six hours ago."

"Six hours is a long time. They could be in Cork by now."

"I doubt it," said Hunter. "They're comfortable over there. Why risk traveling so far?"

"So, what would you do?"

Hunter outlined her idea. "Put watchers on the main road around Donegal. That's a choke point going south and the van might be seen."

Making a small circle on the map about 20 kilometers south of Londonderry, she continued, "And we put our search teams in around here."

"Headquarters would lose their minds."

"No weapons, short duration visit, no more than twelve hours. That's probably all the time he has anyway."

Rhys pondered the map and the length of his career remaining.

"And if you find the van?"

"We call in the *Gardaí*."

"What gave him away? Why did they take him?" Rhys wondered aloud.

"Maybe VIPER saw him. Maybe someone got suspicious of him hanging about. Maybe he had too many and talked too much."

Silence. Rhys stared hard at the map, rubbing his unshaven chin like an art critic.

"Do you have your passports?"

56

"Colin" sat across the table from Stavros once again. Stavros saw there was another man in the room, seated beyond the obnoxious light pointed at his eyes, unrecognizable in the darkness. One of the two goons, Dumbo, stood to the side, his nose bandaged, his eyes surrounded with ugly purple blotches.

Stavros wasn't planning on going anywhere soon. Again, his hands had been tied tightly behind him and he knew he wouldn't be able to work them free.

"Why did you run?"

"You're kidding, right? You kidnap me and expect me to like it?"

"When you run, you tell me you're guilty of something."

"When you put a gun to my head, you say that you're murderers."

"So, you think we're murderers, do you?"

"What would you prefer? Freedom fighters without a conscience?"

Colin snorted. "We do what we have to do, boy. Now, tell me again what you're up to here."

Stavros answered with the now usual irritation he showed, "I told you, I'm trying to do a story about the Troubles and how the insecurity affects daily life and the families."

"You said you were trying to talk to the IRA, why?"

"I wanted to talk to both sides. To get the fighters' perspective, how the conflict affects them and their families." He paused for effect. "You don't know any, do you?"

That sort of answer usually got him in trouble. Colin didn't bother with pain this time.

"We don't need you to give us any perspective."

"My article isn't for you. It's for the outside world."

"The only thing the world needs to see is that the Brits are bastards and our struggle is justified."

"That's a well-balanced view. Not much room for compromise."

"Better than being a penny-a-word writer who doesn't change a thing."

"Now you're going for the jugular."

"What we do has to be done for freedom and along the way some people will suffer."

A voice from the dark behind him spoke. "Get on with it. You're wasting time."

Stavros saw a glint of anger in the Irishman's eyes.

Mad at me? Or the guy in back?

Colin paused for a moment.

"We've done some checking on you and can't seem to find anyone who can vouch for you. Why should I believe you?"

It was a line of questioning Colin had used before. Stavros decided he must be rehashing the same points for the unknown man.

"You haven't asked the right people. Ask the American Embassy in Dublin. I registered there when I arrived. As far as my press credentials go, I don't have any. I'm doing this freelance because I want to write a decent story, not one about St. Patrick's Day in New York."

"What else have you written?"

"Some small stories, nothing major. I did have a fiction novel published a while back."

It was a fact, but the print run was small. Money spent, lesson learned.

"What is it called?"

"*The Long Green Line.*"

Dumbo spoke: "Never heard of it."

"That's probably because it hasn't been on the telly yet," Stavros said.

Dumbo didn't get the joke. Colin suppressed a laugh.

One for me.

From outside there came the crunching of footsteps on gravel. Someone, several people maybe, were approaching. The knock at the door was answered by Dumbo. Rat-face walked in followed by a tall, red-headed guy who was very known and very unwelcome to Stavros.

Neil looked briefly at Stavros and then at Colin.

"Hi Danny, I'm here. What's up?" he said.

Colin aka Danny Monahan nodded toward Stavros. "You're acquainted, I think."

Neil studied Stavros for a moment and nodded: "Yeah, he was in my unit for a while." Turning to Stavros, Neil said, "Hey buddy! Remember me?"

Stavros couldn't believe his bad luck. He held his breath and waited for the shoe to drop.

"What do you have to say now, Yank?"

"I told you I was in the army."

"Kinda strange that you should show up here now, isn't it? Have you been looking for someone, like maybe our boy here?"

"No, I told you why I'm here. Ask the embassy. I have nothing to hide."

"You admit you were in the army together then?"

"I remember him, but like he said, I wasn't there long."

"Long enough, I think," said Danny. He turned to the man in the shadow. "What say you?"

"At this point in time, we can't risk loose ends."

"Loose ends? What does that mean?" Stavros said.

"We could shoot you and make you disappear. Leave everyone to wonder what happened to that Yank journalist. In fact, that's a fine idea. No real problems that I can see, and it would discourage other people from looking into our affairs. I think we could blame it on the loyalists or the army."

Neil said, "We don't need the Americans looking for him. You could give him some words for his article and send him on his way."

Danny gazed at Neil for a moment. "You think we should let him go? Even if he's not working for the English, we haven't handled him with kid gloves, you know."

"He'll get over that."

"Will he now? More important, he's sure to make a story of you being here. That wouldn't be good for your life expectancy."

Stavros said, "He's not part of my story. It's about how the Troubles affect the Irish, not Americans. And I'm willing to let the rough part slide."

"And we should take your word on that?" said the voice.

"Yes."

"Not much of a guarantee."

"I suppose, but fewer problems than the alternative."

"Oh, you won't be a problem, boy. I think we've talked enough about this, don't you?"

***

Neil's heart thumped as Desmond Reilly, the shadow man, stood up.

Reilly said to Neil, "You and the boys, take him out and make him go away." He pulled up a small automatic pistol from his pocket. "This is your problem, you brought him to us. Now you get to fix it."

The two goons pulled Stavros out of his chair and maneuvered him toward the door.

Neil remained. "I still think it's a bad idea. The Americans won't stop looking for him."

"Don't you worry about that. We've done this before and we haven't had any bodies found yet."

Neil had little desire for what was to follow but he also knew he had little choice. The two heavies that were with Stavros would ensure that Neil finished a job that took priority over all else.

Sorry, Paul, was all he could think. *Priorities. There are teammates and there is family.*

He turned and followed the others outside. Pausing in the passage, he heard Danny's voice: "You think he'll do it?"

Reilly said, "It really doesn't matter. We have the bombs. Rourke checked them and says they're ready. But he'll do it; he's a soldier and knows his duty."

"And if he doesn't, we disappear them both."

As Neil approached the edge of the clearing, he saw Stavros already kneeling and one of the heavies putting a hood over his head. The two were acting very carefully. The tall, thin man turned to Neil.

"Worried he'll get away?" Neil asked.

"Yeah, he's a tricky one. Last time we did this, he escaped after he busted us both up. He go through some special training or something?"

"I didn't know him well."

"But you did some of that stuff?"

"Not really. I was a combat engineer. I built things."

"I have it, you're the explosives expert ..." the fat one said.

"Not now, man. We have work to do," Neil told him.

Stavros was motionless, kneeling in the damp grass. His head was bent forward, almost as if he was praying, which he probably was, Neil thought.

"Let's get this over with." Neil held out his hand to the thin man and was rewarded with a small pistol placed in his palm, a .25-caliber Beretta. He sighed.

"Really?" He pulled the slide back carefully and saw the brass glint of a round in the chamber. He let the slide go forward and then checked the magazine. It was empty.

"One round with this little thing? Not very likely. Got anything bigger?"

"No," said the thin man.

"If it doesn't do the job, I'll finish him off," the fat man said, grinning stupidly, a 9mm in his hand.

"Well, move out of the way. This bullet is just as likely to bounce off his skull as anything, so you shouldn't stand in front of him."

The fat man moved to stand next to his partner on the side.

Neil moved closer to Stavros, standing behind him.

Stavros could feel his presence and tensed.

57

"So why did you come, buddy?" Neil asked.

"I thought the questions were finished," Stavros said.

"They are, but I'd like to know."

"I told them. I'm writing an article."

"So, you didn't come here to find me?"

"No one told me about you."

"I'm disappointed. I thought for sure that someone might miss me." Neil looked at the two heavies and winked at them. They seemed to understand his game and smiled back.

Neil stared at the pistol in his hands. *It's a long shot, but worth a try.*

"Will Carolyn miss you? She was your girlfriend in Berlin, right?" said Neil.

"Carolyn from the 'Speakeasy'?" Stavros answered. His head came up. "She wasn't my girl." He knew Carolyn was Neil's girlfriend.

"Too bad. Nobody to miss you," Neil said.

Stavros tensed.

Neil stretched out his shooting arm, pointing the gun at the treetops, and then lowered it to align with Stavros' hood. He looked at the fat man with the gun.

"Ready, mate?"

A nod. The Beretta's safety clicked off.

It was a natural shift, his eyes were already focused on the target. A sharp bark came from the pistol. Blood and cerebral fluid squirted from the fat man's forehead as he tumbled backwards. The thin man, eyes wide, lurched towards his partner's pistol on the ground. With his off hand, Neil pulled a pistol from under his coat and fired once, a muffled spit. The thin man continued down, face first into the dirt, bleeding from a hole in the back of his head. Neil picked up fat man's Llama pistol and fired one more suppressed round into the thin man.

"Okay then. That went well," Neil said as he pulled off Stavros' hood and untied his hands. He handed him the pistol and a spare magazine.

"Thanks for the warning," Stavros said, pulling the slide back to check.

"I wasn't even going to give you one until I thought of Carolyn," Neil said.

"I'm sure Carolyn would appreciate your taking her name in vain."

"It was for a good cause."

"Where did this come from?" Stavros asked, looking at the pistol Neil had given him, an old 1903 Colt with a long, gunmetal-gray suppressor screwed onto the muzzle.

"Stupid fucks didn't search me today, not that they ever did. Anyway, my cousin from Dundalk loaned it to me one day when I lost my minders. I don't think he'll want it back now."

"I'm a bit confused. Why are you in Ireland then?"

"I had an old family thing I needed to set straight and shooting you wasn't part of the deal. Follow my lead, buddy." Neil checked the Llama's magazine and found it almost full.

Stavros hefted the Colt and followed Neil toward the cottage. Reaching the closed door, Neil turned to Stavros and flashed five fingers twice, mouthing, "Follow me in ten."

He turned the knob and pushed the door open.

"It's done. He's no longer your problem," he said, tossing the little Beretta onto the table.

Danny caught the pistol as it slid across the wood and then looked up to see a pistol barrel staring him in the face.

"What's this all about, boy?" said Reilly, looking for anything that might be useful for survival.

"Don't move, Danny. You either, Desmond," Neil said.

Stavros came into the room, holding the Colt with both hands in front of him.

"What the hell?" said Danny. Reilly started to scoot his chair back from the table but froze when Neil pointed the gun at his head.

"Your two minions are no longer with us," said Stavros.

"Who told you my name?" Reilly asked Neil.

"Your friends in the States talk way too much. They wanted to brag about your deeds and when they mentioned Warrenpoint, I signed on."

"Why, what does Warrenpoint mean?"

"Warrenpoint and Lord Mountbatten. You had a twofer, didn't you? You killed them all."

Monahan looked at Reilly. He started to speak.

"Don't say a word, Danny," Reilly said. Then, looking at Neil, he went on, "You said you wanted to help. I don't understand."

"It's a long story and it's about my dad. It started when he joined the British Army in World War II."

"Then he was a traitor!" said Danny.

"Bullshit. My father did not desert Ireland. He fought the fascists, Ireland's real enemy. He survived the war, but you welcomed him back home with hate. When he came home, the IRA forced him to leave. He was betrayed and he went to America. He died homesick."

"Bloody Hell, is that what this is all about?"

"Yes. Mostly."

"So, how does your father involve me?"

"My dad served under Field Marshal Mountbatten in Burma and loved him. I know you planned the hit on Mountbatten."

"So, you came here because of that?"

"Simply put, yes."

"Mountbatten was an oppressor, one of the royal family. He deserved to die."

"You screwed that one up big time. He was an old man, a warrior, and a friend to Ireland. You've pissed off a lot of people," Neil said.

"Some friend, and I don't care about what a lot of people think. And you? Why are you here?" Reilly nodded toward Stavros.

"I didn't come here for revenge, although you've made me very angry. I just wanted to find my friend," said Stavros.

"So Branna was right," Danny said.

"Branna? The girl in the bar?" asked Stavros.

"That's the one."

"Danny, shut up. What now? Do you want me to confess?" Reilly asked.

"No need for that, I know you did it," Neil said.

"What do you want then?"

"My vengeance, retribution, or whatever you want to call it. You use guns and bombs to make holes in people's lives, holes that can't be filled. I'd want to fill at least one of those."

"Spare me your platitudes, boy," said Desmond.

"So you're going to kill us," Danny spluttered.

"We don't have any other option, now do we? Can't just walk away and, after all, you are the bad guys," Neil said.

Danny fingered the Beretta in his hand.

"Don't bother, boyo. The one round that was in there is in fat boy's brain. Paul, do you want to shoot one of them?"

"Nah, I don't feel an overwhelming need unless you absolutely don't want to."

"That's fine. Just wanted to offer you the chance."

Two rounds from the Llama hit Danny in the chest. He staggered back into the dark, knocked the chair away, and slumped to the floor. Desmond Reilly dropped to his knees, pleading, "For the love of Christ …."

Two rounds slammed into Desmond's face, and he tumbled to the side like a sack of rice.

"I hate hypocrites," quipped Neil.

Neil fired twice more as insurance, before he turned to Stavros.

"So, what happened? How'd you end up here?"

"I was out a bit too far," said Stavros.

"That's profound. No, really."

"I was looking for you."

"Officially or non-officially?"

"Officially. Jeff asked me to look for you. You had the Bureau worried; seems they thought you'd gone over to the IRA."

"I did. But I had a good reason."

"I heard, but you probably should have mentioned that to someone."

"If I had, they would have stopped me before I got on the plane."

Stavros found his shoes and rummaged through the items on the table. He found his wallet and checked for the few items he had in it.

"Bastards stole my money." He checked Monahan's and Reilly's bodies and pulled some bank notes out of their pockets.

"They probably figured you wouldn't need cash if you were dead."

"Even more reason for them to pay me back. What do we do now?" Stavros said.

"You accelerated my program a bit, but I have one more small thing to finish. You want to tag along?"

"I wouldn't miss it; these guys pissed me off. That's a nice beard by the way."

Neil looked at Stavros' wrists. "We ought to take care of those," he said, grabbing a bottle of whiskey. He opened it and poured it over the wounds.

"Shit!" Stavros blurted. He shook his stinging wrists. Further care would have to wait as the cottage was ill-equipped for first aid.

"Let's go. We'll take care of my errand and then I can take you wherever before I head to Shannon. I need to get out of Dodge," Neil said.

"We both do."

They walked outside and down a narrow path to a dirt road where a car was sitting.

Neil held up his gloved hands.

"Try not to touch anything."

"I'll do my best," Stavros said. He was trying to remember if he had left fingerprints behind. "I don't think I had a chance to touch anything in the cabin."

"Hopefully not, but you might want to avoid Ireland for the foreseeable future. So, what were you doing in Derry?" Neil asked as he started the car.

"I was waiting for you. When they announced the VIP visit to the bridge site, we figured you might show up."

"And I did."

"I know, I saw you in the plaza."

"That was you on the wall?"

"Yes, and you were with a woman."

"Branna is her name."

"The woman you were with?"

"Yes, I stayed at her place the night before."

"Hold it, the woman who was with you was Branna? When I saw her with you, her hair wasn't black."

"It is black; she dyed it for the day."

"How do you know?"

Neil looked at his friend for a moment. "I just do."

Slightly chagrined, Stavros said, "Sorry, I get it. Never mind."

"What of her?"

"I met her. I think she's the one who set me up to be snatched from the bar."

"She did. I heard them talk about her. She's one of their auxiliaries, a helper. But how did they know you were looking for me?"

"Did they know? Maybe they thought it was suspicious for an American to spend so much time there. I haven't figured it out."

"Maybe it was dumb luck?"

"Maybe, but I intend to find out when I get back to Derry."

They drove on in silence, both dwelling on events of the previous hours. Four men lay dead at a cottage deep in the forest. Terrorists who knew too much, who probably had enemies, and who died violently of copper poisoning. Maybe the *Gardaí* would chalk it up to an internal IRA dispute. Hopefully, but they didn't need to hang around to find out.

***

"We're almost there."

"Where?" asked Stavros.

"The factory. The place where I built some things for the boyos."

"Let me guess, the bombs?"

"Kinda, but I neutered them."

"Then why go?"

"I have to see a man about a dog." The look on Neil's face told him not to ask and when they pulled up to the cottage, he told Stavros to stay in the car. So he did. As Stavros looked at the barn across the field, doors closed, he wondered what secrets were hidden inside. Or not.

When the shot came, the noise was muffled, coming from inside the stone house. Still, Stavros knew it was a shot. A few minutes later, Neil came out and tossed a duffel and a shoulder bag into the back. Settling back into the driver's seat, he turned the key. Stavros watched as Neil closed his eyes for a moment, his hands at his sides. The engine purred quietly, waiting.

"Done," Neil finally declared. "All loose ends tied up. I can go home, and you can go where you need to. You can keep the Colt."

"Where's the other pistol?"

"I left it with the man in there."

"One shot?"

"One shot. That's all that was needed. Where do you want to go?"

"The border. Drop me and I can walk across."

"It's late. You'd be better off waiting until tomorrow."

The drive was longer this time. Neil knew the roads and showed Stavros the checkpoint from a far vantage point before he drove into the village. About half a mile from the crossing, he stopped the car in front of a small bed and breakfast. It was a quiet spot on the street and the traffic, both foot and vehicular, was light.

"So, you'll cross here tomorrow. Perhaps we'll see each other back in the States." There was a certainty to Neil's statement, not a finality but an end-of-episode kind of finish.

"Hope so. I'll let Jeff know you're on the right side so the Bureau doesn't give you a hard time."

"They probably will anyway, just to annoy me. What about you?"

"I'll go see Branna and ask her some questions," Stavros said.

"Keep your head, buddy."

"What do you mean?"

"Branna means 'raven' in Celtic. Ravens are clever. See you soon, brother."

58

Stavros pondered Neil's words as he watched the car drive away. Before he presented himself at the hotel, he found a public telephone to place a call. Shoving a handful of coins into the device, he dialed a long number and waited. A voice, German, heavily accented, answered. No name.

Stavros spoke, "*Hallo, Ich bin's.*"

A pause.

"Paul! *Wie geht's?* I heard you had a bit of trouble," Bergmann said.

"I'm fine." A short cryptic explanation, long in nuance, followed. Neil was okay, clean, returning home, Stavros said. There were a few issues to clarify and he was returning to the North; it would be a few more days before he could return to the city.

"Problems?"

"No, just questions."

"Need anything?"

"Hard to say."

"Do you have to go back?"

"I can't just walk away. Besides, my passport is at the hotel."

"You could go to Dublin. Get a new one from the embassy."

"Too far, too risky. A lot of water under the bridge in the last days."

"When do you go over?"

"Tomorrow, early morning."

"Okay, but be careful and keep me informed." Bergmann rang off.

59

The next morning, he made a second call, fewer coins. It was answered with a number, the same one Stavros had memorized and dialed. He thought he recognized the voice.

"It's Paul. I'm back."

A pause.

"Shit! Where are you?" It was Goose on the line.

"In the city," he lied. He didn't need to meet anyone who knew him at the border.

"We'll pick you up."

"No, I don't know where I am exactly," he lied again. "I'll call you from my boarding house."

"When?"

"Soon. Is everybody there now?"

"Yes, and you're on speaker."

"Listen, I know who set me up. A girl in the bar, I know who she is."

"Who?"

"There's more, but the most important thing is that VIPER is taken care of, he's out of the game. I'll fill you in when I see you."

"When will that be?"

"Like I said, soon. I need to go to my hotel and change. I haven't had a shower in a couple of days."

"Get there quick. We need to debrief you."

"I know. Won't be long."

Stavros hung up and looked at the address Neil had given him. It was somewhere he needed to go.

***

Goose hung up the phone and looked at Rhys.

"The IRA is going to be pissed when they find out he offed VIPER."

The captain spoke, "We'll wait for his call and then pick him up at his place. In and out quick. If we show up early and hang around, we might bring a Provo ASU in on us."

"My people will need to debrief him immediately," said Hamish. "I want you to physically detain him and then my people will get him out of the province and back to England."

"Can't you debrief him here or in Belfast?"

"Not safe enough. He killed VIPER, so we need to get him to a secure location in the homeland. The sooner he's out of here, the better. I'm going to report this to headquarters. Let me know when he calls." Hamish disappeared out the door.

"Why do I get the feeling that SEARCHER is in trouble?" said Hunter.

"Well, at least we weren't over there looking for him. That might have been awkward," Goose said. "HQ made a good decision for once."

"Hamish's HQ, not ours," Hunter replied.

"Let's get serious. If he did escape the IRA, they'll be looking for him and hard," said Rhys.

"What can we do?"

"We saddle up and wait, that's all."

60

Crossing the border wasn't as much of a hassle as Stavros thought it would be. He hefted the small bag Neil had given him and approached the official with a smile he didn't really feel. Explaining that he'd left his passport behind, a call to the hotel confirmed he was who he said he was. He suspected his smell may have accelerated things a bit. With things sorted out, he grabbed a taxi. The driver dropped him a ways from the address. It was a Catholic area and, on this day at least, quiet. He took a long moment to orient himself, then approached carefully, looking for loitering young people and occupied parked cars. There were none.

He followed Neil's directions. Using the rear entrance he quietly climbed the stairs to the fourth floor. Silently, he set his shoulder bag on the floor next to the door, which was slightly ajar. He eased it open, the long pistol suppressor following every movement of his eyes as he entered the flat. A short hallway opened onto a small sitting room, a chair, a tiny desk, with an open Murphy bed that took up the remainder of the space.

A man was standing, back to Stavros, distracted.

Stavros spoke softly. "I thought I might find you here."

Hamish whirled about and was met with the sight of a pistol leveled at his head. His own was useless to him, as he was screwing off the suppressor.

"Drop it," Stavros commanded. Hamish complied, and the Browning thumped on the carpet.

Stavros glanced at the woman spread out on the bed. He could see she was dead, but she was wearing black and her wounds were not visible. Her eyes were fixed open, and blood stained the sheets. Branna.

"Why did you kill her?"

"Her job was finished. She's what we call a supergrass. The IRA would have done it if I hadn't."

"You mean she was a collaborator, a tout," Stavros said.

"No, she was an agent of influence. Those other words are so ugly."

"Why didn't you just ask her where the bombers were? Or for that matter, where VIPER was?"

"She didn't know who VIPER was or where they were. She was a one-way conduit to provide information, rat people out, things like that."

"And arrange for people to be kidnapped."

"That was my plan all along, lad. I knew you would never find VIPER on your own so I decided to help. What better way to trap the rats than to put down some cheese? It was a come-on, just like the bridge visit. That's why I told RAVEN about you. She did the rest, she took you to him didn't she? My gambit worked, didn't it?"

"Not quite. She took me to someone else. But you know what's funny?"

"What?"

"VIPER came over and stayed in this very flat. Branna slept with the man you wanted to find. I bet she never told you."

"She was a whore, an opportunist," Hamish fumed.

"Meant a lot to you, did she?"

"None of them do. They fill a requirement and when that's finished, so are they. It's all about results and results justify the means."

"Do you have a quota?"

"For terrorists? That's a laugh. No, no quota. I'll take as many as I can get."

Hamish embodied the worst of the spy business: the lying, the deceit. Worse still, he seemed to revel in exploiting people. Stavros was willing to accept the necessity of intelligence operations if it served a higher purpose, but he was sure Hamish saw it all differently. Hamish played a zero sum game—I win, you lose, was all he cared about. And there were pawns to be used and tossed aside at any cost.

Hamish continued his diatribe. "England brought civilization to this province. Look what they've done with it."

"I've heard that one before, something about the white man's burden. And you wonder why the Catholics hate you."

"Not all of them do."

"No, I suppose not. Most don't hate Brits, just Brits like you."

"Why do you moan about Ireland? It's not your problem; you high-minded Yanks can't make your own country right."

"That's true, but then we had a good teacher. The English saved America from the uncivilized and ignorant natives, as well as the Spanish and the French. And since then we've had waves of slaves and immigrants who were oppressed and blamed for our country's problems and they still are. All flavors and colors of people came to America and each was resented in turn. That's what you need here: some variety. That way you can pick and choose who to oppress."

"That's the way the world turns, Yank. But you Americans have done us much better since then, haven't you?"

Stavros felt his anger rising. He'd experienced it before. But this discussion would just lead to an endless spiral downward and it wasn't a game he wanted to engage in at the moment. He saw another way out.

"And what do you hope to get out of this?" he asked Hamish.

"I'll get a mention, maybe a promotion, and an assignment somewhere better than this shit hole."

"Because you stopped the bombers by having me kill VIPER?"

"Yes. That was worth all my efforts."

"I see. Except I'll be telling them what actually happened."

"What did happen?"

"When the IRA captured me? Or when VIPER saved me?"

"VIPER? Saved you? I thought you killed him?"

"Seems he wasn't the bad one after all."

"Then they'll be looking for you."

"Not likely. The ones who knew him are all gone."

"Interesting …" Hamish looked at the floor, at his pistol.

"Don't."

"What?" Hamish shifted forward, toward Stavros.

"Don't do anything stupid. I'd like you to face the music."

"They won't believe you. You have no proof."

"Other than the dead woman."

"I didn't shoot her; she was dead when I got here. And, of course, this pistol was taken off a dead RUC constable by the IRA. They killed her. That's the story."

"And me?" Stavros said.

"And you too." Hamish exploded forward, flinging the suppressor he held at Stavros' face, and dropped to the carpet, going for the gun.

Good move but you telegraphed it, Stavros thought as he barely ducked the steel cylinder.

Hamish grabbed for the Browning. He couldn't see his target, looking down, distracted.

Stavros stepped to the side and had a split second to reset, think, and decide. The Colt bucked solidly in his hands three times. Three quiet bullets hit Hamish in the chest as he looked back up.

Hamish, perhaps surprised that he could be shot, looked down at the red spilling across his shirt and collapsed without a sound onto the carpet, not like a tree in a forest, more like a pig carcass hitting the floor in a slaughter house.

Stavros found the suppressor, screwed it back on the Browning, and put the pistol back into Hamish's hand. He pressed the Colt into Branna's and fired a fourth round into the desk, then repositioned the cartridge casings closer to her body.

"You weren't clever enough," he murmured over her. *A shame.*

He surveyed the room for any signs he had been there and, satisfied there were none, backed out, pulling the door closed behind him. In the hall, Stavros peeled Neil's gloves off, picking up his bag before he stepped carefully down the back stairs.

61

Stavros picked up the house phone in the entryway soon after he got back to his tiny boarding house. That was after he explained to Mrs O'Brien, the elderly proprietor, that he'd been caught up in a medical emergency for a couple of days. Not specifying what kind or whose emergency it was probably led the woman to surmise that he'd been hit by a bus, because that's what he looked like. His body was indeed still quite sore.

The call made, he climbed the narrow stairs up to his room, brushing by the faded lace curtains on the windows, stopping to straighten a picture on the wall. He felt lighter now, his job done. All he needed to do was finish whatever end-of-mission business his counterparts wanted to debrief him on and go home. The biggest priority was to pass on the registration numbers and descriptions of the bomb trucks, the info that Neil gave him before they had parted company. That would have to wait until Hunter came for him.

As the first order of business, he pitched his clothes into the trash bin. Somebody would have a use for them and he didn't want to see them again. Then it was time for a shower. He stood in the hot water and steam for what seemed a half hour, but it felt good. Drying off, he stood in front of the mirror staring at the welts and bruises on his legs and abdomen. He knew there were more on his back, but he couldn't see. The skin on his arms, ankles, and feet had been shredded by his escape dash through the brush, vines, and brambles. It would be a while before he could wear a swimsuit in public without scaring people.

Getting dressed with his last clean set of clothes from the small suitcase, he picked up his Seiko and tried to put it on. He couldn't get the strap closed; the abrasions on his wrist hurt and forced him to pocket it instead. But it was a reminder to call Sarah. *I need to know how she's doing, to tell her where I am, that I need her ….*

Then he was back to making mental notes, the clothing he had lost, his anorak and fisherman's cap. Luckily, he hadn't been wearing the watch or his leather jacket. Both had history that couldn't be replaced. Everything else was expendable. His passport came out of its hiding place and went into his jacket. He felt almost human again.

How long has it been? He wasn't sure. Four or five days? Seemed like more.

Mrs O'Brien's voice came, sing-song, from below. "Mister Paul, you have a visitor downstairs. He'll wait for you down here."

She's effectively giving instructions to two people at once, Stavros thought. *Efficient.*

Stavros grabbed his bag and thumped down the carpeted stairs. The sight of Captain Brown was unexpected. Strange to see the boss out on the street; he'd expected Goose, or Philip maybe.

"Rhys! I wasn't expecting you," he said, genuinely curious. He handed an envelope to the woman. "I have to leave you today; something's come up back home."

"Too bad, but maybe you'll be back?" More of Stavros' cash payments would be gladly accepted was her intimation.

"Yes, maybe. Hopefully."

Rhys took the bag, "Thank you, Mrs O'Brien." Her name was on the sign outside. "Let's go, Paul. Everyone's waiting." Concern was evident in his eyes. Stavros felt it but didn't comment. *Wait until we're outside.*

"How you getting along? They'll be wanting all the details, big debrief planned."

"My kidneys are sore," Stavros said. It was all he could manage. Rhys was talking too much.

They stepped onto the path and the lodge door clicked shut. Stavros' curiosity got the better of him. "Something up?"

"We need to move you out of here fast." Rhys threw the words over his shoulder as he strode toward the front gate.

Hunter was on the sidewalk, watching up and down the street. *Goose or Philip must be with the car.*

Rhys pushed open the gate and Hunter moved toward a Ford Cortina to open the door, while Rhys opened the boot lid to stow the bag. Stavros saw that it was Goose at the wheel. Their attention wasn't where it should have been.

Out of the corner of Stavros' eye, he saw two figures in black and white. It took a moment before he registered them. Two Catholic nuns, hands tucked inside their sleeves as they walked directly at them.

"Excuse us," one spoke, a lilting sound, slightly accented. "Would you like to help our orphans' fund?"

"Not now, sisters. We're in a hurry," said Hunter, rushing to climb in the car.

"In that case, don't move." Two .45s came out of the nuns' habits. "We're Americans and we're taking Paul."

A van slid to a halt parallel with Goose's window. A young man with a Heckler & Koch MP5 pointed it at Goose.

"Freeze, mate. Don't do anything stupid and no one gets hurt."

A second man jumped out of the van to cover Rhys.

"Paul, grab your stuff and get in the van."

Stavros looked hard at the nun who had spoken. He knew the eyes. "Rhys, do what they say. They're friends," he said.

"Bloody Hell." Rhys stood with his hands up.

Relieved of their weapons, Goose and Hunter were carefully moved to the van. Then Rhys, hands tied, followed them in to sit on the floor. As his partner secured the three, one of the men spoke to Stavros. "I'm Frank, that's Jerry, we're taking you out of here."

"I can see that."

The van driver urged them on. "Come on, we need to get moving. The neighbors are getting curious." Hans Landau looked at Stavros and winked. "You can call me 'Wolfgang.' You know 'Ruth' already and that's 'Heidi.' All friends. Climb in."

As Jerry put hoods over the heads of Stavros' English teammates, Stavros stared at Sarah, unbelieving.

"Ruth is it? You're my rescue committee?" he asked.

"For this job we are," Hans said. Sarah just smiled.

The van jerked off down the street, the open side door sliding back and forth with each change in velocity, until one hard brake shut it definitively. They sailed down the street, making several quick turns, never quite stopping for the signs, but not fast enough to attract attention. The women peeled off their habits and became civilians, nevertheless dressed for business, jeans, black boots, and dark blue commando sweaters.

Heidi reached out her hand. "Hi Paul."

"How did you know I was in trouble?"

"When the Brits told us you went missing, NCA authorized us to deploy to look for you. The Agency supported us getting into the Republic, but events moved so quickly we were too late to do anything until today. We came across the border last night."

"And your guns came from where?"

"Like I said, the Agency was helpful. Then we picked up chatter from London. When they heard you escaped, someone high up in Her Majesty's Government wanted to give you to the Irish. They were going to blame Neil's death on you. So they told us to try and make sure you didn't get pulled in."

"That's nice of you, but Neil isn't dead."

"What? The British think he is!" said Hans.

"I kinda told them that he was dead, but he isn't. Long story but he needed some time to get out. He should be on his way to the States by now. I told Sergeant Major Bergmann, but he obviously didn't pass that information on to you."

"Bergmann didn't, but then he knows how to play the game better than any of us."

The van exited the warrens of the city and headed north along the river and then broke off into the countryside. The cottages and barns became fewer, the terrain turned rugged, almost desolate, a wild isolated beauty. Stavros looked out the window, mesmerized by the sight and his feelings.

He looked back at Sarah who was quietly watching him, her back against the wall of the van, smiling. Stavros shook his wrist free of his coat and pulled the Seiko out of his pocket. He handed it to Sarah, inviting her into his world. Seeing his wounds, she gently placed the watch around his wrist and buckled the strap. Not too loose, not too tight. He looked at its face, the second hand sweeping around the dial, and saw Sarah in the background.

It was time to go home.

62

Standing on the windswept heath some 30 kilometers or more northeast of Derry, Stavros tried to listen in on the SEAL platoon commander's radio conversation. The rushing noise of the breeze through the grasses made it hard to hear and Lieutenant Sullivan had a hand pressed down hard on his earpiece. Finally, Sullivan looked at Stavros.

"The birds are fifteen minutes out," he said.

Stavros decided it was time and walked over to the British troopers sitting on the ground. He looked at them for a moment before he spoke.

"Let's cut them loose."

A big SEAL with side-cutters snipped the 550 cord and pulled off their hoods.

Freed from their bonds, Rhys, Hunter, and Goose stood up rubbing their wrists and blinking in the light of the day. They looked around at the team in civilian clothing and the ten menacingly armed SEALs who surrounded them—all dressed in dark green camouflage and carrying suppressed Smith & Wesson Model 76 submachine guns. Each had a red, white, and blue American flag sewn on the left shoulder of his fatigues. It was their only insignia.

VOICE
ACROSS

621.38   13485
C597   CLARKE.

Voice across the sea.

DATE DUE		
DEC 12 78		
NOV 24 82		
SL		

By the Same Author

"It's best if you don't move too quickly. You're in protective custody but these guys are still nervous," Stavros said as he gestured toward the SEALs.

"How did you pull this off?" Rhys asked.

"I kept an open line with my command and when things started to look strange, they decided I might need backup. These folks," sweeping his hand to indicate the two women and three men in civilian clothes nearby, "are our equivalent of your Element. The guys with green faces and guns are some friends who just happened to be in the neighborhood. Submarines really are wonderful things."

The SEAL base in Scotland isn't far away. Nor is Holy Loch and the subs … not so far at all.

Rhys looked hard at the American women. "You've ruined my opinion of nuns, you know. I'll never trust one again."

Ruth aka Sarah and her comrade, Heidi, smiled and took that as a compliment.

Then Hunter squared off across from Sarah. They looked like two scorpions about to sting each other to death.

"Paul, is this your partner in crime?" Sarah said, nodding at Hunter. "She looks like a handful. Should I be jealous?"

Hunter looked from Sarah to Stavros and back again. "No," she said. "And now I know."

"What?" Sarah said.

Hunter answered, "Now I know why he ignored me. I was beginning to think he was gay."

Sarah laughed.

"Why I ignored you? What are you talking about?" Stavros said.

"It's obvious, I just now saw how you looked at her. There's a fire there between you two. But Paul, I think you should know that woman would cut you to pieces if you ever get out of line," Hunter said.

"I'll remember that," Stavros said.

"Enough caterwauling, ladies. Paul, why are your people here? Didn't you trust us?" asked Rhys.

"You and your folks I trusted. It was Hamish and his crew that I didn't."

"What didn't you like about Hamish?"

"The girl I met in the pub—she told the IRA that I was looking for Neil. She drugged me and arranged for me to be taken across the border. Her name was Branna. Hamish told me his asset was code-named RAVEN. He must have told her about me after I spotted Neil in the plaza."

"Branna is Gaelic for Raven," Hunter said.

"That's what someone else told me. I think you should walk back the cat and look at the death of William Graham. Hamish may be responsible for him as well."

"Why do you think so?"

"Were you watching me the day before Graham was killed?"

"No, I told you that we weren't," Rhys said.

"Hamish told me you were. What he actually said was 'We were watching you.' I didn't mention it to you because I thought he might have some MI6 personnel working with him that you didn't know about."

Rhys looked at his team. Goose shook his head and looked off in the distance. Rhys turned back to Stavros.

"He may have had some loyalists watching you and they saw you meet," Rhys said.

"That would mean he considered Graham talking to me was dangerous to him."

"Some things are starting to fall into place now," said Goose.

"Like the surveillance run we made across the border? The two boyos your other team took out? You told me an informant gave up the meeting."

"Hamish briefed us. But we didn't take them down."

"I thought the other team snuffed them."

"Remember, I stayed back a bit? I told the boys not to kill them because you were an outsider, a witness. So they just tied them up in the cottage and burned the barn."

"I bet Hamish was pleased. He told me, 'I am going to make sure it's the IRA that are dead.' I think he wants all Catholics dead, IRA or not."

"I didn't tell him that they're still alive."

"I'm beginning to like you, Goose."

"Don't get sissy on me, mate." Goose winced at the thought.

"Well, the news is that I escaped and there are five dead IRA across the border. RAVEN has the pistol that killed a couple of them."

"How did she get it?"

"I gave it to her. Thought she might need it once Hamish finds out about what happened with VIPER."

"You gave her a pistol?" Rhys said.

"Yes," said Stavros.

"After she set you up? You expect us to believe that?"

"My word against hers."

"She won't be having any more words, she's dead," Hunter said.

"Really? How did that happen?" asked Stavros. No emotion visible.

"It looks like Hamish shot her."

"That might have been predictable. Where is Hamish now?"

"They're both dead. He apparently went to kill her and things went wrong," said Hunter.

"That's too bad."

"How did you get the pistol?" asked Rhys.

"The guy that saved me from the IRA gave it to me. Said I might need it because I tend to get in trouble."

"Who was he?"

"Make a guess," said Stavros.

"VIPER?"

"It might have been him, yes, it's possible," Stavros said. *No need to admit anything.*

"Did he kill them?" Rhys asked.

"There may have been an exchange of gunfire, yes. I don't remember, I was under a lot of stress and wearing a blindfold."

"Why was he there?"

"Some family issues, I think."

"What about his bombs?"

Stavros handed Rhys a piece of paper.

"The registration numbers and descriptions of the two bomb trucks. They crossed into the province two nights ago."

"Two nights ago? They could already be in place and ready to go off!"

"Not likely. VIPER sabotaged the firing systems."

"Where is he now?"

"Hopefully he's drinking a gin and tonic somewhere over the North Atlantic. I told you he was worth saving."

After a long silence, Goose spoke, "Too bad, I would have liked to have met him."

"You might yet. I don't think we're quite finished with him."

"How do you expect to get off this island? There'll be a lot of people who are looking for us right now and you can't get far," Rhys declared.

"Far enough, I should think." Stavros turned and looked north.

Far away, two dots were flying low and heading directly for them, getting larger by the moment.

"Our taxi is about to arrive."

"This just keeps getting better and better," Goose said, following Stavros' gaze. He stared at the approaching helicopters.

"Thanks to Churchill, Lend-Lease, and long-range fuel tanks, anything can happen," Stavros said.

"I would like to know how your government will explain this," Rhys said.

SEAL Lieutenant Sullivan spoke, "This is part of a sanctioned NATO search and rescue exercise. It seems one of our pilots had an engine malfunction and ejected around here." Pointing at Stavros, he said, "And we just found him. Besides, your radar coverage up here is lousy when it's being jammed."

"You do cover the bases, don't you? One more question if I may?" Rhys said, speaking to Stavros.

"Sure, we're still friends I hope," Stavros said.

"How did you know we were going to pick you up?"

Hans spoke up, "Because your communications security sucks. Our signals folks have been listening to everything you've talked about for the past couple of days."

"This could cause a diplomatic incident you know," said Rhys.

"Somehow I doubt it. Like I said, we could hear all the chatter, including some things you didn't. Things your government might not want out in the open, like how the UK government was prepared to turn an American over to the Irish for a crime he didn't commit."

Conversation was cut short as the two mottled dark green HH-53s approached, came to a hover, and then settled to the ground nearby. The grass flattened under the rotors' down wash and a cloud of debris—vegetation, dirt, and small lightweight creatures—roiled up through the air. The helos' ramps dropped. The SEAL platoon closed in on the group, still maintaining a good defensive perimeter.

"Say your good-byes. We need to run," said Lieutenant Sullivan through the din.

Hans pulled some keys out of his pocket and tossed them to Rhys.

"The van is yours. Your weapons are under the seats. There's also a blue Rover sedan near Stavros' place. We bought them cash on the barrelhead in the Republic so I'm sure you can confiscate them for your operations. A gift from Uncle Sam."

Then he turned and ran for the helos. The rest of the Azimuth team followed him on board.

Stavros grabbed Goose's big hand and shook it. "Thanks for the cover, mate. I really appreciated your being out there. At least some of the time."

Then he turned to Hunter. Before he could speak, she reached out and pulled him close, hugged him tightly, and for a moment he savored the smell of her hair.

"Let me know if things don't work out with that woman," she said quietly in his ear.

Stavros shivered a bit but was speechless.

She seemed to sense his shock and pushed him back to arms' length. Their eyes glistened a bit in the afternoon light as they stared at each other.

After a moment, she said, "Stay safe, SEARCHER. Come and see me … I mean, come and see us."

"I will, I promise."

Then he faced Rhys, "Rhys, it was almost all a pleasure. I wish you all the best in your long war."

"We'll be fine. What are you going to do next?"

"Find some decent scrambled eggs. I need a real breakfast."

"Ha! Good luck with that one. At least it's a safer quest than this one was."

They shook hands. Stavros stepped back and saluted.

"Take care, sir!" Stavros had a grin on his face as he ran for the nose of the first bird.

"Don't call me sir!" Rhys yelled after him.

Lieutenant Sullivan gave the signal and his team folded in from their positions and loaded up the helos once the precious cargo was on board. The ramp closed and the rotor pitch increased as the pilots throttled up. The big birds rose heavily like giant dragonflies. Then they pivoted ninety degrees in unison, dipped their noses a bit, and barreled off to the west across the plain, one following the other offset a bit, lifting higher in the sky before turning north out over the rocky coastline, a long trail of kerosene exhaust smoke trailing behind. Soon they tacked east, homeward toward their North Atlantic base, flying above the waves of the wine-dark sea.

Acknowledgements

This book is based on historical events and the experiences of individuals present during that period. That said, *Direct Legacy* is a novel and I have taken liberties with some of those facts both to protect those involved, whether innocent or not, and to placate the prepublication review board.

I would like to thank the following:

Casemate Publishers and especially my commissioning editor, Ruth Sheppard, for bringing me on board, Alison Griffiths for her attention to detail, Declan Ingram for the cover design, Sarah Stamp and Daniel Yesilonis for their promotional skills, and all the other staff members who made things happen in this difficult year.

And not to forget:

Ian Fleming for his notes on men's fashion and introducing me to the Walther PPK a long time ago,

Henry Glassie (*All Silver and No Brass*) for his take on Irish tradition,

my English mates who introduced me to the wonders of Wales,

my Irish friends who introduced me to the real Guinness,

Major McHale, who put me back together again.

Most of all, I want to say thanks to all my comrades who stood ready and when asked went into the breach without a second thought.

And my family who have always been there.